DAY BREAK

A POSSESSION POINT MYSTERY

JILL SANDERS

GRAYTON

This is a work of fiction. Names, characters, organizations, places, events, and incidents are either products of the author's imagination or are used fictitiously.

SUMMARY

After spending the last year of her life behind bars for a crime she didn't commit, Chloe is now free. She's also divorced, jobless, homeless, and completely alone in the world. If not for the kindness of a stray dog, she would have just lay down and let the world take the rest of what she had. But that dog showed her kindness and led her to a stranger who opened her eyes to the good in the world. Then the tender-hearted man's grandson steps into the picture and, suddenly, her past doesn't look so terrible.

Lane Robinson comes from a long line of stuck-up, blue-blooded asshats. His grandfather, who is a recently reformed asshat, is the one exception. Since the rest of the family has disowned the ailing man, Lane steps in and does what he can. But then a strange woman shows up and claims that she's his grandfather's caretaker. She causes Lane's libido to spike, but Lane doesn't trust easily. Especially after learning all about the woman's dark and dangerous past.

*To all my wonderful friends and family
who have been with me on this crazy ride.*

*To my husband,
who has stuck with me for twenty-nine years!*

*To my amazing editor,
for hanging in there for ninety books!*

*To my readers,
I hope you enjoy my ninetieth book.*

CHAPTER ONE

*"Our eternal message of hope
is that dawn will come."*
- Martin Luther King, Jr.

I remembered the worst days of my life and stupidly believed that they were behind me. I was convinced that I was going to finally be freed from my enslavement. Freed from the chains that had bound me for all twenty-six years of my life. I'd spent half of that life as a wife, controlled by the monster that waited in the darkness, who caused me to cower in fear every waking moment of my life.

But he couldn't hurt me anymore.

He'd been the beast that demanded everything from me and then required even more, always more. There wasn't enough in heaven or on earth to sate his hunger. Every move I made, he watched.

He had fed on what I was, what I could give, day and night. He'd seemed starved for attention. My attention.

The monster changed over the years, as did the demands, but always he had claimed what he saw as his right. And it seemed I was the only provider of the sustenance he required.

I knew later on that I wasn't the only one who had suffered at the foul demon's hands. Nor, I wagered, would I be the last.

Since I was finally free, at least for the time being, he would be forced to go elsewhere for his nutrition.

"What are you in for?" the woman sitting next to me asked.

I blinked, trying desperately not to let the tears that burned the back of my eyes fall. I knew better than to show weakness. I glanced over at the older woman and ran my eyes over her heavily lined face. I took in her frizzy gray hair and her thin lips. She bit them, and they were chapped around the edges from the cold air that was coming through the open windows of the bus.

I desperately wished to be her. To have her life, no matter how hard it had been.

Instead of answering her, I turned back towards the front and watched the tall city buildings grow farther apart from one another.

I didn't talk to strangers.

I wasn't here to make friends.

I no longer cared what anyone thought of me. Or if they thought of me at all.

I was dead inside.

All of my emotions had perished at someone else's hands years ago.

Would I ever feel anything again?

Why did I even care?

"Hey, sweetie, I didn't mean to scare you," the older

woman said, trying once again to spark up a conversation. "It's a long trip up the river. I just thought we'd pass the time."

I closed my eyes and leaned my head on the window. It was cold. Too cold. Still, instead of jumping away or laying my head against the back of the seat, I suffered. Once again. The iciness numbing my skin was the only reminder that I was still alive.

I must have fallen asleep at one point, and when the bus came to a stop, I jerked awake. Gut reaction. Every muscle in my body tensed, every nerve ending ready for what was to come.

Then I remembered nothing was there.

"Off," someone said loudly.

I stood, as did the rest of the women on the bus. I didn't look to see who I was riding with.

I didn't care.

I felt nothing.

Standing in line, I kept my eyes on my shoes.

Dull gray sneakers. Their white laces had turned a muddy white.

"Sarah Meyers," someone called out.

They said it three times before I finally lifted my head.

"Yes," I said in a low voice.

Suddenly, a large woman with noticeably short hair shoved her face directly in front of mine. She had nice eyes.

"When I call your name, answer me. I won't wait around for you. This isn't some preppy bullshit school. Got that?"

When she talked, spit flew out of her mouth and landed on my nose, eyes, cheeks, and lips.

I didn't care.

I felt nothing.

I nodded and returned my gaze to my shoes.

I was shoved until I followed everyone else as we made our way through tall metal fences. We passed several gates and then went through some doors that swung open and shut once we were all inside. We were crowded into a narrow hallway, then led into a large room.

I didn't even think to look around to see where we were going.

I didn't care.

I felt nothing.

The sounds of the last door shutting behind me would eventually echo in my mind during the darkest parts of the nights. The moments when I was forced to be alone with myself. Forced to own up to my own deep fears. To the anxieties that I had never even admitted to myself.

But for now.

I didn't care.

I felt nothing.

A bunch of items were tossed at me. Since I was still staring down at my shoes, they hit my chest and fell to the floor.

I bent slowly and started to pick them up, but I was shoved from behind and fell headfirst into the table.

Everyone in the room laughed at me. Only the shrill sound of a whistle stopped the laughter.

The large woman was back, yelling at me, inches from my face, spit spewing over my skin.

"What are you? A troublemaker?" she screamed.

I blinked and didn't respond.

Something flashed deep in her eyes. If I had blinked at that very moment, I would have missed it. But I hadn't.

"Pick up your things," she screamed at me, and then she disappeared.

I bent once more to gather the items.

A gray jumpsuit. More gray shoes like the ones I was currently wearing, only with laces that were white and new. A boxed bar of soap. A new toothbrush and small tube of toothpaste. A box of tampons. A Bible.

I held the items to my chest as I was escorted through another doorway.

As we moved through the last gate, names were called out, along with a letter and a number.

Andrés, C2

Clark, C4

Marquez, C5

Meyers, C7

I jumped when someone shoved me from behind.

"You're here," they said.

I took two steps until I entered what would be my new world. When the door slammed behind me, I flinched, not prepared for the sound that reverberated in the small space.

"You get used to it," someone said in the dark room.

I blinked a few times until my eyes adjusted. Then I glanced up and noticed a large Latino woman sitting on the upper bunk. Her hair was dyed a bright yellow and cut so short I could see her scalp in places. She wore the same jumpsuit I had on, only her sleeves were rolled up, show-casing arms that were covered in faded tattoos.

"I won't bite. At least not when we're alone." She smiled. That was when I noticed that one of her canine teeth was missing. The other one was capped. "I'm Lucy." She ran her eyes over me. "Do you have a name besides Meyers?" She mimicked the guard's tone.

"That's not my name," I said quickly.

I knew what she was seeing when she continued to run her eyes over me.

I was skinny, lanky, pale.

My naturally blonde hair was ratted and pulled back into a ponytail. My skin looked washed out, almost translucent.

My blue eyes were no doubt red and puffy, even though I'd held back the tears. So far. They were dead inside, much like I was.

Lucy's eyebrows shot up. "Okay, then what is your name?"

I looked back at my shoes as I stood rod straight just inside the room.

Sarah Meyers was dead. I'd killed her to survive.

I heard the woman moving around in the room but didn't let my eyes waver from my shoes. I could feel the burning behind them grow.

I didn't care.

I felt nothing.

No matter how many times I said it to myself, I just couldn't force my heart to believe those words.

To my horror, tears fell from my eyes and landed on my dull gray sneakers.

Then Lucy's face appeared between my nose and my shoes, blurry from the tears. She must have been bending over and practically upside down so she could see my face.

"You get one night of self-pity. That's the rules around here," Lucy said firmly, her eyes boring into mine. "After that, you gotta put on your big girl panties like the rest of us. Understand?"

I swallowed and closed my eyes as I nodded. When I shut my eyes, I sealed off the rest of my tears. I told myself that was all I would allow myself to shed.

"Good. The bottom bunk is yours," Lucy said cheerfully. She jumped easily onto her bunk. "Those bitches even take that choice away from us."

I set my things on the lower bunk before sitting down. The mattress reminded me of one I'd slept on at a motel long ago. Back when I had foolishly believed that I could fight for my freedom all by myself. The first and only time I'd tried to escape. That move had cost me dearly.

"Hey, not Meyers," Lucy said from her spot on the top bunk. "I'll trade you some smokes for that new bar of soap."

"I don't smoke," I said, looking at the pale green cement wall across from the bunk.

There was a small sink and a toilet in the room. Despite the grittiness of the entire place, the space was clean.

"Hm..." Lucy made a noise above me. "How about some nail polish?"

I looked down at my hands. At my nails. They were cut short. I had never had color on them. It hadn't been allowed.

More expectations forced onto me.

"No, thank you," I answered.

Lucy's upside-down head appeared directly in front of mine.

"Well, what do you want, not Meyers?" she asked, her eyes running over my face again.

I thought about it. In my heart, I knew there was nothing she or anyone else had that would lift the heavy weight pulling me down.

"Do you have any books?" I asked on a whim. Then I held up the Bible that I'd been given. "Other than this one?"

Lucy smiled. "A brainiac?" Her eyes narrowed. "Or maybe you're into smut? I don't got none of that *Fifty Shades* shit," Lucy said, disappearing from my view. "But I do got this." She reappeared holding a small, tattered book.

I looked at the title and for the first time in days, a smile caused the corners of my lips to curve upward.

Somehow, in one of my darkest hours, Byron had found me.

Reaching up, I took the frayed copy of *Don Juan* and then handed my new bar of soap to Lucy.

"Yep, called it, you're a brainiac." Lucy chuckled. "I couldn't get through two pages of that one."

I scooted back until my back was against the cold cement wall, hugging the book to my chest like a treasure. Then I tucked my knees up to my chest and just looked down at the cover. I could barely make out the image on the front, but I knew it so well, I closed my eyes and pulled it into my mind from memory.

No, I didn't need any more tears.

I had my closest friend, the best lover that I'd ever had.

A book.

One that I loved and had read from cover to cover half a dozen times. There were only a handful of books I could say that about.

"Hey, not Meyers. You good under there?" Lucy asked.

"Chloe," I said softly. I could no longer stomach my real name. I didn't want one more person to call me Sarah Meyers. That woman was dead.

Suddenly, Lucy's face appeared again. Her upside-down smile looked strange. Her eyes went over me as if she were trying to figure me out.

"I think we're going to get along just fine, Chloe," she said, before disappearing again.

I didn't sleep that first night. Most of the night, I sat in my bunk, hugging my book to my chest. It was too dark to read. Then they had called lights out and seconds later the entire place went pitch black.

It was so dark that I couldn't even see my hand in front of my face. It took minutes for my eyes to adjust.

I could hear Lucy snoring softly in the bunk above me.

I felt more tears try to come. Instead, I opened my book as if I could see it clearly. In my mind, I tried to run over the words from memory, but my memory wasn't as great as I'd imagined it would be. Instead of each line appearing in my head, only some of the great ones flashed quickly in my mind.

> *"Nothing so difficult as a beginning*
> *In poesy, unless perhaps the end;*
> *For oftentimes when Pegasus seems winning*
> *The race, he sprains a wing, and down we tend,*
> *Like Lucifer when hurled from*
> *Heaven for sinning;*
> *Our sin the same, and hard as his to mend,*
> *Being Pride, which leads the mind to*
> *soar too far,*
> *Till our own weakness shows us what we are."*

This passage played over in my mind until I noticed the first slivers of light. I didn't understand why it stuck in my mind. I had read it more than a hundred times. Memorized it. It seemed to touch something deep in me.

When I heard Lucy stirring above me, I knew that the quiet was about to come to an end.

My very first day in prison was about to begin. Would all the other women I was to be locked up with be as kind as the old woman on the bus and Lucy? I knew it wasn't possible.

After the life I'd had so far, I wasn't hopeful.

A loud buzzing sound caused me to jump again.

Lucy's face appeared over the bunk. Her eyes scanned my face, and then she jumped off the top bunk and landed at my feet.

"If you're shy, turn around," she said before dropping her pants and using the toilet.

I quickly averted my eyes and looked down at my book. It was finally light enough that I could read the words on the pages.

I hunted down the quote I'd been replaying in my head all night and sighed when I found it.

I had remembered it, line for line, perfectly.

"You need to use it?" Lucy asked as she washed her hands in the sink and started to brush her teeth.

"I'll wait," I answered, being too shy to even think about going to the bathroom with a stranger in the room.

There was another loud buzzing sound, and our door flew open.

"Welp." Lucy rubbed her hands together. "I'm going to get in line for breakfast." She reached up into her bunk and grabbed something before disappearing out the door.

I watched several other people pass by the opened door but waited.

When I believed the coast was clear, I rushed to use the toilet, my eyes glued to the open door for fear someone would see me. They didn't. No one passed by.

I washed my hands, only then remembering that I'd given away my bar of soap. I allowed the water to wash over them for as long as I dared.

When my stomach growled, I turned off the water,

stuck my copy of *Don Juan* in my pocket, then slipped on my new shoes. They instantly hurt my feet, and I changed back to the old ones.

Leaving my things on my bunk, I stepped out the door and looked around. I could hear the hum of many voices talking at the same time to the right of me and followed the sound until I stepped into a large two-story room.

There were more than two dozen long tables with attached benches arranged in rows in the middle of the room. Close to fifty women of all shapes, sizes, and ethnicities stood in line in dull gray jumpsuits, holding trays.

I made my way to the end of the line, picked up a tray, and waited my turn.

I didn't speak to anyone.

No one spoke to me.

I ate my tasteless breakfast and sucked down my burned coffee.

It flashed through my mind that I'd be eating tasteless food for the next year of my life, and I gulped in air and bit my lip to try and stop the flood of emotions.

I chanted in my head that it didn't matter, that I didn't care, until the flood of sadness dissipated.

I sat there until only a handful of women were left in the dining room. Most had left in large groups through a door at the end of a short hallway.

Every time the door opened, I could see sunlight streaming in.

When I was done eating, I took my tray to the tray return area and slowly made my way to the outdoor courtyard.

It was early spring in the Northwest, so though the sun was shining, the wind was cold, and I wondered if they would provide warmer clothes.

"Who you?" someone said behind me.

I turned to see a short young woman. She couldn't have been more than nineteen years old. One of her eyes shot off to the outside and was obviously not working properly. The other focused on my face.

I moved out of the doorway, believing this would end the conversation. It didn't. The woman took a giant step towards me, her eyes narrowing.

"I said," she spat out, "who you?"

"Chloe." I turned to move further out of her way.

Suddenly, my long ponytail was yanked back. My chin was raised to the sky as I flew backwards to the ground.

The woman held onto my hair, yanking harder than I'd ever felt before. Several strands popped out of my scalp.

"Who you?" the woman continued to scream as she jumped on my stomach and slapped my face. She scratched my hands and neck, any exposed flesh.

Flashbacks to all the times I'd been pushed, shoved, slapped, and hit suddenly boiled up inside me.

I'd given others everything I was.

Had everything taken from me.

They'd made me feel as if I deserved it. As if it was my burden. My sole reason for existing.

I'd never really learned to stand up for myself.

Well, I was tired of it. This had to stop. It had to end.

A low growl sounded from deep in my chest, and I screamed at the top of my lungs as I shoved the woman off me. I pushed her into the cold dirt and sat on her chest, holding her down just like she'd done to me.

My skin burned from where she'd attacked me, though I barely noticed.

I swung out—clawing, slapping, punching—until strong arms lifted me away.

As I was carried back inside, my eyes were glued to the destroyed copy of *Don Juan* lying in the mud beside the unconscious woman who had just attacked me.

I didn't realize I was still screaming until we passed through the dining room. My loud shrieking echoed in the large space.

I was mad.

I had obviously lost it. At this point, I no longer cared. My sanity was just one more thing that had been taken from me.

That thought had my mind sharpening.

I stilled. My body went limp as I was carried down another hallway and tossed unceremoniously onto a hard floor.

Without a word, the door shut behind me, and I was left in complete darkness. Alone.

I curled up into a tight ball, holding my knees to my chest and rocking back and forth.

I didn't cry.

I made no sounds as I lay on the cold ground, my clothes torn, my bruised body shivering with the chill.

I didn't care.

I felt nothing.

I didn't know how long I lay there. I didn't care. I slept for a while. How long, I had no clue.

My only thoughts were of just how dark it was in the room, twice as dark as my room the night before.

Several times, panic tried to creep into my mind. It screamed warning signs that I was blind. That I would never see again. There wasn't even a sliver of light from under the doorway.

Even though I couldn't see, I could at least still hear. Dull, faint sounds reverberated off the thick metal door.

My ears strained to make sense of the voices down the long hallways, trying to turn murmurs into words that I could understand. I gave up trying when everything outside grew quieter and more distant.

I didn't even try to explore the space. I didn't care how big or small it was. I lay there in the same spot they had tossed me until the door was opened.

My bladder was full thanks to the coffee I'd drunk hours before. Or had it been days? I didn't know how long I'd been in there.

My eyes hurt when I stepped out into the sunlight, and I had to blink many times to get them to adjust. I stumbled against the wall. Hands shoved me, and I walked like a blind person back down the hallway and once more into the dining room.

Again, there was a line. Without thinking, I picked up a tray and waited for my food.

This meal was a slab of lasagna with bread.

Dinner.

When I sat down this time, three others came over and sat next to me.

Two were skinny Caucasians, one old with jet black hair, the other a redhead who was around my age. The third woman was a petite Hispanic woman roughly in her forties.

"That was sure fun watching you take out Crazy Carlie," the redhead said. "I'm Sam, this is Lindy." She pointed to the older dark-haired woman. "And that's Rizzo." She pointed to the other one.

I watched them until she stopped talking, then I turned back to my food.

"Did they stick you in the hole?" Rizzo asked.

I glanced up and shrugged.

"You lose track of everything in there," Lindy said.

The three of them were eating and didn't seem to be too bothered that I hadn't spoken yet. They just continued chatting as if I was an active part of the conversation.

"In case you don't know, it's the same day. Dinner time," Rizzo said.

I nodded and continued eating. I wasn't even hungry, but I didn't know when I'd be able to eat again, so I figured I'd better finish every bite. What I needed was a bathroom. I didn't know if there were common ones or if I had to make my way back to my own room. It didn't matter. I'd been forced to hold it in before.

"Listen, we don't want you to get the impression that this place is all... crazy. Like Carlie. Sure, there are a handful of people you should steer clear of, but for the most part, we look out for one another in here," Rizzo said.

"At least in here, you can pick and choose your fights," Lindy added.

They grew quiet, so I lifted my head and realized they were all watching me.

"You made a statement earlier," Sam said, motioning with her spoon. "Ain't no one going to mess with you. Not after that show you put on. You knocked out one of Crazy Carlie's teeth."

I went back to eating my food as the three of them continued to talk like I wasn't there. Though I appeared to be the hot topic of the hour.

I was thankful they weren't demanding that I take part in their conversation. When I was done eating, I returned my tray and made my way back to my cell.

Thankfully, Lucy wasn't there, and I had plenty of time to empty my bladder and clean up. I flung myself on my bed and closed my eyes and allowed the entire world to drop off. I hadn't really slept in the hole. I'd just gone into a trance.

Somehow, I'd exited the space more tired than I'd been when I'd been shoved inside.

I woke later when something light landed on my chest.

"You should keep track of your things better," Lucy said, jumping up to the top bunk.

I blinked a few times and looked down at the destroyed book. She'd taken the time to clean the mud and dirt from the cover and had even taped the spine so that the book hadn't fallen completely apart.

"Heard you destroyed Crazy Carlie after breakfast," Lucy said with a chuckle. "I knew you'd have it in you to stand your ground." Her face appeared once more over the side of the bunk. "You made your point. I wouldn't go picking any more fights, though. There are a handful in here that you don't want to mess with. Trust me." She rubbed a bald spot on the side of her head before she disappeared up top again.

I sat in the bunk, silently reading Lord Byron until the lights went out.

I had officially survived my first full day in prison. I only had three hundred sixty-four to go.

CHAPTER TWO

> *"Each time dawn appears,*
> *the mystery is there in its entirety."*
> - Rene Daumal

I stood in the early morning sunlight, not quite feeling its warmth. I held the light jacket to myself, trying to keep out the cold wind that somehow blew through my entire body.

I had less than ten dollars to my name.

I didn't have a job.

I had no family or friends.

I was completely alone. Not a single person I knew had stayed in contact with me over the past year. Not that I'd had many friends to begin with.

I hadn't been allowed to have people close to me, lest they see through the web of lies and find out the truth.

But officially, my last name was no longer Meyers.

I was free.

Tossing the small bag with all of my possessions in it over my shoulder, I glanced to the right, then to the left.

Which way to go?

Without thought I turned my body to the sun and started walking.

In the past year, I'd realized that I had no idea where the correctional facility was. I didn't really know the area.

I still didn't care.

I still felt nothing.

I walked until my feet hurt. Then I walked some more. I grew hungry and tired. Thirsty. I continued walking.

When I came to the water, I thought of stopping or turning around. Then I noticed a ferry a few yards down the road.

I paid five dollars and eighty cents to cross Puget Sound and head to Whidbey Island. I'd never been on an island before. But I figured it was as good as any place.

One thing was sure—I no longer wanted to be in the city. In the last year, I'd heard horror stories from others about how bad the homeless situation had become in Seattle.

Women who had no place to go were being raped or killed. Many of the women in the facility with me had been caught on purpose, just to escape the nightmare.

It took half an hour to cross the dark water. By then, the sun had set and the warm spring sun had disappeared, leaving only the chill of the night.

Even if I wanted to go back, I couldn't. I no longer had enough money for the crossing.

I stepped off the ferry and glanced around.

There was a small park to the right, and I noticed a sign for public restrooms under a light. I made my way over there and used the facilities and washed up.

Since I'd showered earlier that morning and had braided my long hair back, it didn't take me long. There was no heat in the small room and somehow it felt even colder than outside.

There was a busy restaurant across the road, but I had no money, so I turned to the right and once more began walking. I didn't stop until I felt a pebble in my shoe. Only then did I sit down in the grass by the side of the road and pull it off.

Once I was off my feet, my body screamed for rest.

Tossing my backpack in the grass a few yards from the road, I pulled on my other jacket and shut down.

One thing I'd learned in the past year was to listen to your body. When it needed sleep, you slept.

I woke to the sound of a rooster in the distance. It startled me at first. I'd never heard it before.

Having lived in a controlled environment my entire life, I'd always believed it was a made-up thing. Roosters didn't really crow at the break of dawn.

Now I knew they did.

Somehow, the sound broke through one of those barriers that I'd been building up my entire life.

For a brief moment, I dreamed of having a rooster just so I could wake to the happy sound each morning.

Then a car passed by on the road, the sound of it jolting me back to reality.

Dusting myself off, I gathered my items and started walking again.

I didn't make it far before a truck pulled over. An older man smiled at me through the open window.

"How far are you going?" he called to me.

I glanced around, as if thinking.

"I'm heading to Greenbank. You can ride with me that far if you want," he called out.

What difference did it make to me? Here? Greenbank?

I climbed in the truck without a word. I set my bag at my feet and enjoyed the warmth of the truck.

"Thanks," I mumbled.

"Sure thing," the man said as he pulled back onto the road. "Everyone calls me Buddy."

"Chloe," I responded.

"Do you have family on the island?" he asked.

I lied by nodding my head quickly.

"Where? In Greenbank?" he asked.

"Further down," I lied again.

The man seemed happy with this answer. "Well, it's a good thing I came along. That's a long walk for a young lady such as yourself."

"I appreciate the ride." I looked out the window.

We passed trees, fields, and some small buildings. The view out of the window assured me that I was no longer in the city.

Less than fifteen minutes later, the old man pulled the truck off the main road and into a parking lot of what appeared to be a hardware store.

"This is my stop," he said, turning to me. His eyes ran up and down me. I'd gotten used to being assessed, only now, it was different somehow.

"Are you going to be okay, sweetie?" he asked me.

Somehow, the small endearment hit me in the center of my chest.

I nodded, no longer trusting my voice.

"Well, since you have a way to walk still..." He reached into the back seat of his truck and came back with a small brown bag. "It's my lunch. Take it." He handed it to me. "I can grab something at the diner." He smiled at me.

I took the bag, not wanting to argue. My stomach chose that moment to growl loudly.

"Thanks," I mumbled again and climbed out before he could see just how much his kindness had affected me.

Once more, I took off walking. I didn't stop until the hardware store was out of sight. Then I sat down on a guardrail and opened the bag.

There was a bottled water that I downed in less than a minute. An egg sandwich, a banana, and some string cheese. I devoured the entire meal in seconds.

If I'd been thinking, I would have saved something, maybe the banana, for later. Instead, I stuffed the empty paper bag into my backpack and continued walking.

By night fall, I hit a roadblock when the road stopped at water.

I had reached the edge of the island. I thought of turning around and walking back the way I had come, but once again made the mistake of sitting down.

This time, I was just past a sign that read Possession Point. The irony didn't escape me, even in my dulled state of mind. I had no possessions. Nothing.

I sat at the top of a small hill overlooking the water and watched the sun disappear. The moment the light was gone, so was the warmth.

I'd never built a fire in the wilderness before. I worried that it would draw the attention of a park ranger or that someone who lived nearby would call the police.

Was being homeless illegal on the island?

Who cared? Maybe then at least I'd be warm.

I pulled on my other jacket and slid on a second pair of pants. Nothing seemed to help.

Wouldn't it be summer soon? Why was it so cold?

I shivered as I lay in the grass with my backpack behind my head as a pillow. Every time I moved, the brown paper bag that the old man had given me crinkled. The sound was a reminder of the food I'd devoured hours ago, and my stomach began to complain.

Giving up, I tossed the backpack to the side. I cupped my hands behind my head and used them as a pillow. I watched the night sky, the stars flickering, the sliver of the moon rising higher into the emptiness of space.

Occasionally, there were blinking lights from planes that flew high overhead. Thankfully, I couldn't hear their engines from this far away.

The only sound was that of the insects buzzing around my spot.

I didn't mind bugs. I never had. I knew that most women hated spiders or crawling things. I didn't.

I had only ever been afraid of one thing in my life, but I was free of him.

"Beat, happy stars, timing with things below, Beat with my heart more blest than heart can tell, Blest, but for some dark undercurrent woe."

I played Tennyson's words over and over in my head as I counted the stars in the clear night sky until I fell asleep.

I woke with a jolt as a wet tongue ran across my face. I almost screamed, but then the dog's happy bark caused me to relax.

I sat up, and the curly haired yellow lab mix took my move as a hint and sat directly in my lap as it continued to lick my face.

Nothing like this had ever happened to me before. I couldn't help but laugh as I was happily assaulted by pure, unconditional love.

I held onto its soft fur, not knowing when my tears had started to fall from my eyes. I buried my face in its soft fur and held on as every last drop of emotion that I'd held locked inside poured free.

When I was done, the dog gave me one last kiss before jumping off my lap and running away.

I hugged my knees to my chest and rocked back and forth as I watched the sunlight dance off the water.

In that moment, I changed my mind. I no longer wanted a rooster to wake me each morning. I now desired dog kisses as my alarm clock.

Hearing some rustling sounds behind me in the grass, I glanced over and saw the dog return. In its mouth was what looked like a bright green ball. It moved towards me and then sat by my side. When it dropped the item into my lap, I stared in amazement at a small green apple.

Since it was early spring, I doubted the thing would be ripe enough to enjoy. My stomach growled loudly, causing the dog to tilt its head and look at me.

When I didn't pick up the apple, he nudged it with his nose several times.

Smiling, I lifted it up, wiped it on my sleeve, and bit into it. It was sweet and quite possibly the most perfect thing I'd eaten in my entire life.

"Thank you," I said to the dog once I was done eating it. I gave him the core, and he gobbled it up as if it was the best treat in the world. Then he turned and disappeared once more.

Standing, I stretched my arms over my head and eyed the water. I knew it would be cold. Yet, the part of me that screamed to be clean won out, and I took my things down the steep hill and started pulling off the layers I'd pulled on the night before.

When I stepped into the water wearing only the cotton bra and underwear I'd been given, I shivered once before diving headfirst into the crisp cold water.

As with the apple, the water felt better than all the showers I'd had on the inside. I untangled my long hair from the braid and used my short fingernails to scrub my scalp clean.

I had a small comb in my bag, the kind that men typically used. It would take me an hour or two to remove all the tangles, but I didn't care. I had plenty of time.

When I climbed out of the water, the sun was high above me. I lay down on the soft grass, letting its rays warm and dry me.

For the first time in years, I was happy.

That inner voice I'd grown to fear no longer screamed at me. I didn't have to fight to fake it. I might starve tomorrow, but today I took the small joy I had.

After a short walk in either direction of my hidden spot, I decided to spend the night there again. I wished for another apple but hadn't found any trees nearby.

Had the dog found the green apple from a tree close by? He hadn't been gone long, but when I looked, I hadn't seen any apple trees. Then again, I wasn't sure what an apple tree even looked like.

I assumed it would be full of green apples that looked like the one I'd had. I did find a bush with sharp pointy dark green leaves that had red berries on it. But when I tasted one, it was bitter, and I spit it out for fear it was poisonous.

What I really wanted was some water. I tried to sip the water that I had jumped into, but it had a funny taste, and I was reminded about a book I'd read once about toxins from big pharma companies being drained into the waterways.

Instead, I popped a button off my jacket and sucked on

it to stimulate saliva. That got rid of most of my thirst. It would do, at least for a while.

Tomorrow, I'd figure something else out.

I sat on the hillside and once again watched the sun sink in the sky. Only this time, once I was engulfed in darkness, the cold wasn't so bad.

Hugging my knees to my chest, I replayed the words from some of my favorite poems. Most of the ones I could remember at the moment were about the stars or the sunrise.

This time when I awoke, the dog was sitting over me, staring down at me.

When I opened my eyes, its tail thumped, and it dropped the apple right on my face. It hit my chin and fell to the grass beside my head.

I sat up and gave the dog a quick hug before cleaning off the apple and enjoying my breakfast. As before, I gave the dog the core and watched as it enjoyed the treat. While it was busy, I snuck a peak and found out that it was a boy.

He had no collar, no sign that he belonged to anyone other than he was extremely healthy and well fed. He was obviously someone's pet.

When he was done with the core, he sat beside me for a few moments before turning and rushing off.

I thought about following him, but I didn't want his owner to know I was there. If there was a house nearby, they certainly wouldn't want a homeless ex-con camping out near their property.

As with the day before, I spent some time bathing in the water. Only this time, I kept my hair dry by piling it on the top of my head. I was not going to spend another three hours trying to get the tangles out of it again.

As I was drying, I pulled out the worn copy of *Don Juan*

and read the book once more. I spent the rest of my day pretty much the same way I had the one before.

By the third morning, I was positive that the dog would be there again when I opened my eyes. When he wasn't, I instantly worried.

I had learned a lot over the past year. The number one lesson had been not to trust anyone. Well, okay, I'd learned that one long before stepping foot into a cell.

Still, I'd been foolish back then. Today, I was no fool.

I knew I needed water and food. I was weak from the lack of both. Whenever I stood up, everything went white for a moment until I blinked and bit my bottom lip so hard that I could taste blood.

I also had to check in with my parole officer by the end of the day, so I'd have to walk some more and find a pay phone.

I waited almost a full hour for my furry friend to show up. When he didn't, I tossed my bag over my shoulder and set off through the thick brush surrounding my hiding spot and back down the road.

It took me almost an hour of walking down empty streets, past the occasional home, before I luckily stumbled upon a convenience store.

They had outside bathrooms and the first thing I did was use the facilities and the hand soap to wash myself.

The tampon vending machine was broken and, thankfully, there were four tampons inside that I immediately shoved in my bag. There were also two rolls of toilet paper sitting on the back of the toilet that I took as well. The soap was in one of those liquid dispensers attached to the wall, so I had to make do with washing myself for the time being.

I refilled the water bottle that I'd saved from the old man's lunch three times and drank it dry. Then I filled it one last time and shoved it into my bag. I instantly wished I had several more bottles to fill up.

But now that I knew the bathrooms and fresh water were only a forty-five-minute walk away, I figured I could make the journey more often.

I spent a few minutes combing my hair and braiding it. I smelled and felt so much better. My reflection in the cracked mirror confirmed that I didn't look homeless. I looked like someone who had just taken a day hike.

Pasting on a smile, I walked into the store. The smell of burgers and fries hit me, and I almost doubled over with hunger pains. Then I noticed that to the side of the small store sat a diner.

Most of the tables were filled with people eating their meals and chatting. The noise was almost deafening after spending the last couple of days alone with only the sound of nature to keep me company.

"Can I help you?" the woman asked, glancing up from a crossword puzzle book. Her eyes ran over me cautiously.

She was middle-aged, slightly overweight. She wore a bright green shirt and had short matching hair. Each of her fingers had at least two rings on them, and her nails were also painted green.

I walked over to stand across the counter from her. "I was hoping you had a pay phone or maybe a phone that I could borrow?" I asked in a cheerful voice.

The woman's eyes narrowed. "There used to be a pay phone out front. I'm not sure it works anymore." She waved her hand to the door. "If not, I suppose you could borrow this one inside. Just as long as it's a local call."

"Thank you, I'll check outside first." I turned to go.

I'd been so excited about using a toilet and washing off, I hadn't looked for the phone.

When I stepped out on the front deck area, I realized why I hadn't seen it. It was at the base of the big sign that held the gas prices. Actually, the small half booth was part of the metal pole holding up the large numbers.

I lifted the receiver and relaxed when I heard the dial tone.

Using my last dimes, I dialed the number I'd been given for my parole officer.

I was only obligated to make the one call. The terms of my sentence stated that after my initial check-in, I wouldn't have to be on any kind of long-term parole. If this first call went well, I'd be good to go, so I'd practiced what to say.

Still, when the man answered the call, a bead of sweat rolled down my back as I lied to him about where I was. Yes, I told him, I had a place to stay. Yes, I had been looking for jobs. No, I didn't need any assistance.

I hung up, relieved that that part of my life was behind me. My last obligation for the crime I had not committed was over. I was officially freed from the hell that used to be my life.

I dug in my pocket and counted my change. I figured I would have enough for something small, maybe a bag of chips or an apple.

When I stepped back into the store, the woman was watching me.

"The phone worked. Thank you," I told her as I turned to slowly walk down each aisle. I was slightly shocked at how much everything cost. A small candy bar was more than a dollar.

Had items always been this expensive?

In the end I picked out a loaf of day-old bread and some string cheese. I paid while the green-haired woman eyed me cautiously. She looked at my change as if she expected it to bite her and then pushed it along the counter until it dumped into the drawer uncounted.

She didn't offer to bag the items for me. Instead, she turned to greet a newcomer who had stepped into the small store.

"Afternoon, Rod," she said with a bored tone. She turned back to her crossword puzzle as I gathered my items and stepped aside.

"Well, well, what have we got here?" a man's voice said, causing me to look up.

A large man roughly my age filled the doorway. His girth blocked out most of the light from the glass doors. I couldn't see his face clearly, but by the tone in his voice, I knew I was in trouble.

The man moved closer to me, his body growing larger and more intimidating as he drew nearer. I hugged my items to my chest and looked for my escape.

He didn't stop until he was a breath away from me.

"You must be new in town," he said. His smile would have appeared friendly if I hadn't seen the spark of something deeper in his eyes. His voice lowered so that only I would hear his next words. "I could show you around town. Maybe have a good time while we're at it?" He wiggled his eyebrows.

I sidestepped and tried to pass him, not wanting to respond.

His hand came up, gripping my arm tightly, blocking my escape. I tried to jerk it free and dropped my items, which he quickly stepped on. Whether by accident or not, my bread was now a smooshed clump inside the bag.

"Why don't you pick on someone your own size for once, Rod?" a deep voice sounded from the diner area.

I glanced over and, to my horror, saw that everyone in the diner was watching the show.

I didn't know who had spoken. I didn't care. Thankfully, Rod dropped his hold on me. I took that moment of freedom and sprinted out the door, minus my bread.

I ran until my lungs burned, until I felt myself on the verge of passing out. Then I ran some more.

Every few moments I'd steal a glance over my shoulder to make sure I wasn't being followed. That Rod wasn't coming after me.

I'd lived through hell once. I refused to do it again.

When I reached the safety of my hiding spot, I collapsed face-first into the soft grass.

I was so busy trying to catch my breath, I didn't see the apple at first. My sides hurt, my head hurt, and I desperately wanted to cry. But I'd told myself long ago that wasn't a luxury I could afford any longer.

Tears were for the weak. I no longer fit that description.

When I'd caught my breath, I rolled over and, seeing the apple, smiled. Suddenly, my heart felt lighter.

I'd never known anyone as kind or caring as the dog I'd befriended. Even though he was nowhere to be found, I knew it had been him who'd delivered the treat.

As I drifted off to sleep that night, I dreamed of him. My Byron. My rescuer. My only friend.

CHAPTER THREE

"Let every dawn be to you as the beginning of life, and every setting sun be to you as its close."
\- John Ruskin

Lane

There were a handful of people in this world who pissed me off. Every single one of my family members, and Rod Clarkson.

My childhood nemesis.

The guy had been a thorn in my life for as long as I could remember. Thankfully, I hadn't had to deal with him in the past eight years or so.

Either way, when I agreed to meet my grandfather, George Robinson, for lunch, I hadn't expected the day to go the way it had.

When I'd spent my summers on the island as a kid, I'd always loved the slower pace of the countryside. The

Robinson family was easily one of the most influential and powerful families in all of Washington State.

My grandfather had been a senator, my dad a judge, my uncle a congressman, my aunt one of the top state attorneys, my other aunt the secretary of the state. Other various distant relatives also held prominent positions that warranted the respect of others. We were the freaking Kennedys of the Northwest.

But behind closed doors, every last one of them was a sniveling asshat. Which was why they were on my shit list.

This last move of my uncles and father had only solidified my feelings for the men I barely had a phone call with once a year.

It wasn't that I was endeared towards my grandfather, George. During my life, I could count on both hands how many times the man had had a long conversation with me.

But then last year I'd noticed a change in my grandfather's attitude. He'd contacted me out of the blue and hired me shortly after he moved back to the island home. At our first meeting, I'd suddenly realized just how frail the old man was. How long had he been like that? My whole life?

A year before, I'd heard through the family gossip chain that my dad and Uncle Bobby, or Robert outside of the family, had forced him to move back to Whidbey Island.

The man was eighty-ish. Wasn't he? It was about time he slowed down.

But I couldn't help but wonder why they had wanted him to move far away. It wasn't as if my father and his brother had ever really taken an interest in their old man, even when my grandmother, Florence Clarkson, had been alive. For that matter, when she'd died from cancer when I was a teen, they hadn't shown much emotion.

Sure, there had been arguments between the brothers

and their sister and some other relatives over some of my grandmother's trinkets. A gold locket with the family's symbolic R on top. A painting. Various properties. A few stocks and bonds.

All of it should have gone to my grandfather, but somehow ended up being distributed among various family members instead.

This was my second visit to the island this week. I'd been here a handful of times since my grandfather had moved back. The fact that it had been less than a week since my last visit had raised a red flag with the rest of the members of my family.

Before the tires of my one-year-old BMW rolled off the ferry and hit the pavement of Whidbey Island, I'd received three calls and six text messages from various family members.

They believed I was, as they put it, brownnosing my grandfather. Vying for an advancement in the line of inheritance.

What I was doing was being pissed that my father and his brother would allow a man of my grandfather's frail constitution to live in such a secluded and massive place all by himself.

I had grown up summering at Possession Point for as long as I could remember. During the school year, my family spent our time in our home in Seattle. The same one my parents still occupied.

The day that I'd been accepted to Harvard was one of the best days in my life, as it meant I could put a great distance between the family and myself.

I don't remember exactly the moment I first thought I wanted to become a lawyer. I know that it had to do with my aunt Kate, my dad's older sister, who was a state attorney. I can't remember any of the details, but I think I was around six at the time.

I was a Robinson, which meant that my grades and schooling had taken priority over everything else in my youth.

It was a family tradition. We had a lot of those. For instance, when a Robinson boy turned sixteen, he received a gold ring with an R on top of it. I was the youngest of the boy cousins and had looked forward to receiving mine for years. Now, the thing sat in a box on my dresser, collecting dust.

When I finally returned to my home state after graduating at the top of my class at Harvard, I breezed into a prime position at one of the biggest law firms in Seattle, where I still worked today.

As I pulled into the convenience store parking lot, I saw a woman in gray pants and a dark blue hoodie step out of the store and glance around as if she were looking for something. For some reason, I watched her walk towards the edge of the parking lot and step into the telephone booth.

It wasn't strange to see someone on the island using the old phone. It was probably the only pay phone for a hundred miles. Still, there was something about her that made me want to watch.

The way she held herself reminded me how long it had been since I'd gone out on a date. It wasn't as if she walked provocatively. But even though her clothes were worn and a little dusty, there was a natural beauty about her that caught my attention. It was like stopping to appreciate the shine and glow from a raindrop as it fell in the sunlight.

My eyes followed her until my grandfather's old truck pulled into the parking lot next to my car. I climbed out to greet him.

Just like every time I saw the man, his frailty shocked me. I rushed over to help him climb out of the driver's side door and instantly wondered if he should be driving himself.

"There now," he said, patting me on my shoulder. "I can manage well enough on my own. Thank you."

I dropped my hands, knowing better than to oppose my elder's wishes.

"Yes sir." I followed him up the wooden stairs. He moved slowly, as if each step pained him.

How many times had I been in the convenience store in my youth? My cousins Phillip and Derrick and I would ride our bikes up here when we were bored. Sherry and Tiffany would try to keep up with us on their pink bikes.

I smiled at that memory and my heart ached. I longed to return to those simple times as we stepped through the glass doors.

It didn't surprise me to see Jessie McGould still sitting behind the counter of the store, working on her word puzzles. What did surprise me was that she didn't look a day older than when I'd been young.

Back then she had been a bored teenager sitting at her parents' business. She had green hair and nails now, but otherwise she hadn't changed much.

When we passed through to the diner area, I noticed her eyebrows draw up slightly with recognition. I decided not to give her a chance to catch up and followed my grand-father into the diner quickly.

Grandfather chose a barstool near the doorway, and I sat next to him. He looked comfortable enough, as if he'd been there many times since returning to the island.

I wanted to ask him how he was, if he had hired

someone to look out for him, but we just ordered our drinks and remained quiet.

But then I heard Rod Clarkson's voice. As memories of all the times the larger boy had bullied me flashed in my mind, I watched the now much larger man use his size to intimidate the woman I'd seen outside moments before.

He scared the woman so much that she'd dropped her loaf of bread and her face had paled.

I don't know what made me jump up from my seat and storm the few feet towards Rod and bark out, "Why don't you pick on someone your own size for once, Rod?"

Maybe it had been the sheer look of terror in the woman's eyes. Or maybe it had been because, despite that, she'd raised her chin just a little, enough that I knew she wouldn't have backed down from a fight if Rod had been her size.

Most likely, it was the memories of all the times Rod had used his size and strength against me, and I'd had no one to stand up for me.

Now, I knew that I could probably punch Rod out, even with his larger girth.

I was no longer the skinny teenager. I was a twenty-eight-year-old man who spent hours in a gym and a boxing ring each week. I no longer feared bullies.

The blonde woman took advantage of the distraction and rushed past Rod straight out the door. I was so occupied watching her go, that I missed the first swing aimed right at my head.

Rod's punch had my head snapping back quickly, and I tasted blood. That just pissed me off. Not because he'd caused me to bleed, but because I had dropped my guard, something I'd told myself I would never do again.

I easily dodged his second blow. The man moved like he

was in molasses. He raised his thick arms and pulled back as his fists bunched. His swing was so wide that it lost most of its speed and strength by the time it passed three inches in front of my face.

I smiled as I ducked the next blows, easily dancing away from the man's reach.

"You've gotten slow in your old age," I teased. Rod's face turned beet red. "You should just give up your lifelong career of being a bully."

"I hit you once and I'll easily do it again," Rod barked back.

"You sucker punched me," I said with another smile as I swiped the blood from my lip. "It won't happen again."

Rod's eyes narrowed. "You and your family were always cocky shits that needed to be knocked down a few notches."

"And you've always been nothing but a bully. Praying on the smaller and weaker just to make yourself feel strong."

Just then, the store's door opened, and two officers walked in.

The island had a handful of police and sheriff departments on it. On the south of the island, there was one of each.

I was slightly shocked to see Alex Everette in uniform. Alex was a few years older than I was, but we'd always hung out together back in the day.

The other man with him, Officer Oliver Whitlock, I also remembered very well. The older man had busted me and my cousins plenty of times back when we'd sneak onto the school grounds to shoot basketballs. It was the only court for miles around, and we had never understood why it wasn't available to us to enjoy in the summer.

Seeing the two uniformed men, I took a giant step away from Rod and lowered my hands to my side, easily dodging

his last swing as the two men watched with both amusement and annoyance.

"That's enough, Rod," Officer Whitlock growled,
getting Rod's attention.

"I didn't start it," Rod complained as he spun around to
face the officers.

I couldn't stop the quick burst of laughter, which I was
happy to see pissed Rod off again.

"He got between me and a woman. I was about to get
her number."

"Rod," Officer Whitlock sighed, "there isn't a woman on
the island that would let you get near her on purpose."

Rod's fist tightened, but he jerked his massive body
towards the door. Officer Whitlock laid a hand on his
shoulder and stopped him from leaving. Then he looked in
my direction. "Since we can all see that he hit you, I have to
ask. Do you want to press charges?"

For a moment, I thought about saying yes. I was a
lawyer, after all. And Rod's family had plenty of money,
which they'd had to use to bail him out of jail numerous
times. I'd heard a few rumors from my cousin about just
how many times he'd been in trouble. But I didn't want to
be labeled as the sniveling big city lawyer who couldn't take
a punch.

"No, not this time" I said with a sigh, and Rod stormed
out the door.

"Well, shit, look who it is," Alex said, slapping me on
the shoulder. "Lane Robinson. I thought that was you." He
flipped the collar of my white button-up shirt with a finger
and added. "It was hard recognizing you in the monkey suit.
Last time I saw you, we were jumping off the pier in our
underwear."

I laughed, remembering the fun that we'd had, then my

smile slipped at the memory of that last summer I'd spent on the island. The one before my childlike innocence had been ripped away and I was forced to grow up very quickly.

"Right." I nodded. "So, you went into law enforcement?" I motioned to his uniform as Officer Whitlock walked over and sat in one of the booths.

"Yeah, after everything... I was drawn to helping others." He glanced over my shoulder, then motioned back to the dining area. I followed him into the dining area. "I hear you went into the law as well, in a different way," Alex said, sitting across from his partner.

I had gone into law, but that last summer I'd spent on the island hadn't really played a factor in my decision to do so. If anything, for years after, I felt discouraged about becoming a lawyer.

I sat down next to my grandfather, who had watched the entire display with curiosity in his eyes. The old man had never been the kind to stick his neck out for anyone, least of all a stranger. At least he didn't berate me like he would have done when I was a kid.

I was only here today because of what he'd said over the phone to me after our last visit, a visit that had troubled me. It was clear to me that the stroke had had a more lasting effect than my family had let on.

I could see that Alex was eyeing my grandfather.

"I hear you're back on the island full time, Mr. Robinson," Alex asked.

My grandfather swiveled the barstool around and narrowed his eyes at Alex.

"You that Everette boy? The one that was always getting my boy here in trouble?" my grandfather asked, and I held in a chuckle.

Alex smiled. "Sure am," he said proudly.

"I see you're on the right side of the law now," my grandfather joked.

My family members weren't monsters. I could tell that my grandfather had meant it as a joke. In the past, there would have been a hint of truth just to cause a slight sting to the recipient.

Everyone laughed, but then the conversation fell away as we all ordered food.

I knew that my grandfather wouldn't have the private conversation we needed with the two police officers sitting behind us. I'd only met him at the diner to try once more to convince him to hire someone to look out for him.

His house was massive and now that he was living there all alone, I worried. Especially since the reason he'd been forced to move was because of the small stroke that he'd had the year before.

My family didn't deal with medical problems well. Not after my grandmother's fight with cancer. They deemed it below them to watch someone in the family suffer. It was like they thought that if they didn't see it, they themselves wouldn't be affected in the future.

It hadn't taken long for my uncle Robert and his wife Reba to move into my grandfather's home in the city. They'd basically taken over the property within days of moving my grandfather into the summer home on Whidbey Island.

My uncle was a congressman, but he would have done whatever was necessary to beat out the rest of my family and take over the home. At last look, the place had an esti-mated worth of more than ten million dollars.

Still, I knew for a fact that the property in the city wouldn't be going to my uncle, father, or aunt after my grandfather's death, which was a huge relief. I was the only one in the family who knew this information, and I kept it to myself.

It had surprised me when my grandfather had contacted me last year and hired me to oversee his financial accounts. I'd heard a few stories about how he'd made the choice after a nasty fight between his three kids about something trivial. I hadn't heard any more details, but the three siblings were still not on talking terms.

The responsibility of updating my grandfather's accounts had put a target squarely on my back for the rest of the family to aim at. In that first month after he'd hired me as his estate lawyer, I'd been contacted by each of my family members, some I had never even met before.

I handled everything except his will, due to the conflict of interest. One of my coworkers in the firm handled that instead. I trusted Lee Steinbeck and apparently so did my grandfather. He'd hired him more than twenty years back, which was the reason I'd looked at working for the firm after graduating from law school.

All of my family members had tried to pry information out of me about my grandfather's wishes and financial status. Some had even tried to convince me to go to the courts and claim that my grandfather wasn't fit to care for himself any longer.

Most of them just called to bitch that I was involved in the matter instead of them.

My grandfather had been an ass for most of his life. Up until that strange phone call last year when he'd hired me out of the blue.

On the call, weeks after his stroke, he'd mentioned that he'd made a huge mistake. He wanted to make things right but didn't know how.

When he'd come into my offices downtown for our first

meeting, we'd had the first real conversation I could remember in my entire life.

Since then, we'd had plenty of others. The more I had met with him, the more I'd seen the changes he'd made.

If I wasn't careful, I'd actually start looking up to the man soon.

"Did you get my last changes?" he asked me as he finished off his coffee.

"I did." I turned slightly to run my eyes over him. He'd opened a new account and had closed several others, moving the money from accounts in the city to the smaller bank on the island. Others in our family had found out he'd moved the funds. I knew this because they had called me about it.

Even though he was old, he was still a damned good-looking man. All of the Robinsons were. It was the jawline. I pushed my empty plate aside.

"Are you sure about this?" I asked him.

"I am." Grandpa nodded. "It's easier to get cash now." He laughed. "Besides, now they won't get their hands on my money so easily. They've somehow had access to it for years. They don't deserve a dime of mine." He looked sad.

I'd sat in on the last meeting between my grandfather and Lee, the one where my grandfather had struck every last family member out of his will with the exception of three people—including me.

"But leaving everyone out," I started, but he cleared his throat, a sign that he didn't want to talk about this in public. I lowered my voice. "They could contest it."

He laughed, a loud booming sound that had me smiling.

"Let them." His eyes met mine. "You and Lee will represent my estate and my wishes. Besides, that's why we moved everything into a trust."

"Trusts can still be contested," I pointed out.

"It'll just be more money for you and your firm to make when they do. Smart people have always made money on the stupidity of others."

I nodded and then decided to change the subject.

"Have you thought about my request to hire someone to come in and lend a hand?" I asked.

"I have and my answer is still no," he said clearly. Then he surprised me by laying his hand over mine. The frailness of it shocked me. His skin was thin and had many freckles on it, no doubt from all the summers he spent out on the water. "I can take care of myself."

"I still think hiring someone to come in once a week..." I dropped off when he raised his eyebrows at me. "Don't look at me like that. I'm worried."

"You're the only one in the family who is." He tapped my hand. "Which is why you're my favorite."

"You can't stand me any more than you can stand the rest," I joked.

His eyes turned soft for a split second before he turned around. "Now, pay for our meal. It's time I got back and had a nap." He stood up.

It bothered me that he wobbled when he stood. I promised myself that I wouldn't go another week without coming up here to check up on him. It was a long drive and ferry ride, but it could be counted as work time because he was technically a client.

In the last few years that I'd worked at Seattle Law Group, I'd thought about leaving. How had I allowed myself to stick around so long?

One year had turned into two, which had turned into more. It wasn't where my heart was, but it certainly paid the bills, allowing me to live in my thousand-plus-square-foot townhouse. Not to mention it afforded me my new ride.

After watching my grandfather's truck pull away, I headed back to the ferry dock. Without thinking, I took the front road instead of the back one I normally took.

When I slowed down at the pond, I knew the reason I'd come this way. Knew in my heart that it was past time I stopped to pay my respects.

The pond sat between the main part of town and the gas station. Most people didn't even really know it was there.

I did and I normally did everything I could to avoid driving by it.

All these years I'd felt guilt and anger, but I now understood that my anger should never be directed at the person who had paid the ultimate price. My sister.

It wasn't her fault I'd suffered all those years ago at my family's hands. I had always vowed that one day I would find out what had happened on that late summer evening. The day that had caused my entire life to change. The reason I'd been charged with murder at the tender age of sixteen.

CHAPTER FOUR

"For each thorn, there's a rosebud... For each twilight - a dawn... For each trial - the strength to carry on, For each storm cloud - a rainbow... For each shadow - the sun... For each parting - sweet memories when sorrow is done."
- Ralph Waldo Emerson

Chloe

Somehow, I survived. Days went by and eventually turned into a full week. Thankfully, I'd found a large blackberry bush not far from my new home. The berries were still red and very tart, but they nourished me, along with my daily apples from Byron, who was my only friend, my steady rock.

I didn't like to think what would happen to me if he stopped coming. If he didn't show up every day. I didn't walk to the store. I wasn't going to make that mistake again. Besides, I was out of money.

I thought of calling my parole officer back and asking for

help. Thought of walking to the local government office and filling out the paperwork I'd heard about on the inside that would give me food, money, a voucher for a place to live for a few days.

I thought a lot about returning to the city. Trying to find a way to get off this island. I knew there was a bridge that connected the island to the mainland, but I didn't have a map or a phone, so I had no idea where it was or how far away it was.

I grew much weaker. At this point, I doubted I could even make the long walk to the little store again.

Thankfully, it had rained a few times, and I'd been able to collect some rainwater. If I rationed it, it lasted me a few days.

I began to lose track of the days. I believed I was on my second week when Byron suddenly showed up in the middle of the day.

He'd been there earlier that morning, and we had shared our apple like always. Now, however, I could tell there was something wrong.

He rushed over to me while I was reading *Don Juan* once again and started to pull on my sleeve.

"What's up?" I asked him, knowing he couldn't answer. Still, I liked to talk to him. My voice was the only voice that I heard every day.

I was shocked at how lonely I had gotten in the silence.

When he continued to tug on my sleeve, I stood up. He then tugged on my pant legs until I took a step forward. Then he did a little jiggle, barked, and started off across the tall grass, stopping occasionally when I didn't follow him fast enough.

I was so focused on following him, I didn't realize I still had my book in my hand until I came to an old iron fence archway. I tucked the book into my pocket, afraid that I'd set it down or lose it.

The wood fence on either side of the archway was newer and stained a warm honey color.

The archway itself appeared to be thirty or forty years old. Someone had built the new fence around the intricate iron gate.

I could see thick vines growing up each side of the arch and meeting overhead. Come spring and summer, there would likely be colorful flowers to appreciate as you walked through the opening.

Byron rushed through the open gate and across a well-manicured lawn. Most of the flower beds were just now starting to grow and bloom. The warmer weather in the past few days had signaled the yard to rebirth.

I stopped at the gate. I knew that I couldn't afford to be caught. If I took another step, I would be trespassing, which meant that I'd be breaking the law. Technically, for the first time.

I turned to go back, but Byron rushed over and grabbed my pant leg again, pulling and tugging on it until I moved forward once more.

"Hello?" I called out as I went. I was hoping to have a chance to explain why I was on someone else's property.

I moved slowly, only taking a step when Byron tugged hard enough. A few steps past the gate, the trees opened up, and a house came into view. I couldn't help it, I gasped at the beauty of the home.

The trim was a stark white while the rest was painted a soft sky blue. Actually, more of a gray mixed with sky blue. Was that called robin's egg blue?

Byron tugged again. and I took another step forward, my eyes focused on the back of the house. I was afraid that at any moment someone would step out and shout at me.

The home reminded me of a cottage, only much bigger. Two stories. I moved slowly past a cute circular firepit with six huge chairs set around it. There was a wide covered patio off the back of the house with a long table and chairs underneath.

Byron was growing more determined and stopped several times to bark at me.

Large glass doors filled most of the back of the home, allowing anyone inside to pretend they were outside without being in the elements.

I tried to push the memories of my own past comforts out of my mind as I stepped onto the stone patio.

Byron stopped pulling and rushed through the opening in the glass doors. Then I heard him bark, only this time he didn't sound annoyed. This time he sounded... desperate.

"Hello?" I called out, stepping up to the glass doors.

It took a moment for my eyes to adjust, but then I noticed the small, crumpled figure on the floor just a few feet inside the doorway.

Crying out, I rushed forward, no longer thinking.

Byron sat at the man's side, watching me.

Carefully, I turned the older man over and noticed a small gash on his forehead. The man groaned and slowly opened his eyes.

"Are you all right?" I asked, running my eyes over the rest of him to make sure he wasn't injured anywhere else.

The man just blinked at me, and I could see that his eyes were adjusting and focusing on my face. I hadn't bathed that day. Actually, I couldn't remember the last time I had washed.

I probably had grass in my hair and dirt on my face and

hands from lying in the field. My hair was so tangled that I'd given up braiding it.

If I'd had a pair of scissors, I probably would have chopped all my hair off.

"Who?" the old man asked, then groaned.

"Easy," I said, looking around for something to clean the blood. "It looks like you had a fall." I found a hand towel on the countertop. I used it to dab at the blood, but it was too dry. "Hang on," I said, standing up to look around. There was a massive sink in the middle of a wood island, and I rushed over and wet the corner of the towel. When I returned, the man was sitting up and leaning against the cabinet. "Here," I said, gently moving his hand aside so that I could clean the cut. "How are you feeling?" I asked, wanting to see if he was coherent.

"Fine," he said with a sigh. "I tripped." He motioned to a pair of shoes. "I should have put them away."

I glanced around, worried that someone else might be home and come in to see the scene. My hands had blood on them, and an outsider might believe I'd hurt the old man.

"Is there someone here that can help you?" I asked, returning my gaze to him. "Someone I can call?"

"No." He waved his hand and looked a little annoyed. "I can tend to myself," he said with a stern voice.

"I have no doubt of that," I agreed. "It's just..." I glanced over at Byron, who sat between us, looking worried. "Byron is worried. I think he'd prefer someone look after you until you can assure him that you're okay."

"Byron?" The man frowned.

I motioned to the dog. "Lord Baron Byron. At least that's what I call him. He came and got me, basically dragged me here. He wouldn't stop pulling or barking at me until..." I suddenly dropped off, feeling stupid that I'd rambled on about the dog leading me to him.

The man looked over to the dog and then surprised me by laughing.

"I suppose that names suits him better than Dog," the old man said with a chuckle. He turned to me, and his sharp eyes ran over my face, my hair, my clothes.

I shrank back a little. Afraid.

Since gaining my freedom, it was the first time someone had looked at me. Really looked. The man's eyes somehow pierced through my outer shell and bore into what was hidden beneath.

I felt tears sting my eyes once more and cursed myself for being stupid.

I knew my time of being undiscovered had just come to an end. I'd have to move on now. Which meant no more daily apples. No Byron to talk to. Sadness flooded me so quickly, so powerfully, I swayed as I knelt beside him.

"Who are you?" the old man asked.

I stood up quickly, ready to leave, but then the old man tried to stand up and almost fell on his face. Moving quickly, I took his arm and helped him into one of the chairs at the table.

"Your name?" he asked. I could hear the energy drain from him.

"Let me call someone to help you," I urged.

He waved his hand. "I have no one who would care." He stilled. "Well, one. But he's too far away." A sad look crossed the man's face. "You." He pointed at me with a crooked finger. "Name?"

I looked down at Byron, who had laid his head on the old man's leg. The old man was gently scratching between the dog's ears, as if this was their normal interaction.

Dogs were excellent judges of character. If Byron thought the old man was trustworthy, then at least I could give him a name.

"Chloe," I finally answered. "Chloe Dawn."

The old man nodded once. "George Robinson." He grew silent for a moment. "What do you think about helping me out? Just for the rest of the day, mind you. I'd pay you," he added after I took a step back towards the door.

My heart leaped. For just one beath. Then, reality came crashing back.

I shook my head and started moving towards the door quickly. I stopped when Byron rushed over and blocked the doorway, almost tripping me in the process.

I heard the old man chuckle. "See, even Byron wants you to stay. Come now, girl. You've said it yourself. Someone should look out for me." He motioned to his head. I could see a trickle of blood oozing from the cut.

"You should call an ambulance," I said, not moving.

The man waved that suggestion off. "I'm fine. I just need someone to lend me a hand. At least for today." His eyes narrowed at me. "You haven't got anything better to do today, have you?"

I thought about returning to my spot. Reading my book once again. I'd lost count of how many times I'd scanned the pages. Was it possible to grow bored reading a story you loved and knew by heart?

"You can start by finishing making my lunch." He motioned towards the kitchen. "While you're at it, make yourself a sandwich too."

At the thought of food, my stomach growled. Loudly.

The old man smiled. George. He'd said his name was George.

"Hurry now, girl. I'm hungry, and from the sounds of it, so are you," he said with a grin.

I lifted my chin. "First, do you have a first aid kit? You're still bleeding," I said, making up my mind.

If he was going to give me a sandwich and not call the police, the least I could do was clean him up and make sure he was all right.

"In there." He waved his hand towards a hallway. "Under the sink in the bathroom."

Taking one last look at the glass doors, I took a deep breath and turned towards the hallway.

The kitchen and living space were connected with a short half wall that sat between them. It was topped with a warm wood that was filled with rows and rows of framed photos.

I moved through the beautiful kitchen with its marble countertops and soft cream-colored cabinets. The middle island was the only surface different than the rest of the space. Its warm wood color matched that of the kitchen table and floors perfectly, as if they'd all been made from the same tree.

Passing by the large stainless-steel refrigerator, I stepped into a wide hallway. To the left was a huge walk-in pantry, stocked with so much food that I felt almost faint at the thought of eating it.

To the left was the powder room. I stepped on the soft gray and white rug that covered the hardwood floor. The walls were painted a cheerful yellow, and there was a large, framed painting of bright purple flowers hanging over the toilet.

I was about to look under the sink for the first aid kit when I caught a glimpse of myself in the mirror and gasped.

No wonder the old man, George, had been staring at

me. I had been fooling myself into believing that I continued to look almost normal. I had known my hair was a rat's nest. But the rest of me...

The only good thing about living outdoors was that my normally translucent skin had a soft glow to it, thanks to those sunny days. I was by no means tan, but at least I wasn't as pale as I'd been the last time that I'd seen myself in a mirror.

I had dirt and grass stains everywhere. My eyes looked hollow and sunken into my face. Dark rings were obvious through my light skin.

I turned on the sink and quickly washed my hands. I didn't want to get the man sick because of the dirt that was caked under my nails. I was shocked at how much dirt washed off and instantly wanted a shower to clean off the rest of the grime.

I knew he was waiting for me, and I was worried about the amount of blood he'd lost already. Leaving my reflection, I gathered up the first aid kit and returned to kneel beside him.

He sat perfectly still as I cleaned up the cut, watching my movements as if he was still trying to figure me out.

Now that I'd seen myself in the mirror, I knew it was obvious to anyone what I was. I was a homeless woman that was half starved, dehydrated, and desperate.

"There," I said after putting a small bandage over the cut. I'd finally gotten the bleeding to stop. "Head wounds always bleed a lot," I assured him when I gathered up the gauze and towels that I'd used to clean the blood up.

"Thank you," he said. "You can toss all that in the trash." He motioned towards the pantry.

I dumped the soiled items in a large metal trashcan. My eyes landed on a box of granola bars and for a split second, I thought of grabbing a few and stuffing them in my pockets. After all, he wouldn't notice if one or two of them disappeared. Right?

Then I closed my eyes and took a deep breath. I was better than that. I didn't break the law.

I took a giant step back and left the temptation.

"I like my sandwich with extra mayo on it," George said from the table.

I walked over to the island and stopped briefly to wash my hands again. There was a loaf of bread, the really good and expensive kind that had the little seeds on the top with the extra crispy crust, and the slices were so thick you couldn't see through them. There was also a small container of real turkey and some really good yellow cheese, American or cheddar. I lifted a slice up and smelled it. It was cheddar. I held in a groan when my stomach growled.

There was a jar of expensive mayonnaise and a jar of chilled pickles. It all sat on the island along with a cream-colored square plate, a cutting board, and a knife.

I made George his sandwich, moving like a chef would, slowly, methodically, until it was a piece of art in front of me. When I was done, I cut it diagonally and placed a pickle slice next to it.

"There are chips." George waved towards the pantry. "I like a handful of the onion and chive flavor." He sighed. "I'll have some cranberry juice too. It's in the fridge. Glasses are to the left." He waved towards a cupboard.

After gathering everything he wanted, I set his meal in front of him and waited.

He looked at the sandwich and smiled. "Perfect. You even cut it right." He looked up at me. "Well, make yourself one. There's no reason I should eat alone."

I moved quickly, afraid that he'd change his mind.

I mimicked his meal exactly, only this time I rushed. When I set my plate and glass down across from his on the table, I looked down at Byron. "What about Byron? Does he get lunch?"

George chuckled. "He's had his breakfast and snack." He leaned ever so slightly towards me. "He enjoys a nice green apple every morning after his meal. It keeps his teeth clean and breath smelling better than most of those dog treats I buy him." He winked. "He takes it off somewhere to enjoy." George's gaze turned towards the glass doors, and I watched sadness flood his eyes. Then he blinked and returned to look at me. "Please." He motioned to the food. "Enjoy."

I swallowed the lump in my throat. Should I tell him that Byron had been bringing me the apples each morning? I looked down at the dog, who was looking up at George as if his world centered around him.

I felt my stomach growl again, so I picked up the sandwich and took a bite.

There had been a handful of times in my life when it felt like the world shifted under me. This was one of those times.

I had never tasted anything as amazing as that simple sandwich. Even the chips, a flavor I'd never appreciated or enjoyed before, tasted amazing.

When I tried the pickle, I had to hold in a groan of sheer pleasure.

Had food always tasted this incredible?

"How long has it been?" George asked me.

I glanced up and then realized that he'd stopped eating and had been watching me eat.

I felt my face heat, my throat close up. It was obvious

what he was asking me. I didn't want to answer. I hated appearing weak.

"You don't have to tell me." He tilted his head. "Are you hiding from a man?" he asked. When I didn't answer, he sighed. "The law?" I blinked, then shook my head.

"Myself," I answered and was horrified as a tear slipped down my cheek and landed on my sandwich. The bread soaked up the moisture quickly as I dashed another tear from my face.

"Do you have a place to stay?" George asked. I glanced towards the glass doors. The room grew quiet. "My grandson has been bothering me to hire someone to help out around here," he said, picking up his sandwich and taking another bite before looking at me again. "The problem is, I can't stand people," he said with a low chuckle. "That is why I got a dog." He motioned to Byron. "They don't demand things from me other than food and attention. And, most importantly, they don't talk back."

I swallowed and folded my hands in my lap, digging my long nails into my palms. I wanted to finish my food but sat still and listened to him as he continued.

"I'm old, but not a complete invalid. But I can see some benefits of having someone around." He took another bite of the sandwich. "Can you cook? Clean? Do laundry?"

I nodded slowly.

He ran his eyes over me again. "There's an apartment, over the garage." He looked down at Byron for a moment. "I have a change of clothes, if you need."

I looked down at my grimy clothes. I'd tried washing them, but since I didn't have soap, the stains hadn't disappeared. I nodded, not meeting his eyes.

"Good, it's settled then. After lunch, you can head up and pick out what you want from the closet upstairs, then go out and get settled. I eat dinner at six sharp. There's plenty of groceries stocked up. Choose what you want to make. I'm not a picky eater." He continued to eat his meal.

When he was done, he pushed his plate aside. "I don't tolerate thievery. But something tells me that won't be an issue. I'm a really good judge of character," he said with a sigh. "Now, if you'll help me to the sofa, I'll take my afternoon nap while you clean up."

He started to get up, and I rushed over to help him stand. He smiled and patted my hand. "See. I'm an excellent judge of character," he said again as I helped him over to the sofa. He grabbed a book from the coffee table and settled down.

I briefly wondered if the bump to his head had caused his judgment to be off, but then I dreamed of showering off and finding some new clothes to wear. The possibility of having regular meals and someone to talk to outweighed my fears at this point.

Leaving him and Byron on the sofa, I made my way back into the kitchen and cleaned up. I put the food back where it belonged. I washed the plates and glasses, dried them, and returned them to the cupboard before wiping down the chop block countertop of the island.

Once I was done, I tucked the chairs in at the table and made sure everything was in order. When I went to check on George, he and Byron were fast asleep on the sofa. The two of them looked so comfortable together, I knew this was their daily routine.

While I sat out in the grass, reading my book, they had been tucked here, napping happily together. That thought made me smile.

George had mentioned there were clothes upstairs but

had neglected to say which room. Should I go poking around?

He'd told me I could stay in the rooms above the garage. I glanced towards the back windows and could see the other building tucked in the corner of the yard. There wasn't a car sitting out front.

The garage sat on the back part of the lot. There was so much of the home I had yet to see.

I glanced around and wondered what to do. I could just barely see the staircase and front door from the living room. There was a circular hallway space with doors on either side that separated the two spaces and opened up to the front of the home.

Leaving the two of them asleep, I made my way to the front of the house and stopped at the base of a very impressive two-story circular staircase. The railing was the same warm-colored wood as the flooring in every space on the main floor of the home.

It was worn in places, like by the front door and at the base of the stairs. The rugs appeared newer and were in soft grays, whites, and deep blues that matched the outside paint almost perfectly.

To the left of the front door sat a formal dining room. A wood table with eight high-back leather chairs filled the space, along with a hutch that matched the top of the table. Windows looked out over the long driveway off the front of the home.

I hadn't realized until now how secluded the home was. I couldn't see a road or any other homes from any of the windows.

To the right of the front door was a large office with a massive wood desk and cabinets. There were comfortable looking black leather sofas and chairs facing the desk. When

I turned to leave the room, I saw the walls of bookcases and held in a gasp.

I ran my fingers over the spines and silently dreamed of reading them. Later, I thought. The possibility of showering and putting on some new clothes had me turning away from the shelves.

I climbed the circular staircase, trailing my hand on the smooth wood banister. At the top, I stood on the highest stair and frowned down at the bright white carpet. Then I looked at my worn sneakers, which were caked with mud and grass stains.

I toed them off and realized my socks were no better. I leaned on the railing to steady myself and pulled them off as well. At least my bare feet were cleaner.

Leaving my shoes on the top stair, I turned to the left and made my way down the hallway, opening each door as I went. The first one was to a large bathroom filled with light colors and bright colorful paintings. The second was to a smaller bedroom that was obviously a guest room and had an empty closet.

The next room had a large dog bed at the side of the king-sized bed and clearly belonged to George and Byron.

Not wanting to disturb his personal space, I shut the door and turned back towards the stairs.

On the other side of the balcony, to the right of the stair-case, sat three more doors. As with the other side, the first door was a bathroom that matched the other almost perfectly. The next two doors were bedrooms. The first was a very male looking space. It looked much like the guest room except this one had several personal items. The closet had male clothes in it, none of which would fit me.

The last bedroom, however, had soft pink walls, a cream-colored bedspread with pink pillows, and several other feminine touches around the space. I made my way to the closet and was happy to discover a closet full of women's clothing.

Instantly, I noticed that it was all an older style, as if it had been sitting in the closet for the past ten years.

Since he'd asked me to stay in the rooms off the garage, I figured I could bring the clothes out there and see what fit. I found a gym bag on the floor of the closet to use.

I took several pairs of jeans, a couple shirts, and a sweatshirt and sweater that I believed would work. I didn't dare hope to find any underwear or a new bra. Those items seemed too personal.

There were, however, several tank tops with sewn in bras, so I grabbed a few of them instead.

I also found a couple of pairs of shoes in my size—white tennis shoes and slip-on sandals—as well as clean socks that had been shoved in a box at the bottom of the closet.

After packing up what I thought would work, I turned and saw a framed picture sitting on the dresser. Setting the bag down, I picked up the white flowery frame and stared at the picture. The two people in it looked like brother and sister.

I could tell the photo was from years ago. The clothing and hairstyles were dated.

The girl, a muddy blonde, had braces and just a hint of womanhood peeking through her girlish charm.

My own youth had been far more controlled than this girl's. Actually, I couldn't remember ever being young.

I closed those thoughts out, pushing them away as I switched to assess the boy.

The brother was obviously older, maybe already sixteen, whereas the young girl was closer to thirteen or fourteen. I tried to block out the memories of what I'd been going through at the young girl's age—changing from sister and daughter to wife, homemaker, servant, slave, prisoner.

In the picture, the boy had already grown into his manly charm. His arm was flung over his sister's shoulder casually, a gold ring on his finger a symbol of his wealth. He had a smile and a look in his eyes that said trouble. His sex appeal was strong enough that anyone not related to him would have drooled and grown weak at the cocky smile.

I swallowed hard, wondering if I would have ever fallen for someone's charms. I'd never been given that opportunity.

Setting the frame down, I turned and looked at the room once more.

Now it was obvious. This was her room. Something told me that she hadn't made it much farther in life than that picture.

I looked at her face once more.

"Thank you for letting me borrow your clothes. If I can, I'll return them to you soon," I promised softly.

Then I picked up my bag and walked out.

CHAPTER FIVE

*"What humbugs we are, who pretend to live for beauty, and
never see the dawn!"*
- Logan Pearsall Smith

Lane

I had never once considered just how conniving
my family was until I received a phone call from my parents
inviting me to dinner one Friday night.

Actually, scratch that. They didn't invite. They
demanded that I show up.

If I'd had anything better going on, I would have
declined. As it was, I wasn't in the mood to argue with them
and accepted the invite.

I had been stuck in meetings for most of the week and
only had one chance to call my grandfather to check up on
him. He'd sounded happy enough, and we had chatted
almost a full hour before my phone buzzed with another
call.

When I parked at my parents' home, the home I'd spent most of my youth in, I took several deep breaths to try and settle myself.

Since returning to Seattle, I'd learned to limit my contact with my parents. There were fewer arguments about... well, everything, this way.

I parked behind my parents' new SUV and rushed through the rain to the shelter of the front porch.

How many good times had I had under this very cover during a rainstorm? Too many. My first kiss was with Laura Summers right here. Or maybe it had been Becca Landry?

Out of respect, I rang the doorbell before entering.

My parents were already in the dining room, sitting at the table sipping wine. They looked at me as if I was late, even though I was five minutes early.

My uncle Robert and his wife Reba were on one side of the table with Aunt Kate and her husband Donnie on the other.

My uncle Robert and my father looked nothing alike, which always threw everyone off. Robert was shorter and had jet black hair and very Italian features. Reba was petite and blonde, with no real features that stood out or offended, as I'd overheard my uncle say many times.

I glanced around and realized they'd left me the open chair across from my cousin Phillip. He was a year older than me and roughly twenty pounds heavier. Other than that, we could have been brothers in the looks department.

Derrick, my other cousin, who was two years older than I was, was currently in Vegas. No doubt selling something.

My only female cousin, Tiffany, was probably at home with her husband Mark and their newborn son, Johnny.

I'd had no clue that the family would be there tonight, which probably meant this was a family intervention of sorts. Most likely a chance for them to gang up on me and complain about how I'd been handling grandpa.

Taking another deep breath, I walked over, kissed my mother's cheek, handed her the bundle of flowers that I was obligated to purchase for her whenever I was invited into her domain, then sat down in my designated spot.

My mother was a beautiful person, at least on the outside. She always wore the top designers and at no point in my memory had she not had perfect hair and nails.

"It's good that you can finally join us," my father said, his eyes narrowing. It ate at me how much I looked like my old man. Twenty-four years from now, I'd look like that.

I opened my mouth to remind him that I was five minutes early but knew better. My father wouldn't let it go if I argued with him. In his house, he was always right. "I ran into traffic," I lied. He smiled and nodded quickly.

"Robert and Phillip were just filling us in on their plan for Robert's reelection," my mother said, her eyes urging them to speak as Lita, my parents live-in helper, started serving dinner.

For as long as I could remember, there had been someone in the house lending them a hand. When I was younger, it was a nanny of sorts that would shuttle me and Sherry to and from school, practices, or play dates. After I'd grown up, she'd become a full-time chef and maid. Now, Lita did it all, organizing everything around the house.

My parents no longer lifted a finger. Hell, half the time they didn't even talk to one another. Lita acted as a go-between. Why they remained married was beyond me. Then again, they'd probably kill one another fighting over how to split their wealth. We were a real *War of the Roses* sort of family.

"Yes." Robert spoke first. "We were just saying that this time, it would help to have Dad's support."

I held in a groan.

"The old man's just rotting away up there on the island," Phillip added as he sipped his wine and then moved aside for Lita to deliver his plate. My cousin didn't even say thank you. Instead, he appeared annoyed about the distraction. "We're thinking about having him do a couple interviews. Maybe showcase his donations, some highlights of—"

"You got grandfather to agree to donate to the campaign?" I broke in.

I knew better. My grandfather's stand on politics had never wavered. After all, he was an ex-senator. Since his retirement from the seat almost ten years earlier, he'd never once wanted to wade into the field again. He'd made that very clear the first time my uncle had run for Congress.

"Well, no, not yet," my uncle said slowly.

"That's where you come in," Phillip said, motioning with his wine glass.

"Me?" I asked, once again holding in a groan.

"Sure. Everyone in the family knows that the old man has a soft spot for you. I mean, ever since—"

I felt the table move and heard Phillip grunt as someone, most likely his mother, kicked him under the table.

"He moved back to the island, a recluse," Phillip continued after a heartbeat. "You're practically the only one in the family that he talks to."

That was the truth. I'd witnessed it firsthand. My grandfather ignored everyone else's phone calls. At least he did when he was around me. I assumed he did the rest of the time as well.

I leaned aside as Lita set my plate down. "Thank you,

Lita. This looks amazing," I told her. She beamed at me, and I wondered if it was the first kind words she'd heard since taking the job. I turned back to my family. "You want me to convince Grandpa to donate to your campaign and then go on several interviews backing your run?" My uncle and cousin nodded at the same time. I laughed and shook my head. "There is no way in hell you could convince me to do that."

I knew better than to curse, especially at my mother's table and under my father's roof. Still, no other statement would have been strong enough to project my disdain for the idea.

"Lane," my mother warned.

"Son," my father said at the same time.

"I told you he wouldn't do it." Phillip sighed as he took another drink.

In the past year, I had come to wonder if my cousin was drinking too much. Every time I saw him, he was either downing a drink or stumbling away from a drink.

"I don't see why you won't just make the call?" my uncle said.

"We've all tried," my aunt Kate added, getting my attention.

"You've all..." I broke off, a little disgusted at the idea that they had all tried to convince my grandfather to give them money and help in promoting his youngest son's bid to remain in the House of Representatives. I knew that two years ago, my grandfather hadn't agreed, nor had he during my uncle's first term two years prior to that. "No." I shook my head. "He has made himself perfectly clear. I won't bother him." I picked up my fork and took a bite of the salmon.

"Now, Lane," my mother said in that tone she always

got when she was about to try and convince me that what she wanted would be best for me.

"No, Mother," I said a little more firmly. I set my fork down. "I don't think any of you understand just how fragile Grandpa is."

I watched a few eyebrows raise at this news. The last time anyone at the table had seen him was almost a year before.

I knew for a fact that no one traveled up to the island to visit him. I doubted they even called him unless they wanted something. Usually, money or for him to endorse them during some crazy endeavor.

Besides the lot of us looking like siblings instead of cousins, the only thing we had common was that we had all spent most of our childhood summers on the island.

While I had gone into law like my aunt, Phillip worked with his dad, only because no one else would have him. He was too lazy for any real job. He lied often and wasn't even good at it. Plus, he was basically the dumbest person in the family. I was convinced his parents had paid for his grades when he'd been enrolled at Washington University.

Phil's hair was longer than my own and he was about two inches shorter. Other than that, we could have been brothers.

My oldest cousin Derrick was at least a little smarter than Phil and, according to many, the best looking out of the gang. Even if he could never commit to a career, he always had a line of women. He spent most of his time hawking whatever product was trending online. He'd join in the noise online to sell or promote it until things fell through, then he'd change to a new product. He was always looking for the next thing that would make him rich and famous. So far, nothing had. Yet, he always managed to drag most of the family into his scams.

The three of us boys were each a year apart from one another. I was the youngest, which had put a target on my back for the older boys to aim at. I had been thankful when they finally graduated and left me alone.

My youngest cousin Tiffany was the real genius in the group. She'd graduated top of her class and had started medical school, only she'd fallen madly in love with her husband Mark, whom she'd met her first year at college. The pair had quickly married and when she'd found out she was pregnant with Johnny, and she'd dropped out of school to support Mark so he could continue his education. Instead, he'd flunked out of school and sat around playing video games most of the time.

Even though Tiff was beautiful, petite, and easily the nicest one in the family, I suspected Mark was having an affair, possibly many of them. I'd tried to warn Tiffany, but she would always change the subject.

Phillip had been married briefly to Olivia, who had taken almost everything from him. He'd moved back in with his parents, and the divorce was another reason he was now working for his dad.

"Just how fragile is the old man?" Phillip asked.

I glared at him. "Don't count your inheritance just yet," I warned.

No matter what my grandfather hired me to do, there was no way I would let it slip who was inheriting what. I didn't really know all the details, but I knew enough. Besides, it was far easier on me to let them all think they would each get a slice of the pie. One way or another, I'd have to deal with all that eventually.

"Maybe I should head up to the island and have a lunch

meeting with the old man myself?" Phillip said, rubbing his hands together.

"He won't see you," my dad said firmly. "He won't see any of us. I've tried."

Phillip just shrugged and poured himself some more wine.

At this point I was over the conversation and tried to eat as much of the good food as I could. I wanted to leave and knew I wouldn't be allowed to if my plate wasn't cleaned. I continued eating while my family argued the pros and cons of trying to visit the island themselves. They all acted as if it was a trip around the world instead of a fifty-minute drive.

Hell, most of them probably drove longer to get a cup of coffee.

When my plate was cleared, I finally broke in.

"I'm heading up there next week." Everyone stopped talking and turned to me. I knew that if I didn't promise to say something to my grandfather that he would most likely be bombarded with visits he didn't want. I didn't believe that they would wear him down, but I was worried about what all the stress would do to his health, so I reluctantly added, "I will mention that you are looking for his support."

My uncle smiled and nodded. "Thank you, Lane. I knew I could count on you."

I stopped myself from rolling my eyes. I remembered the time my uncle had shouted words of accusation at me over all the others. Then there had been his harsh whispers and small jabs aimed at me for years after. I'd learned long ago to ignore them, which somehow made my uncle seem proud, as if he'd gotten away with the hurt.

My cousin had never imitated his father's behavior, but had instead always looked at me strangely, almost as if he believed without a doubt that I had been guilty. As if it gave him some great joy to believe I was capable of something so horrific.

Actually, the rest of my family had acted like that around me too. Ever since that summer day.

After I agreed to talk to my grandfather, the conversation changed to gossip, another thing my family did well.

I excused myself not long after and drove back through the city to my townhouse.

In the past few years, work had been my mistress. I went out on the occasional date, but I hated dating apps. Hated trying to arrange to meet someone only to find out they had only gone out with me because they'd found out who I was and how influential my family was.

When I pulled up outside my place, I held in another groan. Amber Morris stood just outside my townhouse, leaning on the door and looking bored.

We'd had an on-again, off-again relationship for over a year, and I'd officially broken things off with her almost three months ago. We'd continued to be physically involved when convenient. Tonight, was neither convenient nor wanted.

"Amber," I said, getting her attention. That was another thing about Amber. She was into social media too much. Her parents were wealthy, and she deemed herself a star online. Everything we'd done when we'd been dating had been for show. She would take so much time setting up photo shoots of our food that it would be cold by the time I took a bite. Hell, one time I caught her taking a picture of me in the shower. Thankfully, I'd been able to stop her before she'd posted it. If I hadn't forced her to delete it, I was pretty sure the entire world would have seen my junk.

"There you are, Lane," Amber purred. She smiled at me as she tried to wrap herself around me.

Okay, so she was still sexy as hell. No one would blame my dick for responding quickly to someone it had enjoyed many, many times. Still, my mind wasn't on the same wavelength as my dick, so as I unlocked my door I said, "I have an early meeting."

Not once since moving into the place had I given out my door code or key. I didn't trust easily, and, in this area, I was very strict. I stopped Amber from following me inside. "Sorry."

She pouted and then stomped her foot slightly. "I already tagged that I was staying here tonight."

"So untag," I added dryly. "Goodnight."

I didn't feel bad about shutting the door in her face. Not when I knew she lived a few blocks away and most likely would call an Uber to take her to her next boy toy.

After locking myself into my own private space, I felt like kicking something.

My grandfather's constitution might be strong as a horse, but I was a freaking colt with no backbone. My family had known that if they threatened to visit my grandfather, I would intervene.

I should have kept my mouth shut. After all, I would wager that none of them wanted to make the trip up to see him. My parents hadn't been back to the island since...

I sat down on my sofa and held my head in my hands.

Sherry. They hadn't been back to Whidbey Island since Sherry's murder.

Closing my eyes, I rested my head back on my worn leather sofa and stared at the ceiling.

I didn't know what hurt more, remembering my younger sister's smile and laughter or the last memory I had of seeing her—broken, bloodied, her skin the color of ash. Her eyes had stared up at me up at me, hollow and pale.

Shit. I jerked up off the sofa and went into my closet to change into my gym clothes. I jumped on my treadmill and ran until I almost collapsed.

It was the only way I could get those last images out of my mind. To rid my memories of those days behind bars, having to explain and re-explain where I'd been while someone violated and murdered my sister. Explain how, even though she hadn't died by my hand, it had been my fault anyway.

The rest of the week I worked longer and harder than I normally did. That was usually the case after I'd had a run-in with my family. I was thankful that at least there wouldn't be another request for dinner from them for a while.

I arrived home one night the next week to see Derrick sitting outside my place. I wanted to turn around and get back in the car, but I agreed to go to a bar down the street and have a few drinks to listen to his latest sales pitch.

"I tell you, man," Derrick yelled over the band that was playing in the corner of the bar. "This is the one. This is how I become rich and famous." He slapped me on the back and waved to the waitress so he could order more drinks.

I remained quiet, knowing how Derrick worked. His pitch windup took most of the night while the actual throw lasted seconds and always fell on deaf ears, as I'd stopped listening hours before.

I wasn't looking to invest in anything Derrick had going. Ever. I had, to this date, never invested a penny in anything he sold.

As he droned on about the company and the product, he kept drinking and his self-esteem grew. This was typical of my family. They loved themselves more than anything or anyone else. Add a dash of liquid confidence to the mix, and you had a Molotov-cocktail effect.

By the time I helped carry him to the cab, he was ranting about becoming the next Elon Musk or Bill Gates.

I sent him on his way and walked the block and a half back to my own place. I thought about spending the next few days on the island. I had enjoyed a few nights up there since my grandfather had moved back after we'd worked late hashing out details of the changes he had made to his estate.

In the last year, we'd moved all of his assets into a trust, a smart move for someone as old as he was and for someone with so much wealth and property.

The following morning, I woke up at dawn, packed a small bag, and hit the road. I stopped at my favorite coffee place on the way and grabbed a box of apple fritters to munch on during the drive and to share with my grandfather when I arrived.

During the ferry ride, I received a couple of text messages I didn't respond to and some emails I did answer before turning my phone to do not disturb. I tried to do that whenever I stepped foot on the island.

I wasn't there to work. I went there to escape.

I parked in front of my grandfather's garage and noticed that the yard work had been recently done, which must mean it was officially spring.

Seeing the yard pruned and clear of dead leaves reminded me even more of my summer days there.

I remembered lying under a large oak tree, the smell of the salt water, and the sound of the waves lapping the shore, and was transported back to my youth.

I'd really had a great time here each summer. Maybe I'd

talked myself out of it because the last days here had been tainted.

Facts were facts. I loved this home. When the time came and grandfather was gone, I was really going to miss coming here.

I was walking from the garage to the back door, which was almost always unlocked and the way I usually entered the house, when I heard a woman's laughter. The rich sound was followed by one quick happy bark from my grandfather's newest addition to the household, Dog. Then I heard my grandfather's laugh and tensed.

Who was with him? He didn't normally have anyone over.

I followed the sounds down the pathway that led through the tall grass and exited on the beach.

There, near the water's edge, my grandfather sat in a beach chair under an umbrella. Dog was running around chasing a blonde woman, who was laughing and tugging a rope, trying to get it away from the dog.

The sound of my grandfather's laughter had me frowning. I couldn't remember hearing that noise since that last summer. I had talked myself into believing the man didn't know how to laugh and that any memories I had of the sound had been a dream.

Dog spotted me first. He immediately stopped playing to race across the sand and jump up on me. I'd worn jeans and a T-shirt, so I didn't mind. I was normally there in a suit and would limit our interaction to pats on the head.

"Hey, buddy," I said, giving the dog attention.

"There you are, my boy," grandfather said cheerfully.

I straightened when Dog went back to racing around the sand. Keeping my eyes on the blonde woman, I moved over to stand next to my grandfather.

"Grandfather," I said. I motioned to the woman, who was standing still, her eyes shielded behind a pair of sunglasses.

It was then that I noticed she was wearing familiar clothes. The bright pink T-shirt with the words Kim's Last Stand had my fists clenching. I even recognized the jeans she was wearing. The hole just above the knee was from where Sherry had fallen off her bike that last summer. I'd had to help her remove the material from her bike chain.

"What the hell," I said, storming towards the woman. "Who are you?" I demanded. "And what in the hell are you doing in my sister's clothes?"

I would later play over the encounter in my head many times and realize my mistakes. How the woman's face had paled. How she'd been too thin, too tiny, too fragile.

But for now, I plowed through angrily at this stranger for breaking into my sister's room and taking her things.

I barked at her and threw my hands up in the air as I accused her of things that I was ashamed of even then.

In the end, what made me stop was seeing her crumple at my feet and land in the sand.

"What have you done?" My grandfather got up from his chair and marched across the sand. "Help her."

I glanced between my grandfather and the small pile of woman at my feet. Dog stopped racing around the sand and rushed to the woman's side, licking her face and trying to wake her.

I knelt and shifted her easily into my arms, only then realizing that she weighed less than she should. Far less. There was no way she was over a hundred pounds. Why the hell was she so skinny?

"Bring her back to the house," my grandfather said. "Hurry, get her some water. I'll be along."

I paused, worried about him walking across the sand and through the tall grass, but he waved me away. "Go," he said sternly with a wave.

I marched back through the tall dune grass, across the freshly cut grass in the yard, and in through the open glass doors.

I laid the woman down on the sofa and ran my eyes over her. She looked vaguely familiar. Where had I seen her before?

Her long blonde hair was tied back in a braid that lay over her shoulder. Maybe the familiarity was because she was in my sister's clothes?

She was pretty, there was no denying it. Gorgeous even. Her eyelids were closed, showcasing long lashes that I realized were long without the aid of extensions or mascara like all the other women I knew. Actually, she wasn't wearing any makeup whatsoever. She was a natural beauty.

How many women in my past could I say that about? Many times I'd woken the morning after hooking up, feeling like I'd been catfished the night before.

It was a great mystery to me why so many women piled on makeup and clothes to make them into something they weren't. Another reason I'd been off the dating circuit in the past few months.

My lack of trust in people was now bleeding into my sex life.

However, this woman was different. Even though she was too skinny for my taste, there was something that immediately pulled me in. And it wasn't the fact that I'd yelled at her until she'd passed out. That vulnerability somehow pissed me off. How had she gotten this way?

More importantly, what was she doing hanging around

my grandfather? Most importantly, what was she doing in Sherry's clothes?

When she stirred slightly, I stood up and headed into the kitchen to get a glass of water and returned just as she was sitting up.

"Easy," I said when she flinched and jerked away. I held out my free hand, then slowly held out the glass of water towards her. "Who are you?" I asked after she'd taken it and took a sip.

"I..." she started.

"She's helping me out, like you suggested. I needed someone to do some things around here," my grandfather said from the doorway.

CHAPTER SIX

*"Night is always darker before the dawn
and life is the same, the hard times will pass, everything will
get better
and sun will shine brighter than ever."*
- Ernest Hemingway

Chloe

When I watched the man cross the beach, my heart stopped. It was instantly obvious to me who he was. I'd stared at the picture of him and his sister so many times over the past few days.

He was older now. More masculine, more handsome, more... powerful.

Something that instantly put me on guard.

In the past two weeks, I'd enjoyed my time with George and Byron. The older man was no burden to care for. His company was easy, much like that of the dog. His kindness was more than I'd ever felt from another human being before.

The cut on his head healed quickly, which assured me his health was better than I'd expected.

After the first few meals, he'd thrust more responsibilities my way. I now arranged and managed the grocery lists and deliveries as well as delt with the landscape maintenance crew that had come earlier that week to care for the yard.

I'd found a small patch of tilled dirt in the corner of the yard, and George informed me that there used to be a garden there. Long ago. The sad look that had crossed his eyes hinted that it had been his wife, Florence, who had tended the land.

George often got that same look when he mentioned his deceased wife. I had yet to learn much more about her death, or that of the young sister whose clothing I was borrowing. I didn't like to pry and worried whenever the sadness overtook George, so I would quickly change the subject to something happier.

I didn't know what had caused me to pass out when George's grandson had berated me. Maybe I hadn't eaten enough that morning? Maybe my body just needed to shut down for a while? That morning was the first time my body had relaxed enough that my period had started again.

It had been almost six months since I'd had it. The doctors that I had seen had seemed annoyed that I was concerned and hadn't tried to find the reason. They'd blamed stress or had tried to convince me I was just looking for attention.

Either way, I was happy to know that, at least in this area, my body was getting back to normal.

Then the grandson had yelled at me and suddenly everything had narrowed, like I'd been going into a tunnel.

I have never passed out before and now, sitting on the sofa sipping a glass of water, I realized I never wanted it to happen to me again.

It was obvious that he'd carried me all the way back to the house from the beach, which was humiliating. I didn't like being vulnerable.

Then he'd asked me who I was. Thankfully, George had appeared at the back door and answered for me, since I was having a difficult time piecing any words together.

"Chloe, this is my grandson, Lane. Lane, Chloe. She has been kind enough to deal with me for the past two weeks and I rather think we're getting along wonderfully." George moved into the house to sit at the table. "Fetch me some water, boy." I moved to get up, but George shook his head. "No, you stay put. Since my grandson seems to have plenty of energy, he can tend to me until you're feeling well enough again."

I relaxed back and watched Lane walk into the kitchen and get George a glass of water.

"You hired someone?" Lane asked softly, no doubt wishing the conversation between the two of them was private.

I wanted to retreat to my room above the garage but felt strongly that I didn't want to be pushed out. What if Lane convinced George that he didn't need me? What would I do then?

Even feeling as weak as I did now, I knew that I would fight for myself, for the job, if I had to.

"I did and our arrangement is none of your concern," George said firmly. "Now, are you staying for the night?"

I tensed at that thought.

Lane was quiet for a moment, and I felt his gaze almost burning my skin.

"I'm staying for the weekend," Lane answered quickly.

"Good, then you can cook tonight. I believe Chloe added some steaks to the last grocery delivery…"

"I did," I answered quickly.

"Good." George smiled. "Then you can grill out tonight," he said to Lane. "For now, why don't you go and help Chloe up to her room. I'm sure she needs the rest after the scare you gave her."

Lane opened his mouth, no doubt to argue, but George gave him a look and he shut it, then nodded.

When he moved over to stand next to the sofa, I stood, hating that I wobbled slightly.

Lane's hand came out and gripped my elbow to steady me. I wanted to jerk free, but I doubted I could stand without the help.

"Here," George said, holding up a green apple as we passed by him. "This will help you feel better."

I smiled and took the apple. "Thank you. If you need—"

"My grandson can tend to me. You rest and feel better," George interrupted. He touched my hand briefly.

We made our way outside and across the pathway that led to the garage.

"You're staying above the garage?" Lane asked.

I nodded. "Your grandfather wanted me close," I lied. Well, actually, it was the truth. The older man had schooled me on what to say to any of his family members should they come knocking.

That seemed to pacify Lane, who remained quiet as we climbed the outer stairs.

I'd been shocked that first day when I'd walked outside and had seen the rooms George had offered me. I'd been expecting a small bedroom, like the guest rooms upstairs in the main house. Instead, what I had been greeted with was an entire apartment, complete with its own kitchen and small sitting area.

There was a king-sized bed with a soft down comforter in bright blue colors. The old leather sofa in the sitting area was so comfortable, sometimes I took naps there instead, falling asleep while reading one of the many books George had allowed me to borrow from his study.

Even though the bathroom didn't have a bathtub, I spent a lot of time taking very long showers and sitting on the tile bench, just letting the water flow over me.

Thankfully, there were large bottles of shampoo and conditioner, which helped with the untangling of my hair.

I'd thought several times about cutting my hair, but then worried that I'd botch the task. I had never cut my own hair before. I would have never been allowed to cut it.

When we stepped into the apartment, I stilled, hoping Lane would return to his grandfather's side and leave me alone. Instead, he followed me inside and glanced around, as if looking for proof that I'd done something wrong. Maybe proof that I'd stolen more of his sister's things.

"I only borrowed this outfit because George insisted," I told him.

Lane's eyes jerked back to mine. He seemed to take in my words, and I watched him visibly relax.

"I didn't mean to scare you." He pushed his hands through his hair.

It was the one thing on him that had changed drastically. Instead of a muddy blond color that had matched his sister's, his hair had darkened into a rich warm brown. He wore it shorter on the sides and longer on the top instead of the shaggy style of his youth. He also had stubble on his face, as if he hadn't shaved that morning.

I wasn't sure how to respond to him, so I nodded and sat on the sofa. I hadn't expected him to continue standing by the door, watching me.

"Later, when you're feeling better, I'm going to ask you for your work history. Even though my grandfather has made it very clear to me that it's none of my business. I will also warn you," he said, as he moved slowly towards me.

Shivers ran up my spine in fear of another bombardment of words from him. Instead, he sighed heavily and closed his eyes for a brief moment, as if trying to get himself back under control. Almost like he was afraid he'd scare me again. But I probably misread that. No one had cared about that before in my life.

"My family can be... difficult. If any of them come here, I'd like you to contact me." He reached into his pocket, pulled out his wallet, and handed me a business card. "If possible, without my grandfather knowing," he added as I took the card.

I nodded once and held onto the card as he turned towards the door. Then he stopped, his hand on the doorhandle, and looked back at me. I could tell he was about to say something else, but then he shook his head and said, "I'll see you at dinner."

When I was alone, I set the card down on the table, placed my feet up on the sofa, pulled the blanket over me, and fell fast asleep. I was drained. The short time I had spent playing with Byron on the beach had sucked what little energy I had.

Even though I'd been there two weeks, my body kept acting as if I wasn't getting enough food. My energy level was less than it had been when I'd only had an apple to eat each day.

Since there wasn't a scale in either the house or the garage apartment, I had no clue if I'd gained or lost weight. I was betting the latter, as the pants were much looser than when I'd first put them on.

My health was no longer something I had the leisure to worry about. After all, affording a doctor's visit now was as possible as me going to the moon.

When I woke a few hours later, I showered and dressed in dark gray cotton pants and a white blouse, which were once more taken from Lane's sister's closet.

It was funny. In the time I'd been there, George had never mentioned his family. Never talked about them except to say that only one of them was deserving of his time and kindness.

I now assumed that was Lane.

The way George had talked to him earlier was evidence of that. Sure, he'd been stern, but underneath his tone, there had been kindness. Much like the way he talked to me.

I took a little longer doing my hair, drying and curling it with the blow dryer and iron that I'd found in one of the upstairs bathrooms.

There had been makeup there too, but most of it was too old to salvage. But I had found some lip gloss and mascara that was still good, and I applied some before heading down for dinner.

Lane stood on the back patio at the grill in shorts and a T-shirt. The smell of the steaks hit me, and I felt my stomach growl. Thankfully, I was still out of earshot of them.

"There she is," George said cheerfully. "How are you feeling?"

"Rested," I answered with a smile. "I'm sorry if I worried you." I sat next to George, who was sipping on a soft drink. He'd told me that he allowed himself one a week, but this was his sixth soda since I'd been there.

"Lane, get Chloe a soda." George waved his hand.

"I can—" I started to get up, but George put a hand on my arm. "Sit, let me have a look at you." He turned towards me, running his eyes over my face. "You're too thin," he said as Lane set a cold soda in front of me.

"I know." I sighed. "The last time I saw a doctor, they didn't seem too worried. Then again, it was a male doctor and some of the things I was worried about..." I suddenly realized I was giving too much away and shut my mouth. "They didn't think it was an issue."

Both men were looking at me, waiting for me to say more.

"Those steaks will help," I joked, wanting to lighten the mood.

Lane turned back to the grill as George patted my hand again. From there, thankfully, George began asking Lane a series of questions. I had no idea who they were discussing.

Byron came and laid his head on my lap and then spit out one of his balls. I tossed it across the yard until the food was set on the table.

Steaks as big as my head filled the plates, along with baked potatoes and grilled asparagus. I ate every single bite.

It was only after I was finished that I realized Lane hadn't accosted me with questions. George must have warned him not to bother me. Or maybe he felt guilty about me passing out earlier.

Either way, I wanted to assure him that it had nothing to do with him. Well, maybe a little, but not enough that he should be afraid to talk to me.

For the entire meal I could tell he was actually avoiding talking to me, even though I could feel his eyes on me whenever I wasn't looking in his direction.

After everyone was done eating, I got up and started clearing the dishes. George excused himself to head up to bed, leaving me along with Lane. I tried to busy myself by cleaning up, but as I started washing the dishes, he appeared beside me and took the wet dish from my hands and started drying it.

I was shocked. I'd never seen a man willingly lend a hand around the kitchen. I had seen men grill meat over an open fire, but never had any man in my life so much as washed a dish, let alone dry or put them away.

"What?" Lane asked with a slight frown on his lips.

"I..." I blinked a few times and tried to swallow the shock of the situation.

Lane shrugged. "You look as if you've never seen a man doing dishes before."

"I haven't," I answered too quickly.

Lane smiled. "The magical dish cleaning fairy that comes to my place each day doesn't fly out this far," he joked and, suddenly, I was more relaxed around him.

We worked side by side cleaning up, and I had to admit, when he dried the last dish and put it away, I was sad and worried at the same time. Now what?

I'd never had an easy time being around attractive men. Okay, truth. I'd never had an easy time being around any man.

All the men in my past had caused me pain and made me feel small. My past experiences should have warned me away from all men, but they hadn't. I still felt my heart flutter whenever Lane's hand brushed mine. I still laughed at the jokes he tossed in my direction, jokes that weren't meant to belittle me, such as was the case in my past.

"I saw some brownies in the fridge," Lane said, leaning against the counter. "What do you say we grab one each and head out to sit around the firepit?"

I watched him serve up two huge portions of the brownies that I'd made earlier that morning, then he took a bottle of red wine from the wine rack that was built into a cupboard and grabbed two glasses.

"You take the brownies, I'll grab the wine," he said as he motioned to the plates.

I took each plate and followed him to the door. He nudged the glass door open, and Byron followed us outside.

Lane set the wine and glasses down before turning on the gas firepit, then he sat down next to the chair I'd taken. He poured the first glass and then said, "My grandfather has requested that I not ask you any questions." He handed her a glass.

"And?" I asked, before taking a sip.

"And," he said, slowly as he sipped some wine. "It's been years since I've gone against his wishes, but I have to know some of the basics."

I'd expected as much. After all, the past two weeks had been more wonderful than I could have ever imagined. If it ended now, at least I had some money to get back to the city. What I would do then, I had no clue. "Okay," I finally said. He could ask, though I may not answer.

He leaned back in the chair and watched the fire for a moment.

"Do you have any experience caring for the elderly?" he asked.

"Yes," I answered easily.

"Is this your profession?"

"No," I answered as I took another sip of wine. So far so good.

"What is your profession?" he countered.

"I've been both a cook and maid," I answered, only hiding a little of the truth. I had never been paid anything for my time. Actually, I'd never been paid for anything I'd done in the past. That hadn't been allowed. The tasks had been my duty. The only thing I'd been made for.

Lane seemed to take my answer in and toil over it for a moment.

"How did my grandfather find you?" He shifted slightly until he was almost facing me.

I took a deep breath. "He didn't. Byron did." I motioned to the dog. "He pulled me off the beach, and I found your grandfather lying face down on the dining room floor. He had a small cut on his forehead." I touched the spot on my head. "I cleaned it and patched him up. When he refused to let me call someone, he agreed I could stick around so I could watch him for the rest of the day."

While I conveyed this, Lane sat up straight and set his wine glass down. Worry flashed behind his eyes.

"Why didn't you call an ambulance?" he asked, his tone sharp.

"Your grandfather wouldn't let me. He's very persuasive," I added, not wanting to give him the whole truth. That I'd been afraid to call anyone for fear of what would happen to me. "Then he offered me a job tending him."

"What exactly does that entail?" Lane asked.

"Cooking, cleaning, laundry, managing food orders and yard maintenance. He's asked that I take that patch of land and do a small garden. I plan on planting a few things this weekend."

Lane was frowning now. "Are you proficient in all of those tasks?" he asked.

"Sure, none of it is really difficult." I sighed and looked into the fire. "I'm most concerned about his health. He doesn't like fresh vegetables. He needs them in his diet, so I've come up with a few menu items where he won't even know he's eating them." I smiled. "He had a spinach quiche the other morning." I chuckled remember how much George had enjoyed it. "He asked for seconds."

Lane was quiet for a moment. "Why are you wearing my sister's clothes and staying in the rooms above the garage?"

I looked down at the outfit. "George asked me to stay close to him. The clothes..." I bit my lip and thought about lying. Then gave up. "The clothes I had were ruined," I finally said. "He offered. I do plan on using my first paycheck to purchase my own clothes," I assured him. "I'll return everything that I borrowed then."

There were long periods of quiet as we both sipped our wine, listening to the crickets and the hiss of the gas firepit.

The stars were out, and I looked up to the half-moon, remembering how just two weeks ago I was sleeping under it not a couple hundred feet away, unaware of how close I had been to giving up on life.

Byron rushed over and started to get up on the chair with me. I set my wine down and pulled him into my lap. He snuggled down and laid his head on the arm of the chair and fell asleep.

"He likes you," Lane said softly.

"We were friends long before I knew George," I said with a sigh. "He would bring me apples," I said softly, unaware of what I was giving away.

The wine had made me feel as if I was floating. I couldn't remember the last time that I'd had a glass.

"Why are you and my grandfather now calling him Byron?" Lane asked.

"Because he is Lord Byron to me. Your grandfather was just calling him Dog." I made a hissing sound and waved my hand. "What kind of name is that? That's like calling your kid Human." I chuckled.

When Lane didn't respond, I glanced over to see him watching me.

"What happened to your sister?" I asked, turning the tables on him.

"She died."

"I surmised that," I said. "What was her name?" I asked when he didn't say anything else.

"Sherry," he answered softly. The way he said her name, I could hear the love and the hurt.

"I'm very sorry," I said suddenly.

Then Lane surprised me and smiled. "She used to annoy me a lot." He laughed. "She used to drive all of us nuts. Teenage hormones, I suppose. She even threatened to expose to the world all the terrible things we'd done to her— me, my parents, aunts and uncles, and my cousins. Her entire life she'd kept a diary. My parents have boxes of them in their attic." He shook his head and sighed as he looked out over the yard. "I lost count of how many times I broke into her room trying to find the red leather books she used to write in."

He suddenly looked towards the house. "We never found her last one."

I followed his gaze and suddenly felt worse for borrowing her clothes.

His eyes met mine and for a moment I believed he was

going to say something more about it. But then he looked away.

"You don't live around here, do you?" he asked softly.

I turned away from him and took a deep breath. "No."

"If you're in some trouble, I'm a lawyer," he said.

I tensed. "I don't need a lawyer."

"Are you married? Kids?"

"No," I answered. "I'm tired. I think I'll head up to bed." I started to get up. Byron jumped off my lap with a groan. "Goodnight," I said, leaving my glass for him to take inside.

CHAPTER SEVEN

"Faith is the bird that feels the light when the dawn is still dark."
- Rabindranath Tagore

L**ane**

I watched Chloe walk down the pathway across the yard to head up the stairs to the apartment above the garage.

The dog followed her to the base of the stairs, then returned to sit by my feet with a groan.

"Lord Byron," I said, and the damned thing glanced up at me as if to say. "Yes, what? Can I help you?" I chuckled. Okay, so the name suited him. The dog was even smarter than my grandfather had let on. Whenever I visited, I seriously questioned who was in charge, the dog or my grandfather.

I lost track of time, sitting out by the firepit and thinking of the past. It didn't hurt so much being here, remembering Sherry.

Looking around the dark yard, all I could think of was the good times we'd had together. Later, after I'd crawled into the bed that I'd slept in most of the summers of my childhood, the dreams flooded my mind and jolted me awake.

An hour before sunrise, I finally gave up trying to sleep and took my laptop downstairs. I wanted to see the sun rise as I worked, something I couldn't in the city, as my townhouse was surrounded by other buildings.

I pulled on some jeans and a sweatshirt and when I stepped into the kitchen, Chloe was there stirring something that looked like bread dough in a huge white bowl.

"Morning," she said cheerfully, looking up from the mixture.

"Morning." I had expected to have some time to work uninterrupted. The sun wasn't even up yet, and she was cheerfully working.

She ran her eyes over my computer bag, then back up to my face.

"If you want, I can get you some coffee and you can work in peace. George and Byron won't be up until around eight, so I try to bake quietly." She turned to the coffee maker.

It was then that I smelled the rich scent and felt my stomach growl.

"Thank you," I said, motioning towards the back door. "I'm going to sit outside."

"Go, I'll bring it out." She glanced over her shoulder at me.

I sat at the patio table and had just logged into the system when she set a tray on the table next to me with a mug of hot coffee, a container of creamer and sugar, and a plate of what appeared to be steaming hot coffee cake.

I looked up. "You didn't just make that, did you?" I asked.

"I've been up for a while," she answered with a smile. "Let me know if you need anything else." She turned and disappeared back into the house.

I poured both creamer and sugar into my coffee and took a sip before trying the bread. It melted in my mouth. Like, literally. The dab of butter she'd put on top of it had melted in, causing me to moan with delight.

The last time I'd tasted coffee cake this good was... I tilted my head and tried to think. Then my eyes ran to the back corner of the yard, and I realized the truth. The last time had been when my grandmother had made it.

Taking the plate with me, I walked into the house.

"Where did you get the recipe for this?" I asked, holding out the plate towards her.

Chloe frowned at me and took a step back. "I... it was your grandmother's. George gave me her recipe book." She held onto the wooden spoon in her hands. "Is something wrong?"

I took a couple deep breaths. "No, it's just..." I ran my free hand through my hair and then took my fork and ate another bite. Yup, this was just like my grandmother used to make. "It reminds me of her," I said. I felt totally stupid at this point, so I turned and walked out of the house without waiting for a response.

I finished the cake and the coffee and had yet to even look at my computer screen. Instead, my eyes ran over the yard, remembering what it had been like when she was alive. The only woman who had shown me any kind of love.

Sherry had loved me too, but in a younger sister kind of way.

My mother had never shown me an ounce of maternal love. She'd never shown Sherry any either. We'd been left to fend for ourselves. The only person we'd ever gotten that from had died when I'd been ten. Then Sherry had been taken from me too.

I closed my eyes on the pain that always came thinking about the only two women I'd ever loved. One had left at the end of her full life, the other before she'd even really started to live.

"Are you okay?" Chloe asked.

I jerked my eyes open and to my horror realized a tear had slipped down my cheek. Wiping it away quickly, I turned so that she couldn't see it.

"Yes, just... enjoying the country. I don't get up here as often as I used to."

She stood there, looking at me.

"George will be out here soon. Do you mind if I join you?" she asked.

"Please." I waved to the empty chairs.

She smiled and set a covered tray on the table.

We talked about my job. I could tell she was trying to make small talk, but the deepness of my mood grayed out everything.

My grandfather and Byron came out five minutes later.

"How'd you sleep, my boy," my grandfather said cheerfully.

"The country air always helps. That and the quiet," I said, trying to sound happy.

I noticed that Chloe's eyes narrowed slightly at my white lie.

"How did you sleep?" I asked my grandfather after he'd settled and had a plate of breakfast and a cup of coffee.

"Like a rock. Moving out here was the best thing I could have done. I'm glad I decided to finally do it."

I frowned at this. "You? I thought my dad and Uncle Robert forced you out?" I said, only realizing after the words were out of my mouth that my mother had asked me not to discuss the situation.

I was surprised when he laughed and slapped the table. "That's rich. The day my sons can force me to do a damned thing is the day I let Byron drive me to the city and buy me a beer."

I smiled. Somehow, this bit of news relieved me. I didn't like thinking of my grandfather living out here against his wishes. He had always seemed to enjoy himself out here.

The house had been theirs long before they'd moved to the city full time. Every summer, my dad and aunts and uncles would fight over who got to summer there. When I was close to eight, my grandfather had bought another house down the road so that the arguments would stop.

That was when we'd taken over this place and Uncle Robert's family and Aunt Kate's split their time at the other one.

Which is why the rooms upstairs still had my and Sherry's things in them.

My grandfather turned to Chloe. "What crazy plans do you have for us today?"

"I suppose we could always take Byron to the beach again," Chloe suggested as she sipped her own coffee.

My grandfather smiled and leaned back in his chair, then glanced at me. "What about you? You didn't come up here to work all weekend again, did you?"

I thought about the emails and cases I should deal with

over the weekend but then heard myself saying. "No, no work this time."

"Good." My grandfather clapped his hands. "First things first." He drank the rest of his coffee. "There, now, you two kids can clean this mess up while Byron and I head up to put on our shoes."

Once again, I worked alongside Chloe and cleaned up.

When we were done, we all set out across the yard following Byron, who led the way.

Chloe had brought along a large beach bag. It looked like it weighed as much as she did, so I took it from her and carried it.

The dog had a green apple in his mouth and carried it as if it was a great gift to be saved for the right time.

I helped my grandfather set out a blanket in the sand and, since there was still a chill in the air, handed him another blanket as he settled down to enjoy the scenery.

Chloe and Byron sat at the edge of the water and, to my slight amusement, shared the apple. The way the two of them were with each other, I could easily tell they had been friends for longer than the two weeks she'd been working from my grandfather.

I sat next to my grandfather and rested my elbows on my knees as I watched the pair of them. Chloe was softly chatting to Byron, who appeared to be listening intently.

"What do you know about her?" I asked my grandfather.

He glanced sideways at me, then shrugged.

"Other than the fact that she saved me and that Byron loves her? Not much." He sighed. "I trust her. At my age, that means more than anything else." I thought about it for a moment, but then he added, "Boy, think about it. All of my kids have very impressive portfolios." He turned slightly. "Would you trust them to take care of me?"

"Hell no," I said quickly.

My grandfather nodded and slapped my knee. "Exactly." He turned his eyes to Chloe again. "Whatever's in her past, the pain outweighs anything else. She's been hurt. That much is obvious. So much so that I'm pretty sure she came to the beach to die." He turned back to me. "Alone. If Byron and I give her reasons to hang on a little longer, and she lightens our days, then I'm all in."

Those words played over and over in my mind for the rest of the day. I watched Chloe closely as she laughed and joked with my grandfather. There was no fakeness here. Not like I could easily see with each of my family members.

Still, it nagged at me to think that she might be in this for other reasons. I get that my grandfather didn't want to pry into her past, but I wasn't built that way. I'd grown up in a family that I didn't trust so trust didn't come easy for me.

I was still determined to find out as much as I could about the pretty woman. After all, people who looked like her didn't just appear on beaches. At least not in the real world, I thought, as I remembered an old movie that I'd watched about a mermaid washing up on shore.

Before dinner, I tried to get as much information as I could out of her without letting my grandfather overhear me. That became a lot easier when he and Byron disappeared for their mid-afternoon naps.

I suggested that we sit out on the patio in the sunlight, where it appeared she felt more relaxed.

"Did you go to school?" I asked her, trying desperately to sound casual. When she didn't respond right away, I added, "I went to Auburn public schools."

She turned slightly to look at me. "I thought you grew up here?"

"No, we summered here every year until..." I dropped off, feeling my chest tighten as it did each time I tried to talk about my past or about Sherry.

"How about we play a game?" she asked suddenly.

"A game?" I asked, confused.

"Sure. It's obvious you want to know more about me, to ensure the safety of your grandfather. I've got some questions of my own that I've tried to get answered by him and have hit a brick wall. What I'm proposing is an answer for an answer sort of deal."

I thought about the things I wanted to keep a secret in my past. Things I had sworn I would never talk about and wanted to turn her down. However, I doubted she would ask me anything so specific, so I nodded.

"How did Sherry die?" she asked me.

"She was murdered," I answered, feeling my gut twist.

Chloe was quiet for a heartbeat. "I'm sorry."

I nodded. "Who are you running from?" I asked quickly, not wanting to miss my chance to ask her a question.

"No one," she answered, and I heard the sadness in her voice. "No one is out to get me or looking for me."

I believed her. It was the hollowness in her tone that assured me she was telling the truth.

"Why doesn't your grandfather trust anyone but you?" she asked.

I laughed. "Because everyone else in my family is an asshole."

The corners of her mouth rose slightly. "I know that feeling."

"Your family?"

Her eyes snapped to mine. "Are assholes too."

"I mean, are they around?" I asked.

She shook her head. "No."

"Why aren't you—"

"Nope." She chuckled. "It's my turn."

"Sorry." I motioned for her to go ahead.

"Did they catch who murdered Sherry?"

I tensed. "No," I said between clenched teeth.

Chloe frowned. "I'm so sorry," she said softly.

My last question seemed senseless now. I stood up and walked towards the little garden area. "What are you going to plant here?" I asked instead.

I could see that she'd cleared all the weeds from the little garden area and had raked the soft dirt into rows.

Chloe moved to stand next to me.

She motioned to one area and said, "Strawberries." My heart jumped at the memory of the strawberries that I'd planted for Sherry once a long time ago. "Carrots, peas, tomatoes, potatoes, onions, and pumpkins for the fall," she continued.

I glanced at her. "So, you are planning on sticking around that long?"

She shrugged. "If your grandfather will keep me around."

I turned to look at the house and ran my eyes over the place. It was more home to me than my parents' house or my townhouse in the city.

"He likes you. That is powerful enough to keep you here until something changes."

"What about your family? George seems to think they'll eventually show up and bully me out of the job," she said, twisting her fingers together.

"Don't let them," I answered quickly. "My grandfather is in charge." I turned to her. "I assume he's paying you."

She nodded. "I..." She bit her bottom lip. "I don't have a bank account. I haven't been able to cash my first check."

It wasn't too strange that she wouldn't have a bank account. After all, I'd represented several clients that only worked on a cash basis. Most of them had been recently divorced or recent US citizens.

"Tomorrow is Sunday. I can change my schedule around and drive you into town on Monday. There's the bank there that my grandfather uses," I suggested.

She bit her bottom lip. "I... don't have a driver's license."

"What do you have?" I asked.

She frowned.

"I can help you print whatever you need." I turned and saw my grandfather open the back door. Byron raced out the door and to a bush. "Later tonight," I finished.

"I'd better get dinner started," Chloe said when they moved back over to the table.

An uncomfortable look had crossed her eyes when I'd offered to help her, and I knew that's why she was leaving.

Whatever secrets her past held, it was obvious she hadn't had anyone kind in her life. Much like my own child-hood, with the exception of my grandmother and Sherry.

"What did you do to spook her off, boy?" my grandfa-ther asked, slapping me on the back.

Then I realized that I did have someone new in my life who cared. Whatever had happened last year to my grand-father, his behavior towards me had done a complete one-eighty.

I smiled at him.

"I didn't do anything. She only left when you arrived. It must have been your ugly mug that scared her away."

My grandfather burst out laughing.

"Why don't you head in and see if you can lend her a hand. Me and the dog... Byron"—he wiggled his eyebrows—"will toss the stick around."

I glanced through the windows and with the lights on in the kitchen, I could see Chloe getting dinner ready.

"I don't think she wants any help." I turned to him. "What changed last year?" I asked suddenly.

My grandfather's eyes went dark, and he turned away from me and tossed a stick to Byron, who was patiently waiting.

"All sorts of things changed."

"Your attitude towards me," I said, knowing he understood.

He took a deep breath and then motioned to the chairs. I followed him and sat beside him while he gathered his thoughts.

"I was made aware of... certain things I hadn't known before." He turned slightly towards me. "Things I'd been lied to about."

"Me?" I asked.

He nodded. "My sons... kept some vital information from me."

He leaned back while I reached down and picked up the stick Byron had dropped at my feet. After tossing it, I asked, "What information?"

He waved his hands. "I'm not going into any of that now." He glanced towards the house, and we both watched Chloe suddenly move around as if she were dancing.

The strangeness of such a carefree move when our discussion had been so deep and dark made us both smile.

"That girl reminds me of my Florence," my grandfather said, surprising me. Then he glanced over at me again. "And our Sherry." I felt my heart kick as I frowned. "She deserves happiness. Whatever happened in her past, she deserves it. I can tell."

Neither of us wanted to return to the deep topics, so the conversation turned towards the weather and sports.

We sat around the table and ate the chicken lasagna that Chloe had made. The fresh bread she'd baked was the best I'd had in years.

After dinner, I helped her clean up again while my grandfather went into the den and watched the news.

I went upstairs and retrieved my laptop and sat at the table replying to a few messages while Chloe disappeared into her rooms for a while.

"I can help you print out whatever you need for the bank," I suggested when she came back.

I watched a look of fear cross her face, and she gripped her hands together so tightly that her knuckles turned white. I was instantly afraid that she was going to pass out again.

CHAPTER EIGHT

"For the mind disturbed, the still beauty of dawn is nature's finest balm."
- Edwin Way Teale

Chloe
My fear burst into me when Lane offered again to help me print out my paperwork.

If he helped, he would know my name. Know things about me that I wasn't ready to share. Ready to admit to anyone just yet.

Thankfully, at that moment, George came in asking for dessert. I busied myself getting each of us a slice of the apple pie that I'd made the morning before along with a scoop of ice cream. I also made a fresh pot of coffee, since I knew George liked half a cup after dinner. He usually took it with creamer and claimed that it helped him sleep better.

We sat around the table chatting about a storm that would be coming in late the next day.

I was very thankful the conversation remained light-hearted. The ease of conversation between George and Lane allowed me to relax and joke with both of them about sports, something I had always enjoyed. But because sports were a "man thing," I'd never been able to share my love of it with anyone else.

I had learned over the past year that I'd been kept from a lot of wonderful things in my life. Things I hadn't known I'd been missing out on.

I was raised with sternness and taught that faithfulness and devotion were my only good qualities. Then, being married so young, I'd continued to live by the rules that had been ingrained in me.

I had been, in essence, a slave with no rights.

This last year had opened my eyes, and there was no way I was returning to the darkness. I was free. In every sense.

"When are you heading back to the city, boy?" George asked.

Lane glanced at me quickly, then answered, "Late Monday. I've got a few things to deal with here. Chloe needed a ride into town, and we need to discuss a few things as well. Which can wait until tomorrow."

I liked the way George called Lane *boy*. Each time he did so, the corner of Lane's lips curved up ever so slightly. I wondered if he knew that.

"You can always take the truck," George said to me.

"I..." I took a deep breath and decided to tell him the truth. "I don't have a license."

George narrowed his eyes at me. "Well, I'm sure they can update..."

"I've never had one," I admitted, knowing that it might complicate things.

Both men were frowning at me now.

"You're what? In your late twenties?" George asked.

"Twenty-six," I told them, not wanting to let on that I wasn't even sure of my age. I had no proof of a birthday. No real way to tell just when I'd been born or even who my biological parents were.

The room was silent for a moment.

"I suppose, living in a city, most people wouldn't need one," George said, turning his eyes out to the dark windows. "There's that storm we're supposed to get." He motioned.

I glanced over, thankful for the change in conversation, and saw several bolts of lightning flash in the distance.

"Well, I'm going to head up," George said, standing. Byron jumped up from his spot, where he'd been fast asleep. George stopped in the doorway. "Thank you for a wonderful meal and dessert." Then he disappeared down the hallway towards the stairs.

"I don't think I've ever seen my grandfather move so fast in my entire life," Lane joked. I stood up and started cleaning the table. "He didn't mean to pry," Lane added.

I glanced over and nodded. "I know." I turned and started washing the dishes.

"There is a dishwasher," Lane pointed out.

"I like cleaning them by hand. It gives me time to think."

Lane set his dishes on the counter beside the sink and leaned against it, his eyes running over me.

"Why have you never had a driver's license?" he asked.

"I never had a reason to drive," I answered, truthfully.

Lane was quiet for a moment. "Do you have a birth certificate?"

I swallowed and felt a dish almost slip from my hands.

"I... have documentation of my baptism," I answered, skirting the conversation.

"Chloe." Lane took my shoulders and turned me slightly until we faced one another. My soapy hands dripped between us. I'd never felt anything like I felt being close to him. My heart was pounding so fast, I could hardly hear his next words. "Why? What are you hiding?"

I took a deep breath and then blurted out, "I was raised by and married into very religious families." Maybe being so close to him was causing my mind to shut down. The hold I'd been so careful to place over my past was slowly slipping away around him. Being around George had been a lot easier.

"Okay, but everyone has a birth certificate," he said, slowly.

"I don't. I have a baptism certificate."

Lane's eyes narrowed slightly. "Is that all?"

I closed my eyes and was about to nod, but then I remembered the document that had been sent to my new email several months ago. One of the great things Lucy had convinced me to do was file for divorce. Even though the courts couldn't find Elliott, I had received a default judgment from the courts. She'd even helped me set up an email account, something I'd never had before.

"And a divorce certificate," I added.

Lane was quiet for a moment, then he nodded. "I'll get my laptop while you finish up here. Then we can print both documents for you to take to the bank Monday."

He released me and stepped away.

I turned back to the task of washing the dishes and was thankful for something to occupy my hands while I thought.

I had never been around someone so... manly before. Elliott had been a great deal older. Even though he'd been physically powerful, far more than I had been, he had never been emotionally strong enough not to hurt me.

When Lane talked to me, his words weren't like tiny knives striking out. His eyes were filled with questions and kindness. Like George's were.

All my life I had feared men. But with George and Lane, it was different. Something told me they wouldn't use their physical strength against me. Which is why I hadn't been reduced to a puddle at Lane's feet just now.

I heard Lane return and glanced over my shoulder as he set up his laptop at the kitchen table. I wanted to delay what was going to come next, but all the dishes had already been dried and put away.

I poured another cup of coffee, then asked him if he wanted more. He shook his head, so I moved over to sit beside him.

He turned the laptop towards me. "You can log in to your email, and I'll show you how to print what you need."

When I just looked at the screen, he added, "I've logged you in as a guest. It won't store any of your information." He motioned to the top right of the screen.

It was the same browser I'd used on the jail's computer, so I could tell he was telling the truth. I relaxed a little.

I went to the email website and typed in my account information and wasn't shocked at all when there were only two emails in the inbox.

Two pieces of proof of my existence. I opened the first email, and my baptism certificate filled the screen. I'd gotten a copy from the court documentation. I glanced over at Lane, who was frowning at it. Then his eyes turned to me, and I watched as understanding flooded them.

My shoulders sank slightly as he turned the laptop towards him and printed the document out. Thankfully, he didn't speak. I watched every step he made so that I could repeat it for the next document.

"I know you believe that this changes things, but it doesn't," he said, turning the computer back towards me. "I know a lot of Mormons."

I nodded. "Yes, there are a lot of regular Mormons," I said, taking a deep breath. "I was born into a smaller sect. The kind you see and read about in the news." I kept my eyes on the screen as I opened up my divorce papers. I quickly printed them out without showing Lane the screen.

The truth was, I didn't mind him knowing about me being born into the FLDS. What I did mind was him knowing who I had been married to. My ex-husband's name would lead to the knowledge of where I had been for the last year.

"Okay, the cult kind?" Lane asked slowly. "FLDS?"

I glanced over at him and gave him a quick nod. "We moved here from Utah about ten years back. After our sect was raided. We... escaped," I said, standing up. "Where is the printer?" I asked.

"In my grandfather's study." He motioned to the room I had been thinking of as the library.

As I moved across the space, memories flashed behind my eyes, as if I was watching my life on a screen in my head. The moment my mothers, aunts, cousins, had bathed me, braided my hair, dressed me in my white wedding dress, and placed the thin veil over my face. I'd been twelve. Twelve years old. Yet, that night, I was called wife for the first time.

I'd been lucky. My new husband, a man who already had three wives and was more than three decades older than I was, had decided that first night that he had too much business to attend to to lie with me.

That next night, I hadn't been as lucky. Years would go by as I lay there, unsure of what was really going on before I was finally enlightened. I can't remember what actually caused the scales to fall from my eyes. Maybe it was after one of his many beatings or after one of his bed sessions, as I had come to call them.

Suddenly, I knew without a doubt that everything was wrong. Everything he did to me. Everything around me. The fact that I didn't even know who my parents were was wrong. The fact that I was surrounded by children who were married and having babies. That I had been married off as a child bride. It was all wrong.

Then the compound in which I had grown up and in which we still lived had been raided. I remember running in the darkness. Hiding. Being shoved from behind by my husband because I didn't move fast enough as we snuck away in the middle of the night.

As we disappeared into the darkness, I realized that I had been separated not only from my family and the only life I'd ever known, but from any help I could ever hope to get. I would never escape the madman that I'd been given to.

I wasn't sure how I had avoided becoming a parent to dozens of children like all the other wives I spent my early days working beside. I didn't really understand the reproductive system of my own body, let alone that of a man's. I never looked at my husband's form when he came to me. Never wanted to.

Over the years, he grew older and larger, as life at our new home was very easy for him. He spent most of his time on a computer in the large room we called the home office. There were more than a dozen computers in the cool space.

I was only allowed in there to serve him food. He

worked on his laptop day and night. Sometimes he'd disappear for days at a time, leaving me all alone.

When he was there and things didn't go well, he'd hurt me. When things did go well, he'd hurt me in other ways. Ways I'd learned to block out for so long.

Almost ten years after escaping the New Haven compound to Washington State, I was once more ripped from my home in the middle of the night. Law enforcement officers with guns and bright lights busted into my home and searched the massive house that we'd lived in for years by ourselves. This time, I had been alone, and everything Elliott had warned me would happen did.

"Hey?" I jumped at the deep voice behind me, shaking me from the memories.

I hadn't realized I'd been standing in front of the printer, staring down at the printed pages through blurry eyes. Quickly, before Lane could see my tears, I wiped them away. I grabbed the pages and held them to my chest.

"Are you okay?" he asked, his eyes searching mine.

"Yes." I turned to go, but he stopped me by putting his hand gently on my shoulder.

I hadn't allowed myself to think about my past for a long time. The papers in my hands were to blame for the memories. Seeing my old name. Seeing my past. I was ashamed of it all. Ashamed of who I was, even now.

"Are you okay?" Lane asked again, this time a lot softer.

I looked up at him and, to my horror, another tear slipped down my cheek.

His hand moved slowly off my shoulder, and he wiped the tear away with just his fingertip.

I'd never felt my knees go weak before. Never thought it was possible that a man could cause so many different feelings inside me at the same time.

Elliott had never stoked so much as a spark in me, ever.

Lane's eyes moved to my lips, and for a split second I let my gaze drop to his. I wondered what it would be like to brush my mouth against his. Would his lips be soft? Would he taste of coffee and apple pie?

What would his body feel like? I wanted to know. I needed to believe that physical interaction between two people could be so much more than what I'd experienced thus far in my life.

Without thinking, I lifted on my toes, my papers still held to my chest, and brushed my lips across his.

My eyes were locked on his until his closed and he slanted his mouth over mine. In that moment, when his hands returned to my shoulders, everything else dropped away.

I felt my entire world tilt.

The papers I held floated to the floor as I reached up and gripped Lane's strong arms. My nails dug softly into his shirt as his tongue played slowly over my lips. I opened my mouth, needing to taste him.

It was as if I'd been hit with a bomb. I swayed. His arms wrapped tighter around me as we explored each other's tongues, lips, mouths. I had never felt anything this powerful in my entire life.

For the first time, I felt alive. Really alive.

I felt his hard body press against mine, and I melted against his chest. My hands never shifted. My nails still dug into his shirt as his hands moved up. One was buried in my hair, holding my face to his. The other shifted down to my waist, pressing my body tighter against his.

I felt something jump next to my hip, something strong, hard, something that scared me ever so slightly. Memories. I tried to force them back, but it was too late.

I pushed him back, gulping for air as I doubled over. My vision grayed. I felt my fingertips tingle. My lips were still warm from his but were now numb as well.

"Easy," I heard him say as my body lifted.

I closed my eyes more tightly, wishing he would just go away and leave me alone. I could recover if he wasn't there. At least I kept telling myself that.

He laid me on the sofa and put a warm blanket over me.

"Breath," Lane said softly next to my ear.

"Water," I managed to croak out. I was incredibly embarrassed and just wanted to disappear into the soft cushions.

I heard him get up and leave the room.

I didn't want to face him. I jerked my eyes open and, seeing that the coast was clear, I jumped up and sprinted out the back door.

I didn't stop until I was leaning against the inside of the door to my room, breathing so heavily I doubt I would have heard if he'd called out after me.

I locked the door and crumbled to the floor.

I had made a promise to myself that there wouldn't be any more tears. But now they flowed from my eyes, soaking the knees of my jeans and the sleeves of my shirt.

This was a mistake.

All of it.

I should go.

Thoughts of packing up my backpack flew into my mind. Then I remembered the promise that I'd made to Lane to return Sherry's things. Everything I had was hers. I still had nothing.

I'd tossed out my old clothes. Two pairs of jeans, a jacket, some T-shirts. Even my underwear. All of the things

I'd been given at the prison before I'd been released were gone. They'd been pretty much destroyed.

I hadn't wanted any part of those memories.

I had nothing. Once again.

I lay there on the soft carpet just inside my door, my body too tired to cry any longer. I stared up at the dark ceiling as shadows played over the space. Dark thoughts rolled over me, around me.

Then I heard a soft whining and knew I had to move. I reached up, unlocked the door, and opened it.

Byron rushed in, sniffing my face as I nudged the door closed with my foot. He licked the salty tears from my cheeks before turning in a circle and curling up next to me. He propped his head on my elbow and just looked at me.

His dark eyes searched my face.

"I'm okay," I told him.

He whined softly.

I closed my eyes and took a deep breath.

"Okay," I said, running my fingers through his soft fur. "I'll stay," I promised him.

Hearing these words, he seemed to relax. Within minutes, he was snoring.

Since I didn't want to wake him, I lay there, looking up at the ceiling, trying desperately to push thoughts of my past to a deeper place in my mind. One where they wouldn't surface so easily next time.

How was I going to face Lane in the morning?

What could I say to excuse my behavior?

Oh god! Tomorrow was going to be hell.

CHAPTER NINE

"The morning steals upon the night, melting the darkness."
- William Shakespeare

Lane

I sat out on the patio, watching the sunrise and glancing towards the garage stairs. I was worried.

The night before, when Chloe had kissed me, I'd been thrown off kilter. Hell, I'd been wanting to kiss her but had refrained. There were too many factors telling me it was a bad idea. In instances like this, I usually went with my gut instincts.

Then she'd had a full-blown panic attack.

I knew what one looked like, since I'd had so many as a child after Sherry's death.

And then she'd bolted on me. I had wondered if the panic attack had been a ruse, but why would she do that?

I'd followed her up the stairs and stood outside the door,

listening to her cry. The sounds I'd heard coming from her had assured me that she hadn't been faking it.

I'd leaned my head against the door, wishing I could help her. I lost track of time until I heard a noise behind me. When I turned, Byron was standing at the base of the stairs, looking up at me with worried eyes.

I had motioned for the dog to come up the stairs and then stood back as he scratched at the door.

When the door opened, Byron had rushed inside, disappearing into the darkness. Instantly, the crying had stopped.

I waited for a while. When I didn't hear anything more, I snuck back down the stairs and inside the house.

I had been about to head up the stairs when I noticed the papers on the floor.

I picked them up and was about to set them on the kitchen countertop when I noticed the name on the divorce certificate and stilled.

Sarah Chloe Elliott Meyers.

Sarah Meyers.

I knew that name.

Hell, every lawyer who had lived in the state of Washington for the past two years knew that name.

How was it this woman had come to be here?

One thing was clear now. I had to get her as far away from my grandfather, from my family, as I could. And quickly.

The following morning, I sat at the table on the patio and did a little research. I glanced up when I heard the apartment door open. Byron rushed down the stairs and quickly relieved himself on a bush.

Then Chloe stepped outside. She took a deep breath, lifted her arms to the air, and closed her eyes as she faced the rising sun's warmth.

She hadn't seen me yet. Hadn't noticed I was watching her.

I couldn't stop the wave of lust I felt just watching her. Hell, who wouldn't feel it? She was beautiful. Even though she was still wearing my sister's old clothes, there was just something... mesmerizing about her.

She had a deeply buried sexuality that would call out to any man. The sexy way she moved, her hips swaying, would drive any man mad.

Plus, the slowness of how she talked, as if she thought about each word before speaking. It reminded me of how Marilyn Monroe used to talk. Each word dripped of sensuality, whether she meant them to or not.

I wondered if she knew what she was doing. How just that kiss last night had caused me more sleepless hours than finally knowing the truth about her had.

I'd dealt with criminals before. Hell, it was my job. Some I trusted, others I hadn't.

I knew she wasn't the violent type. I could remember reading about her case shortly after she'd been sentenced.

From what I did remember, she'd been found in a massive mansion, alone. There had been a large room with computers and servers that had been used to funnel money from unwitting victims. So much money had been taken and never found.

Instantly, all fingers pointed towards her husband, Elliott Meyers. Unfortunately, the man had been absent, and Sarah had been unwilling to cooperate with police.

The news report I could find from the previous year showed a grainy photo of Chloe, which had confirmed it was really her.

The case had gone viral because several of the large banks who had taken a hit had gone under. So many people had lost their retirements, their savings, their lives, thanks to Chloe's husband. The anger towards her husband had bled over to her when she had refused to speak or even lift her head in court. That had sealed her fate.

Her court-appointed lawyer had taken the first plea deal. She'd apparently refused to divulge her husband's whereabouts and had been charged with obstruction. One year behind bars. Which meant, for the past year, she had been locked up in a state-run women's facility about an hour from the island.

I couldn't remember any mention of there being anyone else that they were looking to peg the crime on, other than her husband. Ex-husband.

Nowhere in the news articles about the case had it mentioned that she had been a member of the FLDS.

From what I knew of the sect, women weren't allowed to hold positions of power or even work outside the home in any capacity.

I had wanted to stay up all night to do more research but had needed my sleep. I'd woken up early again and was sitting outside enjoying another sunrise.

On my laptop screen was a detailed article about the Fundamentalist Church of Jesus Christ of Latter-day Saints or FLDS. Most of the articles were written by ex-members.

I'd read details about how most of the girls were married off at ages as young as twelve. Now, after a few raids by the FBI, the group had supposedly agreed that eighteen would be the legal age to marry, but it was rumored that the heinous practice marrying off children was still being practiced.

No, Chloe wouldn't have a birth certificate or even a wedding license. If she had been born and raised in the cult,

I doubted she would even know who her real birth parents were.

Had she been her husband's only wife? From what I had read, most men had three or more, depending on their status in the church. She hadn't mentioned anyone else, thus far. Actually, she hadn't even once said her husband's name.

What did that mean? Normally, it seemed, divorces weren't granted to ex-FLDS members. But I knew the laws of the state, and divorces could be granted without the spouse's signature under special cases.

How had she obtained hers? Had they found her husband? Did the man know where she was? Is that why she was hiding out on the island?

Just to be safe, I had made digital copies of both of the documents she'd printed out the night before. I put them in a file on my hard drive for safe keeping.

I knew that a lot of the FLDS members used the same names or took over other's names when in trouble. Half the girls were called Sarah, and Meyers was one of the dozen or so last names that were popular. There was bound to be more than one woman called Sarah Meyers.

I was still watching her when she lowered her arms and turned to head down the stairs. She almost tripped when she noticed me. I smiled and tried to act casual. I'd decided to wait and find out as much as I could before driving her as far away from my grandfather as I could.

"Morning," I said, trying to sound casual.

"Morning," she said as she gripped the railing and slowly walked down the stairs. "I wasn't expecting you to be awake this early."

I motioned to my laptop on the table. "Work." I shut the

window with the article and flipped my laptop screen down. "Did you get some rest?" I asked.

She moved to stand on the other side of the table, her hands gripped together. "Yes," she said. "I... I'm sorry I over-reacted last night."

I smiled. I'd had plenty of time to figure out how I was going to respond to her. Still, seeing the worry in her blue eyes had me responding with a quick nod.

"I'll head in and make breakfast," she said.

"No, don't bother. My grandfather won't be up for a few hours. For now, I can make do with these." I motioned to the tray of muffins that I'd brought out. I'd also carried out a thermos of coffee so I could refill my cup without having to go back in for seconds. I'd even brought out another mug for Chloe. I wanted some time to talk to her before my grandfather woke.

I was on my third cup of coffee and was completely wired.

"Sit." I motioned to the chair opposite mine. "We have some time." I poured her some coffee and nudged the plate of muffins towards her, then took another one for myself, hoping it would counter the effects of the coffee a little.

Chloe's eyes were glued to mine as she sat, her hands spread out on the table.

Before I had a chance to speak, she jumped in.

"You know." She took a deep breath. "Don't you?"

I waited, tilting my head slightly, unsure of what to say. What did I know? Her past? Where she'd been for the last year? Who she was? What she was?

"I'd hoped to tell George myself." Her eyes darted towards the house and her shoulders slumped. "I can go." Her eyes moved from the house to her fingers spread out on the table.

She hadn't touched the coffee or the muffins yet.

I waited.

"I was going to tell him. I was going to tell you." She glanced up but didn't lock eyes with me. Instead, she looked at a spot on my chest. "I... had hoped to..."

"What?" I asked when she didn't finish. "Prove yourself?"

Her eyes jerked up to mine and held. "Yes," she said, and I saw the sadness behind her blue eyes. Sadness and truth. "I'm not a criminal."

I tilted my head slightly, running my eyes over her. No, I didn't think she was. Then again, half of my clients who claimed to be innocent were probably guilty.

"Why don't we—" I started.

Just then Byron let out a happy bark, and we both turned to see a sleek black Jaguar pull in and park behind my car.

"Shit," I groaned. Then I turned quickly to Chloe. "Later. For now, keep your secrets. That's my cousin Phil," I warned, standing up quickly. "Get inside. Make breakfast. Wake my grandpa."

I met Phil halfway up the pathway as Chloe slipped into the house.

"You old sneak." Phil laughed and slapped me on the shoulder. "I should have known you'd bring someone up here to while the weekend away." He nodded towards the house. "Why'd you send that sweet thing off?"

"That sweet thing," I growled out, "is Grandpa's new caregiver."

Phil's eyebrows shot up. Then he laughed again. "Right," he said slowly.

"What are you doing here?" I asked, trying to block his path to the house.

"What?" Phil looked shocked and hurt. "Can't I come up and see my grandfather? Or are you the only family member who can schmooze the old man before he croaks?"

I felt my back teeth grind and had to consciously relax.

"Grandpa's sleeping still." I glanced at my watch. "It's not even eight."

"I know." Phil slapped me on the shoulder again. "I rented the old house for the summer. It'll be like old times." He laughed. "Thought it'd do me some good. All this fresh air." He took a deep breath and then easily moved past me into the yard.

It didn't escape me that Byron avoided my cousin. Phil had hated dogs for as long as I could remember. He claimed it was because he'd been bitten once when we were kids. The funny thing was, I couldn't remember anything like that ever happening.

"You rented your old place?" I asked, a little shocked.

The house my grandparents had owned and lent out to the family for most of our childhood sat less than a mile away, closer to town. I'd spent my summers riding my bike back and forth between here and there to hang out with my cousins.

Grandpa had sold the home shortly after Sherry's death. The fact that Phil had paid to rent the home for the summer had me on edge.

There was no way I was going to let him be this close to my grandfather for that long.

Then I heard dishes and pans banging inside the house and felt my stomach roll. Shit. Okay, correction. There was no way I was going to let Phil be this close to my grandfather and to Chloe for that long.

Just then, my grandfather stepped out onto the patio.

"Well, this is a surprise," he said dryly, his eyes

narrowing slightly. "I have half of my grandkids over for breakfast." He poured himself a cup of coffee and took a muffin.

Phil sat beside our grandfather.

"You'll have me around for longer than that. I've rented the old place for the summer," Phil said.

I watched surprise flash on my grandfather's face, followed by annoyance. It was obvious to me that my grandfather knew that Phil wanted something and was ready to settle in until he got it.

I noticed how much more guarded my grandfather was around Phil than he was around me. He also didn't use endearments with Phil like he did with me.

Half the time, my grandfather didn't even acknowledge Phil.

"Interesting," Grandfather said, then he leaned down and gave Byron half of his muffin.

"Lane has told me you hired someone..." Phil glanced into the house.

My grandfather sat up quickly, a frown on his thin lips. "Chloe. She's not to be bothered."

The warning was clear, and anyone else in the family would have understood. Phil, however, just smiled and I watched his interest grow.

"He means it," I added in a low tone.

Phil turned towards me. "Aren't you going back to the city today?"

"No," I said quickly. "I'm sticking around."

"For how long?" Phil asked.

"A while," I added. "Excuse me, I'll go see if Chloe needs any help." I stepped inside without waiting for a response, shutting the door behind me.

Chloe was dicing some fruit and putting it in a bowl

next to a container of yogurt.

"What's he doing here?" Chloe asked.

"He's staying on the island for the summer," I hissed. I leaned against the counter as she pulled a pan of cinnamon rolls from the oven. "Did you just make those?" I asked. She'd only been inside for a half hour, tops.

"No, well, yes. I mean, I made the dough a while back and had it in the freezer. I thawed it out last night to bake this morning." She shook her head. "He's staying?"

I nodded, letting the smell of cinnamon and sugar fill my lungs until I could almost taste the sweets.

I could see the worry almost consume her. "Hey." I touched her arm. "I'm staying too."

I didn't know how I was going to swing it, but there was no way in hell I was going to leave either of them alone with Phil around.

"You are?" I watched her perk up. "For how long?"

I turned and watched Phil's hands swing around in the air as if he was explaining something to my grandfather. As if he was trying to persuade him of something.

"Shit." I groaned. "He's only here to get my grandfather to agree to back his dad." I closed my eyes.

"For?" Chloe asked as she started mixing frosting for the rolls.

"He's running for Congress again," I answered absently.

"Your uncle is a congressman?" Chloe asked.

"Yes." I turned back to her. "Which is why it's imperative that I stick around."

"Why?" she asked me with a slight frown. "Why can't your grandfather support his son?"

I looked out the windows and thought of all the many reasons it was important for him not to.

"There are too many reasons to go over right now." I

turned back towards her. "After he leaves"—I lowered my voice as my grandfather and Phil headed towards the glass doors— "we have things to discuss."

While we ate breakfast, Phil rattled on about his father's campaign. I was thankful that Chloe chose not to sit at the table with us and instead disappeared outside with Byron until my grandfather was finished eating. Then she magically appeared to clear his plates.

It was very obvious to me that she had experience caring for others. I had read what life was like for female members of the FLDS. They were forced into very strict gender roles. From a young age, girls were trained to wait on the men—cooking, cleaning, serving.

In my research, I tried to find more information about her directly. Her divorce certificate lacked an official marriage date. Had Chloe been a young bride?

She was currently twenty-six. Two years younger than I was. From the sound of it, she'd been married for some time.

Whatever the facts said about her in the many articles I'd read, the woman I watched cleaning up after breakfast wasn't defined by what was written about her by strangers. I couldn't imagine her being so conniving.

Then I remembered the night before. How she hadn't even really known how to print the documents she'd needed. If she had taken any part in the cyber scam that the media claimed she had, surely, she'd know how to print out two simple documents.

I had so many questions, but while my cousin was there, consuming all of my grandfather's time, I wasn't able to get to the bottom of anything. Shortly after lunch, my grandfather excused himself for his afternoon nap and finally Phil left.

I helped Chloe finish with the dishes then suggested we head into town to open her bank account.

The surprised look that crossed her face told me that she had either forgotten about it or that she'd assumed I had changed my mind about helping her. I had put the two documents in a folder and as I drove us into the small town about a mile away, she held them to her chest.

"Does my grandfather know where you've been for the past year?" I asked as I pulled out of the driveway.

She remained silent until I glanced over at her.

"No," she finally answered softly. "At least I don't think he does."

"I'm taking a chance here," I said, trying to relax my hands on the steering wheel.

"I understand that," she said. "I... appreciate it."

"My family may not be so grateful or gracious," I said. I was trying to warn her, but I realized it came across more as a threat.

"I understand," she said a little more softly.

I parked in front of the bank and killed the engine. "Do you need me to come in with you?"

"No," she answered quickly. "I'll be just a moment."

"Take your time. I'm going to head next door to get a few things." I motioned to the general store next to the bank.

"I'll meet you over there, after. I have to grab a few things too," she said.

I waited until she disappeared inside the bank before pulling out my phone and calling my boss. Taking the summer off from work wasn't an option, but working remotely was. Someone would have to fill in for me at court, but at least I could do all the paperwork myself.

After explaining to my boss that there was a family emergency, Stephine finally agreed that I could work remotely.

Since I was going to be sticking around the island all summer, there were things I would need. I'd only packed for the one weekend, and a lot of the clothes in the closet were too small.

I hung up the phone with my boss and headed to gather what I would need from the store. I grabbed a cart and picked out some socks, underwear, T-shirts, and shorts while I waited for Chloe.

When she came in a half an hour later, I could tell instantly that something was wrong.

"Everything okay?" I asked her when she found me.

"I... they wouldn't let me open an account. They cashed the check but took ten percent since I didn't have an account with them," she answered with a frown.

"Why wouldn't they open an account? You have enough paperwork to prove who you are."

"I have no banking history." Her shoulders slumped. "That and the fact I don't have a driver's license..." She shrugged. "At least I got some of my money." She sighed as she patted her pocket.

"Don't you have a purse? A wallet?" I asked, stupidly.

She shook her head and glanced around. "Not yet." She strolled away.

I'd gotten everything I'd needed and had been wasting time looking at some electronics, so I followed her across the store.

She picked out the cheapest purse and wallet she could find and placed them in the top part of the cart. Then she moved over to the clothing section.

Watching her shop and try on clothes was oddly the most entertaining thing I'd witnessed in years.

For all of my life, not a single member of my family had ever looked at the price tag of anything. It had never mattered. We'd never had to put something back because we couldn't afford it.

Even now, as I looked down at the items that I had tossed in the cart, I realized I'd unwittingly picked the most expensive items I could. I hadn't looked at the bargain socks or underwear. The shorts and jeans I'd tossed in the cart cost more than the dozen or so items she'd placed in the top section of the cart.

Guilt caused me to swap some of the items out while she was trying on a sundress.

When we walked out of the store, she'd spent a little over half of her paycheck, and I'd easily spent double that amount with far fewer items.

On the way home, I thought about how it had almost appeared as if Chloe was shopping for the very first time in her life. She'd had me go through the checkout line first and when I looked up, I realized she was watching the entire process as if seeing it for the first time.

Much like she'd been watching me print the documents the night before.

I pulled up the driveway and cursed under my breath when I saw my uncle's car parked by the house.

"Who is that?" Chloe asked.

"My uncle. It appears my cousin isn't the only one staying on the island for the summer." I turned to her. "Go, put your things away." I sighed. "I'll try to head off my family.

"Lane?" Chloe stopped me from getting out of the car. "Thank you. For today."

I nodded. "I'll tell my grandfather to pay you in cash from now on. You shouldn't have to give ten percent to the bank next time." I climbed out of the car. "Not when the government takes about that as well."

CHAPTER TEN

"One may not reach the dawn
save by path of night."
- Khalil Gibran

Chloe
What had Lane meant by that? I climbed out of the car and grabbed the four bags of items I had bought. I had spent more money on them than I had ever seen in my life.

Items I had earned myself. Items that were now mine.

As I climbed the stairs, Lane's words played over in my head. What did he mean the government would take my money?

I had felt embarrassed in the bank, trying to explain why I had never had a bank account anywhere. Why I didn't even have a driver's license.

When the clerk had looked down his nose at me and

told me there would be a ten percent fee for cashing a check, I hadn't wanted to argue. I'd just wanted to escape.

I figured I could deal with the next check George gave me when the moment arose. For now, I was just happy I was able to afford underwear and feminine products. By my calculations, my period would start up again soon. My body was now back on its natural course, thanks to the steady diet and exercise that I was getting.

It had been so easy to lose track of time before. Now, with my daily tasks to care for George, I had gotten good at keeping track of schedules. Food deliveries. Medicine deliveries. Even the daily newspapers he had dropped off on the doorstep reminded me of the passing of time.

I'd been so afraid at first when I'd seen Lane's cousin Phil. The man had looked at me like several men in my past had.

I might have been naive as far as lust and sex went, but that didn't mean I couldn't tell when someone wanted something from me. Phil definitely wanted something.

Then I remembered my kiss with Lane the night before and felt my face heat. Okay, so I'd wanted something from him. But Lane didn't look at me like a wolf stalking a sheep. He looked at me with kindness. Like I was a puzzle he wanted to solve.

I knew I couldn't keep my secrets from everyone forever. Eventually, George would find out who I was. His family would as well. I had no doubt, on that day, I'd be out of a job.

I just hoped that I would have enough money saved up by then to get by.

I dropped my bags on the bed and took my time hanging up each of my new items. I put my money in the wallet and tucked it and my two printed forms of ID into my purse.

Then I changed out of Sherry's clothes and pulled on new undergarments, a cream-colored button-up blouse, and a black knee-length skirt. It was the best attire I could afford that looked like a uniform.

The bra was instantly uncomfortable. It was far too loose, but I'd been too embarrassed to try it on in the store with Lane watching me. Thankfully, the underwear was comfortable enough.

I slipped on my new black flats and, before I headed down to the kitchen to start dinner prep, I tossed all of the clothes that I'd borrowed from Sherry's closet into the washing machine with hopes of returning them by morning.

When I stepped into the kitchen, I gasped at the sight of Lane lying on the floor with a bloody lip and nose while a larger man stood over him.

Both men jerked their gazes towards me, and for a moment I thought of running away. Then I saw Lane smile as he stood up and shook himself off.

"I think you've worn out your welcome," he told the man. "Leave now, before Grandpa comes downstairs." He wiped the blood from his face with his sleeve.

"Screw you," the other man growled out. "You can't keep me from him. He is my grandfather."

Lane's eyebrows rose slowly. "I'll pass on your message. If he wants to talk to you, he knows how to get in touch." Lane jerked his thumb towards the door. "Go. Before I have Chloe call the police."

The other man glanced between me and Lane, then jerked around. I shrank away from him and moved aside just in time for him to storm past me.

"Are you okay?" I asked, rushing forward and grabbing a clean towel to help Lane clear the blood from his face.

"Yeah," he said, sitting down on a barstool. "I let him hit

me. Son of a…" He dropped off. "If I had been the one to throw the punch, he'd no doubt have me locked up for the night."

I dampened the corner of the towel and then gently swiped at the small cut on his lip.

"That was my other cousin, Derrick. I guess my entire family is staying at the old house for the summer," he said with a groan as I cleared away most of the blood.

"I'm going to get the medical kit." I turned to go, but Lane took my hand in his, stopping me.

"I'm okay. Really. My cousins used to do a lot worse to me when we were kids," he said with a half-smile.

"That doesn't make it right," I pointed out. "Besides, you could get an infection. Let me clean you up."

He finally nodded, so I disappeared into the bathroom and retrieved the medical kit George kept there.

I'd used it that first day when I'd found him on the floor. Now, as I cleaned the small cut on Lane's lip, I assessed the similarities between the men.

Aside from their looks, they both had kind and patient eyes. George was decades older, of course, but that just allowed me to see into Lane's future.

That had me thinking of my own parents. Who were they really? Growing up, I had known at least two dozen women that could have been my mother and three men that could have been my father.

Once again, I was thankful I had never gotten pregnant. My husband had believed it was my fault. Over the years, every time I failed to add to his brood of children, he would use it as an excuse to lash out and hit me.

The three wives he'd had before me had not produced any of his children either, to my knowledge. They had children prior to marrying him, but none had come after.

He'd married several more wives with children of their own, and not one had ended up pregnant after.

From day one of my marriage, I had silently prayed my periods would remain steady and had been thankful when they had.

"There," I said, pulling back to assess the damage. For such a small cut, there sure had been a lot of blood.

Lane's hands brushed the back of my hand.

"Thanks," he said softly.

I swallowed the rush of desire that flowed from the simple contact, consuming my entire body in a wave.

I didn't feel as if I could get myself under control around him. Why?

I didn't like sex. I didn't like being this close to a man. I never had before.

"Chloe," Lane said, but then he glanced over my shoulder.

I looked around and saw George frowning at us in the doorway.

"What's happened, boy?" he asked.

"Phil isn't the only one staying on the island this summer," Lane said as he stood up.

While I cleaned up the soiled gauze and towels that I'd used to clean the blood from Lane's face, Lane filled George in on his cousin's visit.

After that, I busied myself making dinner and preparing several desserts for the coming days. Rolling bread soothed the desires and worries and caused them all to fade away.

George and Lane had stepped out on the deck to talk, but since it was now raining, they stayed under the overhang of the porch.

Byron lay at my feet while I put the final touches on dinner. I'd made braised ham, rice with a sweet caramel sauce, and an avocado salad. For dessert, I'd made monkey bread.

I knew how much George liked his sweets after dinner and since baking was one of my true joys, I didn't disappoint him.

It had been over a year since I'd been given free rein in a kitchen. I found it both soothing and therapeutic.

Shortly before I was done preparing dinner, two cars pulled up outside.

George stepped in while Lane waited to greet the newcomers.

"It appears we're going to have more for dinner," George said with a sigh. "Tell me there isn't enough for everyone, and I'll turn them away."

I thought about it, then answered, "There is plenty of food. I was going to use the leftovers for lunch meat this week."

George nodded. "You'd best take your meal in your rooms. You can clean up after everyone's left." He turned and greeted the new people.

I tried really hard not to stare at his family.

Besides Phil and Derrick, who looked so much like Lane it was uncanny, there were two older men. One looked almost identical to Lane. The other was blond and looked nothing like the others. Of the two women, one had Lane's warm brown hair and features, and the other looked nothing like the rest. I assumed one couple was Phil's parents and the other Derrick's.

I wondered vaguely if Lane's parents would be joining us soon as well.

After setting the large dining table and making sure the food was all ready to be served, I stood around and helped out where needed.

For the most part, the family treated me as if I was invisible. I was thankful for that.

Only Lane and George really talked to me. Everyone else barked orders in my direction.

I was pouring one of the women a glass of wine—I think her name was Reba, the blonde that didn't look like the rest of the family—when she jerked the glass slightly, causing me to spill a few drops of wine on her blouse.

"Really, George. Where on earth did you hire this woman? You really should vet your workers better." She glared up at me.

I stood there shocked and unsure what to say or do. "I'm sorry," I heard myself croak out.

The woman sighed and ran her eyes over me. "You know, there's an agency you can hire from. I'm sure they can send someone more suitable." Her eyes moved over my clothes as if they were rags.

I felt my spine straighten.

"Cheap labor is only good for one thing," Derrick said, his eyes zoning in on my breasts.

"Enough," George said. "Leave her be." Then he turned to me. "Thank you." He nodded towards the doorway with a slight smile.

"We'd better keep our eye on this one," Phillip said as I turned to go. "She snuck in under the radar. For all we know, she's just here to get her hands on the family money." His eyes narrowed at me.

Without saying another word, I set the wine bottle down on the credenza and rushed into the kitchen. I feared they would hear me, so I stepped into the pantry as the first wave of panic overtook me.

My hands gripped the shelf, my nails dug into the soft

wood as I took several deep breaths, trying to settle my nerves.

"Hey." Strong arms rested on my shoulders. "Are you okay?"

I nodded, not wanting Lane to see what that woman's words had done to me.

"She's a bitch. They all are," he said softly. "Besides, everyone at the table saw my aunt jerk her glass away." He turned me until I faced him. "She's not worth crying over. My cousins are snakes and idiots. None of them are worth the tears."

"I know that," I said, dashing the tears away and cursing myself for it. How many times had I promised myself that I'd shed my last tear? Too many. I was an emotional fool, and I had no clue why.

"Why the tears then?" he asked.

I closed my eyes and shrugged. "I suppose I'm just tired and hungry."

"Go, take a plate for yourself and head up to your rooms. We can pour our own wine and get our own dessert," he said with a smile. "Hell, if it will get me away from my family, I'll even do all the dishes myself."

"No," I jumped in. "Don't. I won't have them thinking I'm not doing my job around here," I said quickly.

Lane's smile grew. "All right. But don't bother with any of it until after you've had something to eat yourself."

I nodded, then held in a gasp when he leaned down and brushed his lips softly over mine. He turned and disappeared.

Since I didn't want to be gone too long, I made myself a plate of food and ate it in the pantry. I could hear the voices raise several times and was almost curious enough to poke my head out to hear what they were arguing about.

The very first time that I'd been around a fight between others was that first month that I'd been behind bars.

The rumbling from the other room reminded me of a fight between Lucy and another large woman. Lucy had spent close to a week in the infirmary.

At first, I hadn't thought much about it. At least I had the room to myself for that whole time and didn't have to sneak back in there during the day to use the bathroom.

However, I quickly figured out that Lucy had been my shield of sorts. With her around, no one had dared messed with me.

At the very first meal I had after Lucy had been carted away, three large middle-aged women sat down at my table, one on either side of me, caging me in. Their leader, who went by the name Foxy, sat directly across from me.

Even Lucy's friends Sam, Lindy, and Rizzo steered clear once they saw the new interest in me.

"How you doing, baby girl?" Foxy asked, her eyes running over me.

I had never experienced as much anxiety as I had then. For weeks, not a single person had talked to me besides Lucy and her group, and I'd liked it that way.

I think I nodded or made some sort of movement. Honestly, I couldn't remember. Seconds later, my arms were grabbed by the other two women. I was held in place as Foxy leaned across the table. From close up, I could see the age on the woman. Deep wrinkle lines crossed her forehead, and crow's feet disappeared into her mud-colored hair. She was shorter than I was, she but had more than a hundred pounds on me.

"Yeah, without your bitch Lucy protecting you, you're in the shit now," Foxy spewed, her voice almost a hiss. "I'm your protection now. And it's about time you paid up." She tilted her head. "Whatcha got?"

I had shaken my head, not understanding. Protection? From? They were the only ones I felt threatened by.

"Carla." Foxy motioned to the larger woman on the right of me. The woman immediately stuck something sharp in my side. I hissed and jerked, but since they were holding me firm, I had no way of escaping.

"Since you're new, I'll ask again. Make no mistake, baby girl, I won't do it again. Whatcha got?" Foxy hissed.

I pulled out the only thing I had of value. The only thing that was keeping me sane. I laid the book on the table, and Foxy glared at me.

"What's this?" she asked.

"The only thing I have in this world," I admitted.

The three of them laughed. The echoes of their cackles would haunt me for months.

Then Foxy nodded and the sharp object dug further into my side.

"This is how it's going to go down. You work for us now. Whatever you get, it's mine." Foxy slid the book towards her. "You have nothing." She narrowed her eyes at me. "You are nothing."

What Foxy and the other women didn't know was that this wasn't anything new to me. I had never been anything.

I snapped back to reality when I realized that it had grown quiet outside of the pantry. I'd finished my dinner and figured that the rest of the family was done arguing and eating.

I poked my head into the dining room and noticed that some of the family was still inside, drinking wine and talking quietly.

I started cleaning up and doing the dishes. I was putting

one of the large pans back in the pantry when I felt someone behind me. I jumped slightly, caught off guard. I turned to see Derrick leaning against the closed pantry door.

"Well, I have to say, you are an improvement around here. Glad we hired you to take care of the old man. Gives us something nice to look at, you know." He smiled at me, and I felt my skin crawl.

Even though I'd technically been married, that hadn't stopped a lot of other men from looking at me the same way Derrick currently was.

"Did you need something?" I asked, trying to remain still. I knew that words could push men away. Especially since several of Derrick's family members were just in the other room.

Derrick's eyes slowly went up and down me and suddenly I felt dirty. Like the simple outfit I was wearing wasn't enough coverage.

All my life I'd been forced to wear huge dresses that covered everything, with their long sleeves, high necklines, and pastel colors. Now, the short-sleeved blouse and shorter skirt made me feel as if what I was wearing was the problem. Like somehow, I'd brought this upon myself.

He moved forward until my back was up against the shelving on the farthest wall. Then his hands moved up and rested on the shelves on either side of my head.

"There's a lot that I need," he said in a low tone.

It shouldn't have felt much different than when Lane got close to me. Really, I mean, the men were practically identical in looks. But it did feel different.

My flight instincts kicked in, and I tried to duck under his arms and escape, but he shifted slightly until I was completely blocked in.

"We're going to have a fun summer." He pushed his body fully against mine. I felt his erection against my stomach, and I jerked back, knocking several items over on the shelves behind me. For some reason, that caused him to smile and push against me even more.

I was about to shove my knee into his groin when a deep voice sounded from the doorway.

"I'd back off now, if I were you," Lane warned.

The anger was obvious in his tone, and Derrick jerked away. Using that temporary distraction to my benefit, I escaped the trap and rushed past Lane. Not wanting him to see the fear in my eyes, I kept my gaze on the floor until I stepped outside, and the cool air hit me.

It was raining again, so I stood at the farthest point on the covered patio, wrapping my arms around myself and willing my heart to stop banging against my ribs.

"Are you okay?"

I jumped, then glared over at Lane as he moved closer to me in the darkness.

"Sorry," he said, tucking his hands into his jean pockets. "I didn't mean to scare you."

I shrugged and then jumped when lightning flashed in the sky, lighting up the entire yard.

"They're leaving." Lane motioned behind him. "At least for the night. If you want, I'll wait out here with you, so my snake of a cousin won't slither out here and scare you again."

I smiled and instantly felt the tension retreat.

"Thanks. I was just very unprepared." I wanted to promise him that it wouldn't happen again. That now that I knew that both Derrick and Phillip were snakes, I wouldn't allow them to corner me like that again. But the truth was, I knew it was probably going to happen again.

After all, even after Lucy had returned, Foxy and her gang had still been able to push me around, right up until the final moments before I'd been released.

We stood in the darkness, watching the rain until both of the other cars pulled out of the driveway. Then Lane helped me clean up the rest of the dinner mess, and I returned to my own rooms.

The following morning, after folding Sherry's borrowed clothes, I headed up the stairs and returned the items I'd borrowed to their rightful place.

I wondered what would have become of me if I'd grown up in a house like this. If I'd had Lane as a brother. Then I frowned remembering the rest of his family. Lane had hinted that even George had been like the rest of them and that something last year had changed him. Lane didn't say, but I assumed it was after his stroke.

I couldn't see George being anything but kind. The old man I worked with every day was nothing like the rest of his family.

I was putting the shoes back on the floor of the closet when I noticed a loose floorboard. There was a red ribbon attached to something underneath the worn wood.

I glanced over my shoulder to make sure I was alone and tugged on the string until the board popped up.

Inside sat a small shoebox and a worn red leather book.

I sat down on the floor and pulled the items out of the hiding spot. I put the book on my lap and set the box on top of it.

Inside the shoebox was a young girl's treasure trove of items. A gold locket with an R on top and a faded picture. It was so faded that I couldn't make out who it was of. Maybe Sherry and a boy.

There were a few other pictures, mostly of Sherry and

another girl I assumed was her cousin Tiffany, whom I'd heard about. A few pictures of a dark-haired girl. Several of the three of them together.

There were movie stubs, concert tickets, and some wrist bands from what appeared to be shows or parties. I almost missed the single joint that lay at the bottom, underneath some dried flowers.

Putting all the items away, I tucked the box back into its hiding place and then opened the book. On the front page it said "The Diary of Sherry Joy Robinson" in delicate hand-writing in red ink.

I flipped to the first page and read the first entry.

"There is no one on this planet that I hate more than my family. They actually think that they can tell me who I can fall in love with. I don't care what they say, Eric and I are in love. But since they have an ongoing feud with Eric's family, they are all saying that I can't see him. I'm fourteen, or at least will be next month. I can see whoever I want. I hate them all. My family sucks balls."

I heard movement in the house and jerked the book closed. I was going to replace it, but curiosity won, and I shoved the book in the inside pocket of my jacket, hoping I could sneak it up to my rooms before breakfast. I don't know what drew me to hold onto it. I told myself that I'd give it to Lane. Later.

I replaced the wood floorboard, shut the closet door quietly, and snuck out of the room.

For the rest of the morning, I thought about what it would have been like growing up with a normal family. Even as screwed up as Lane's was, they at least had one another.

I had... no one. I couldn't even contact the people I'd thought of as parents for help. We'd been excommunicated.

Outcasts. Apostates. From the moment we'd escaped into the night, turning our backs on the rest of them, we'd been blacklisted.

I doubted even the woman who'd given birth to me cared where I was now.

CHAPTER ELEVEN

"Not knowing when the dawn will come,
I open every door."
- Emily Dickinson

Lane

Something with Chloe changed in the coming days. She was less accessible around the house. Whenever my family stopped by, she disappeared, and, honestly, I couldn't blame her.

My cousins were acting like vultures, as if Chloe was the last woman on earth and they had to have the prize. Honestly, it was unnerving to watch.

There was no denying that even I felt a physical pull towards her. She was, after all, incredibly beautiful.

The more time I spent around her, with her, the more I realized that all she wanted was a place to be. A job. A purpose.

I worked in my grandfather's study most days and could

overhear how she spoke to him. How much she cared for him and Byron.

The only times I came out of my hole to interact during the day was when a member of my family showed up. I was not going to let them strongarm my grandfather into anything.

Time flew by quickly and as the weather grew warmer, my family grew less patient. Their little day trips grew more frequent and soon they were spending the entire day at the house, using Chloe as their personal servant.

When I caught my aunt yelling at Chloe one day, in the upstairs hallway, I jumped in.

"What in the hell is going on?" I growled at my aunt Reba.

"Oh!" Reba jumped, her hands over her heart. I could tell I'd scared her, but Chloe had been facing my way and had seen me coming. "Nothing that concerns you." Reba had recovered, then she'd turned back to Chloe, dismissing me.

"It does when grandfather has requested that we all leave Chloe to tend to her business," I answered.

Reba turned slowly towards me, her hands on her hips, her eyes narrowed.

"I'm simply telling"—she waved her hand at Chloe, as if she didn't even know her name— "her that she ruined one of Robert's shirts and that the cost of it will come out of her pay."

I wanted to throw a line of curse words at my aunt, but instead asked, "How? How did she ruin his shirt?"

Reba's eyebrows shot up. "She washed it on warm."

I slowly shook my head. "Why would Chloe be washing Robert's anything?"

Reba made a tsking noise.

"Since last week, I've been taking care of their laundry," Chloe said firmly.

Her hands were gripped together so tightly that her knuckles were turning white.

"You..." I took in a deep breath. "What the hell?" I turned to Reba. "She is not your maid. She's not your dry cleaner. She's not your cook. She is not your employee. She works for my grandfather and no one else." I said all of this very slowly.

"I don't see that it's any of your business. We can all benefit from her employment. She can cook and clean up after all of us while we're here." Reba waved her hand and turned back towards Chloe. "She's only an employee after all."

"I agree," I said, suddenly. I watched surprise flood onto Chloe's face. "While we're here, under grandfather's roof, he has agreed that Chloe is in charge of the house. This house," I added, making my point clear. "That doesn't include any of your personal stuff. Your dirty clothes are not to be brought into this house. They are not part of this house."

"She's been in Sherry's old room." My aunt's eyes narrowed slightly, changing tactics. "God only knows why. What if she's taken things from there? There is no reason for her to be snooping about. None."

"Her tasks involve dusting. Besides, it's past time we cleaned out the room." I glanced over to Chloe. "It is a task that is way overdue."

"It's disrespectful," my aunt hissed.

"She was my sister. I doubt she'd want the place to remain a shrine forever." I was growing even more irritated. "Now, if we're done here, I'm sure Chloe has work to get back to."

My aunt's eyes narrowed slightly. "I will expect full reimbursement for the ruined shirt," she said firmly, turning to leave.

"Did you personally pay Chloe for the work that she's done for you?" I countered.

My aunt opened her mouth, but then shut it again and left.

I suppose I shouldn't have been shocked to find out that my family had convinced Chloe to do all their laundry. They were all manipulative and selfish. They wouldn't let a chance go by to utilize something someone else was paying for.

From what I could tell, my family had carted load after load of their dirty clothes over to the house in large bins in the back of their SUV. Chloe explained how she would then carry them up the stairs and into the laundry room in her own suite.

"This stops now," I told her. "They are not your employer. My grandfather is. Does he know about this?" I asked.

Chloe looked down at her hands and shook her head. "They were very persuasive."

I lowered my voice so that only she would hear me. "They don't know, do they?" I was suddenly worried that they were holding her secrets over her head.

Her eyes jerked up to mine, then she shook her head quickly. "No," she said softly.

"Then why?" I asked, needing to know more.

Chloe just shrugged her shoulders. "If you don't mind, I have things..." She motioned towards the stairs. "I have to change the sheets in your grandfather's room."

I closed my eyes and took a deep breath. I wanted her to know that she didn't need to do anything my family demanded of her, outside of my grandfather. "Go," I said, firmly. But she didn't move. "We will discuss cleaning Sherry's room out later. Maybe when I have some free time." She nodded, and her eyes searched mine for a moment. "Go," I said a little more softly. She turned and headed back down the hallway.

The rest of the day I was too distracted to work, so I took Byron on a walk to the beach. School had been out for a few weeks, so the beach was full of locals and even a handful of tourists.

Whidbey Island didn't get a lot of tourists, but there was a resort on the other side of the island and the beaches here would get plenty of visitors.

Today, Byron and I walked more than two miles before turning around and heading back. When we had almost made it to the entrance of the beach, Byron barked happily and rushed over to Chloe, who was sitting in the sand with her knees up and her head resting on them.

She appeared to be crying. When Byron sat next to her, she wrapped her arms around him and hugged him, burying her face into his soft fur.

"Hey, is everything okay?" I asked, sitting beside them.

Chloe glanced up at me and wiped the tears away with the back of her hand.

"I had a run-in with your uncle, Robert." She sighed. "Then another one with your cousin, Derrick. How do you handle them?"

"I take long walks," I advised her with a shrug. "Normally, I avoid them. I see them about once a month, once every other month if I'm lucky."

She sighed and rested her chin on her elbows. "I used to think everyone else was lucky to have a family."

"Until you met mine," I said dryly.

She glanced over at me, then nodded slightly. "You and George are nice. I'd believed..."

"What? That the rest of my family would be cool?" I laughed. "Sorry to disappoint."

"What happened?" she asked.

I leaned back on my elbows and thought about it. "We used to be fine." I took a deep breath. "Then Sherry was killed."

Chloe opened her mouth but then shut it quickly and remained quiet for a moment. "I'm sorry. I seem to keep bringing up things that remind you of her death."

"No," I said with a sigh. "This place reminds me of her. Not just her death, but of her." I looked off over the water, and memories of so many summers spent here, playing in the sand with Sherry, flooded my mind. "We had so many good times here, before, when my family was... different. Maybe I'm the one who changed?" I shrugged.

A memory of Sherry and my father burying me in sand played in my mind, and I burst out laughing. I'd fallen asleep, the summer sun warming me after I'd worn myself out swimming all morning. I was sleeping deeply enough that I hadn't woken until I was completely covered with sand and sticks.

"We had good times," I said again. I think it was to reassure myself that they weren't all fake memories. They really did happen.

Chloe remained silent next to me, and I turned my head and looked at her. Byron had fallen asleep, his head resting in her lap as if she was his human instead of my grandfather.

"Did you have any? Good memories?" I added, suddenly feeling stupid. Of course, she did. Didn't everyone have at least a handful of good things that had happened to them in their childhood? Surely, she had dolls or friends. Parents that loved her. Right?

Instead of answering, she looked off over the water, then down at Byron. She'd been absently running her fingers through his thick curly fur.

"The day Byron brought me an apple," she said with a sigh. "The day you took me shopping." She looked at me and my heart sank. Then she smiled. "The first time I stepped foot in the library at the prison."

"Books are important to you." I knew she'd gone through more than two dozen of the titles in my grandfather's library that week already.

"Books are my escape," she admitted. "I can be or do anything I want."

I nodded, understanding completely. "You read a lot of classics."

"What kind of books do you like?" she asked me. "Besides all of those law books I've seen you looking at."

I chuckled. "Those are work and, yeah, a bit of an obsession. For fun, I like anything with mystery."

We sat in the sand, talking books, until Byron jumped up and raced back down the pathway towards the house.

"I wish we could stay out here, like this, all the time," Chloe said as I started to get up and dust my shorts off.

"Afraid of my family?" I joked.

"Some of them, yes," she said with a smile.

I held out my hand to help her up from the sand. Once she was standing, I continued holding her hand, enjoying the way it felt. The way she felt. She leaned into me and our eyes locked.

For one magical moment, our breath caught as we held that moment between us. It was broken when my cousin called out.

"This is fun," Derrick said, walking over and stopping beside us.

Chloe took a step away from me and dropped her hands to her side.

"No wonder you warned us to steer clear of her. You want the fun all to yourself." Derrick narrowed his eyes at me.

"I..." Chloe glanced between us, then jerked her head towards the pathway. "I'd better start on dinner." She turned and quickly retreated to the house.

"What's your game, cousin?" Derrick took a step closer to me.

"No game," I answered easily. I wasn't in the mood to fight again. From the moment they had all shown up, they'd done nothing but try to convince my grandfather to bankroll their plans.

For my cousin Derrick, it was his latest business venture. For my uncle, it was his run for Congress. They didn't even care if they were borderline belligerent towards anyone, including my grandfather. Did they really believe they could strongarm him into giving them millions? It was a joke. At this point, he wasn't even willing to give them a dime.

I started to walk past Derrick, but he stopped me by placing a hand on my shoulder and digging his fingers into my arm.

"If you keep getting in our way with the old man"—he moved closer and shoved a finger into my chest— "things are going to get ugly."

I rolled my eyes and started to pass him, but he grabbed my arm. I thought about jerking it free but wanted to hear what he had to say next.

"What do you know about that woman?" He jerked his

head towards the pathway where Chloe had just disappeared. "The family is talking. We're thinking of hiring that PI Marcus Colter to track down some more information on her."

"Don't," I warned him.

Derrick's eyebrows shot up. "Oh? Do you know something about her?"

"Yes, she's probably the most decent person on the island," I growled. "Leave her be. Besides, as I mentioned, she works for our grandfather. It's his business."

"Yeah." Derrick chuckled. "But the old man is losing it. I mean, he lives here full time now. This place was good when we were kids, but now it's just... pathetic."

"Then why are you here?" I said, not missing a beat.

Derrick looked annoyed. "To do a job. To protect my future." He finally dropped the hold on my arm, then he stepped closer. "As I said, it would be best if you stayed out of the family's way." He walked past me, bumping my shoulder as he went, something he always did when he wanted to show me that he was bigger than I was.

I wasn't small. But my six-foot-two frame was less bulky than his and Phil's. Neither of them had ever gotten into fitness like I had. Instead of swimming, running, lifting weights, and boxing, they'd just stuck with weights and sucking down beers, by the look of their belly fat. I could probably outrun them both, and when it came to power behind punches, I probably had them beat there too. Not that I ever used it. The last time I'd punched one of them had been before Sherry's death.

I waited until Derrick disappeared down the path before heading back to the house. It pissed me off that they had always been able to intimidate me.

With anyone else, I could usually get the upper hand, but with my family...

When I stepped into the kitchen, the house was quiet. I passed through the kitchen and heard a grunt and something bang in the hallway. Then I heard Chloe's voice and rushed into the pantry, afraid one of my cousins had cornered her again.

What I found was her standing on a small stepladder, reaching for a jar on the top shelf. The cream-colored shorts she was wearing exposed her sexy legs, and my eyes ran over them.

She was up on her toes, her arms stretched high above her head, and damned if she didn't look very appealing.

She'd gained some weight since I'd first seen her on the beach. Just enough that her hips and other fun parts had filled in.

I hadn't thought, just moved. Quickly, my hands wrapped around her tiny waist, holding her. She gasped, then smiled when she realized it was me.

"I thought you were..."

"My cousin?" I smiled. "Nope. If you needed help..." I dropped off.

"You weren't around," she said, finally getting a hold of the jar she wanted. "And I was not going to ask anyone else to help me. I've already been cornered by your cousins enough for a lifetime."

I frowned at this thought, but then she turned in my arms and my entire body went on guard. We were so close, our bodies brushing up against one another's.

The jar was sandwiched between us as Chloe leaned down slightly and placed her lips over mine.

"I was starting to believe I'd imagined it," she said, when she pulled back slightly.

"What?" I asked as she rested her forehead against mine.

"The way you make me feel. The way my body reacts to yours. How perfect your lips are."

I smiled at that. "My lips? Do you even know how soft yours are? How perfect your body feels against mine? You're so pretty it hurts."

I'd expected her to smile when she pulled back, but she was frowning and there was a small crease between her eyebrows. "What? Did I say something wrong?"

"No." She shook her head quickly. "It's just... I've never had anyone." She took a deep breath. "I've never had a man tell me how pretty I am."

I jerked back and frowned at her. "Seriously?"

She nodded and shrugged, then I helped her step off the ladder.

Instantly, I missed having her at eye level and looked down at her.

"You were married," I pointed out.

"Elliott was..." She glanced around as if searching for the right words.

"Unappreciative?" I suggested.

She nodded after thinking about it for a moment.

I could tell she felt awkward talking about her past. Someday, I hoped to get more information from her, but since I knew she usually wanted an answer for an answer, I didn't think that the pantry was the best place for this conversation.

"What can I do to help you get dinner ready?" I asked. I knew I'd thrown her off, and my stomach had been growling since before I'd left the beach.

"Do you know how to bake bread in the oven?" she asked. "You can do that while I make salad dressing."

I didn't know how to bake bread, but how hard could it be? I followed her back into the kitchen.

"You're making salad dressing? Like, from scratch?"

She chuckled. "Yes. The dough is in the pantry in the large ceramic bowl with the cloth over it. You can put it into that pan." She motioned. "Season with that." She pointed to a can of seasoning. "Butter it." There was a small bowl of melted butter. "Then stick it in the preheated oven."

"Simple," I said. However, in the next few minutes, I had to ask her three times if I was doing it right. In my defense, I'd never made homemade anything before. My cooking skills were limited to opening cans, putting pre-made items in the oven, chopping vegetables for salads, and grilling meat over a fire.

When I finally slid the pan into the oven, it was oddly satisfying. I couldn't imagine how she felt knowing she'd made the dough herself.

Since she was done making the dressing, I helped her make the salad and red sauce for that night's meal.

She had made so much food, and I realized that the simple task of caring for one old man had grown into a monster. Now she was cooking for eight people instead of just one and that didn't even include her.

"My grandfather isn't paying you enough," I said once we were done setting the table.

She chuckled and waved her hand. "He's paying me plenty."

"No. You're caring for the whole family now instead of just him. This isn't right."

"I really appreciate what you're trying to do, but I'm fine. Really." She touched my arm, but my mind was already made up. I was going to go find my grandfather and convince him to at least double if not triple what he was paying her. At least while my family was around.

"Lane." Chloe touched my arm, stopping me from marching away to find my grandfather. "I don't want to cause any more problems between the family. Everyone already thinks I'm some sort of gold digger. Like Anna Nichole Smith. As if I'm trying to move in on your grandfather." She shrugged. "I'm not. I don't want anything other than a job and to be left alone. Please." She shook her head. "I'm perfectly happy with doing the extra work for what I'm being paid."

I nodded slowly. "For now," I said. "But doing any extra work for my family stops. You're not their dry cleaners, maid, or private cook."

She smiled and nodded. "Agreed."

CHAPTER TWELVE

"I felt a wish never to leave that room - a wish that dawn might never come, that my present frame of mind might never change."
- Leo Tolstoy

Chloe
In the first weeks after Lane's family's arrival, I was too busy to have any time to myself. Mornings after breakfast were filled with laundry and cleaning. After lunch, when George and Byron took their naps, his family found things to fill my time with, and Lane locked himself in George's study and worked. He appeared to be the only one in his family who did so. I wondered if anyone else had a job. In the evenings, after dinner, I did all my meal prep and baking.

By the time I finally made it to my rooms, I was exhausted and went right to sleep.

Since George was now paying me with cash, my purse

was full of it. I hadn't gone into town again and was dying to purchase a few more items, things I'd always wanted to buy for myself.

By my last estimate, I had close to a thousand dollars now, more money than I'd seen or thought I'd see in my lifetime.

I had no idea what to do with so much money. Even if I bought twice the amount of clothes I had last time, there would still be so much left over.

I planned to ask Lane to drive me into town again on Sunday, since George had given me Sundays and Mondays off.

Not that I'd taken the time off. Last weekend, I'd headed to the beach with George, Byron, and Lane for a picnic. The following day, I'd slept in an hour later than usual before getting up to do my own laundry and cleaning. Then I'd taken a long walk before heading in to make lunch for everyone because I was so bored.

Once I had cleaned up after breakfast, and before the rest of his family showed up, I went into the study.

Lane normally set up his laptop at his grandfather's old desk. He'd made the room his workspace and had moved a few things around. The room looked a lot more functional now.

When I stepped in, Lane glanced up at me.

"Do you have a minute?" I asked. I didn't know why I felt nervous. I suppose because I was asking him to do something for me again. I hated not being able to do things on my own.

"Sure." He motioned for me to sit down. I sat in one of the high-back leather chairs across from the desk. "What's up?"

"I was wondering if you'd drive me into town again this weekend," I practically blurted out.

Lane's eyebrows shot up. I could tell he was thinking.

"My family has said that this weekend they're all going to be off the island. I was going to return to my place in the city to grab a few things," he started.

I felt my shoulders sink at the thought of having to wait another weekend. But I'd waited this long, so what was another seven days?

"You haven't really taken any time off since you started," he continued. "What would you think of heading into the city with me? I have a spare bedroom at my place. That way you can hit different shops instead of just buying things at the general store in town."

I thought about leaving George all alone for the weekend and was about to decline when Lane added, "It's just one night. We can be back before noon the following day."

"Okay," I answered before I could back down. I hated the city, really. But the chance to go to some real clothing stores thrilled me.

Lane smiled at me. "We'll head out later this week."

I frowned. "My days off are Sunday and Monday."

"I'll ask my grandfather to move your days off so we can be back here before the family returns," he said, just as his phone rang.

While he answered it, I left to attend to my tasks. I was practically floating all day as I dreamed of the things that I would buy myself this time. I wasn't normally a materialistic person but having the freedom to get what I wanted was exciting.

I was upstairs changing the sheets on George's bed when Phil stepped into the room. At first, I didn't think he was going to bother me, but then he shut the door behind him and leaned on it, watching me.

"Can I help you?" I asked, my voice wavering slightly. When he heard the weakness, he smiled and moved closer.

"I know your secrets," he said in a low tone.

My heart skipped, then it felt like it stopped all together.

I held still, the dirty sheets held in my arms.

How? was my first thought.

What would happen now? was my second.

Since I hadn't said anything yet, Phil moved even closer to me until he was less than a foot away. His eyes ran over my face, down my body, as if he could see me behind the pile of sheets I held and all of my clothes. I shivered, which only caused his smile to grow.

He lifted a hand and nudged a strand of my hair out of my eyes. Then his hand snaked behind my head until he had a firm grip on my ponytail. He yanked my hair back hard, holding the chunk of it firmly in his fist as he moved closer until our bodies were pressed tight. His face was less than an inch from mine.

I dropped the bedding and moved my hands to shove him away, but they were trapped between our bodies.

"Did you think we wouldn't find out?" he hissed, his eyes narrowing slightly. He chuckled when I didn't say anything.

"I..." I started to say, but his fingers tightened in my hair, so I shut my mouth.

"You're not what you want everyone to believe," he jeered. "You can't even open a bank account because you don't have a license." He laughed. "What do you think my grandfather will do once he finds out?"

Hold on. Is this what he'd found out about me? That I

can't drive or open a bank account? George already knew that. It's the reason he was paying me cash.

When I'd told him, he had sat me down and told me a story of when he and Florence had met. How they'd been too poor to even go out on a proper date at a restaurant. He'd explained that they hadn't been able to open a bank account until three years after their marriage.

"He already knows," I said firmly as I shoved hard against his chest. "It's not against the law to not have a driver's license." I shoved again, and he let go of my hair, but his fingers still dug into my arms, holding me still.

"You have other secrets," he said, jerking my body forward.

I felt like a ragdoll. I couldn't stop him from jerking my body any which way. I felt powerless. Once again.

"So do you," I said firmly, my eyes boring into his. "Your entire family does."

I was shooting in the dark. Still, I could tell they were all hiding something. They all tiptoed around one another, when they weren't shouting and fighting.

Phil's hands dropped away as he locked eyes with me.

"What do you know?" he hissed.

Instead of answering, I retreated quickly from the room, leaving the dirty sheets on the floor. I would retrieve them later, when I knew it was safe.

I didn't stop running until I was in my own rooms and safe.

It had been over a year since I'd felt so helpless because of a man.

There had been plenty of times in prison that I'd felt so, thanks to Foxy and her gang. Still, I hadn't feared that much since they'd only threatened to kill me. Death, I had figured, I could deal with.

Phil and Derrick wanted something more from me. Something I doubted I could recover from. At least not mentally. In this area, I was already so fragile. One man had taken everything I was in that arena. I'd grown strong enough to block most of what he'd done to me from my mind.

Elliott hadn't cared if I was mentally present or not. But something told me these two would care. They'd demand more from me than I could give.

Since I had some time now, I flung myself on my bed. I would not let the tears come. To keep my mind from them, I reached over to get whatever book I'd last been reading from my nightstand.

I was slightly surprised that it was Sherry's diary. Still, I shifted and settled in and started reading again.

"My brother almost caught me sneaking out last night. I don't know what he would do if he knew that I'd agreed to meet Eric on the beach. I was so excited and scared as I tiptoed through the house. My parents are deep sleepers, we all know that. I tiptoed down the hall, past Lane's room. I could hear him on the phone with his girlfriend, Chelsey. She and her family are supposed to come up for the weekend soon. She's boring and stupid and only likes my brother because we have more money than she does. Anyway, when I was finally free of the house, I sprinted to the beach, excited to see Eric. Only, he didn't show up. I don't know why. I'm mad and sort of relieved. I know he wanted things from me. Things I'm not ready to give. I'm only fourteen. Okay, the real reason I was thankful he wasn't there is... the thought of sex grosses me out." You and me both, sister, I thought with a sigh. Then I read the next sentence and froze. *"Especially after all the sex that has been forced on me already."*

I sat up and reread the entire paragraph several times. I

was a firm believer that it was taboo to skim ahead in a book. Any book. Even a dead fourteen-year-old's diary. The desire to do so was strong, but I put the book back in my nightstand. I figured I'd waited long enough that Phil had probably found someone else to torture.

I didn't know what the family did during the day. Most of the time, everyone just sat in the living room, talking to George.

I'd overheard a few conversations and from what I could understand, they all wanted something from him. Lane had mentioned that Phil and his dad, Robert, wanted George to publicly back him in his Congressional race.

Robert had only spoken a handful of words to me and spent most of his time on his phone, either making calls or looking at the screen. I was quite sure he was playing games but hadn't had the opportunity to see the screen.

His wife, Reba, however, had plenty to say to me. At first, she'd complained about everything I was doing. My cleaning wasn't good enough. My meals weren't of a high enough quality. I had missed dusting an item or had not gotten a stain out of a tablecloth. She acted as if I worked for her.

She was the one who had coerced me into doing the family's laundry and making and packing dinners for them when they weren't going to be at George's house.

The woman had threatened that if I wanted to keep the job, I'd comply.

I honestly hadn't minded. Until she'd accused me of ruining her husband's shirt and demanded I reimburse her four hundred dollars for the item. Who in their right mind would pay four hundred dollars for a stupid white button-up shirt?

Thankfully, Lane had stepped in and saved me from

paying her. I doubted I had the skills to stand up to the woman. After all, the entire year I was behind bars, Foxy and her crew had had me waiting on them hand and foot. Even after Lucy returned.

Derrick's parents, Kate and Donnie, were a little easier to deal with. Still, they were both demanding and reminded me of children when they didn't get what they wanted.

Kate refused to eat several of my salads because they had the wrong dressing on them. After complaining, she would demand I make her an entirely new meal. If Lane was around, he would step in and tell his aunt to just not eat the salad and enjoy the rest of the meal.

Somehow, when he talked, everyone seemed to listen. The power he had to control his family was something I wished I could learn.

Kate's husband Donnie was... well... a man baby. Most of his time was spent in the television room, watching movies or playing video games. Yes, video games. He was constantly talking about computers but didn't even really know how to hook up a game console to the television.

He'd brought along a set of headphones and was often yelling into them as he played a very detailed shooting game.

The graphics were so crazy that, once, when I was cleaning his spilled chips and drink and happened to glance up, I almost threw up at the amount of blood gushing from a character. Donnie was laughing as his character repeatedly stabbed the other until the screen turned all red.

I felt nauseous for almost an hour after that and vowed to never glance up at the screen again. Sometimes Derrick or Phil would join in the games, and the three of them would drink beer and yell at one another, all while the rest of the family sat around watching.

All except Lane, who was locked in the front office trying to work, and George, who would usually sit outside with Byron or head upstairs to nap.

At first, I didn't know why his family came over every day. They could have spent their summer at the house they'd rented. After the first week, I realized I was the reason they hung around. Not because they assumed I was out to steal George's money. No, the reason they drove over here every day was because I was free labor. Their slave.

When they wanted a soda from the fridge, all they had to do was call out and demand it. When they wanted snacks, I was there. Their dirty dishes magically disappeared, their messes were cleaned, their favorite foods and drinks were ordered and replaced weekly without them so much as batting an eye. They hadn't even had to pay for it all, since it was George's shopping orders.

I hadn't minded at first. But then their requests changed from soft tones to yelling. Sometimes they were so loud about their demands that Lane came out and argued with them to keep it down since he was going to be on a call.

I knew that he was trying to help. For a while, it seemed to. Hours would go by without them yelling or demanding anything from me.

The following day, however, it would start all over again.

I was actually looking forward to having a full day off, away from them. Away from the crazy family and a break from all the work.

No matter what was going on in my life, I'd stayed busy through it all. The hardest times were when I couldn't, such as in one of my many visits to the isolation rooms in prison.

For my own mental health, I needed to stay busy. Idle hands and all that.

Since Lane hadn't come out of the office for dinner, I made a tray of food and carried it into him.

He was busy on the phone but motioned for me to set it on the desk as he moved his laptop aside, then he waved towards the chair for me to sit and wait until he was done with the call.

Moments later, he hung up. He rubbed his forehead and smiled over at me.

"How was today?" he asked, lifting the lid on the food.

"Good," I said, automatically.

His eyes ran over my face and, as if he could sense my worries, he frowned. Then his eyes moved down, and I saw him visibly tense.

"Who did that?" he asked between clenched teeth.

"What?" I asked, looking to where his eyes were locked.

I hadn't noticed or I just hadn't looked. In the same spot Phil had grabbed me upstairs were four perfect dark bruises where his fingers had dug into my skin.

Seeing them, I gasped slightly. They weren't the first bruises a man had put on me, nor, the way my life was going, would they likely be the last.

"I..." I started, but I stopped when Lane stood up quickly and started to leave the room.

I jumped up and rushed to stop him. Thankfully, I caught him before he left the room.

"Don't," I warned softly. "Please don't fight."

"Someone hurt you," he said, his eyes glued to the door.

"They're leaving for the night," I said, still holding his arm. "They'll be gone in a few minutes."

Lane visibly relaxed. He closed his eyes and took several deep breaths.

"Who?" he asked softly.

For a split second, I thought about not telling him. But

then I realized he'd probably do whatever was necessary to find out anyway.

"Phillip. He somehow found out that I don't have a license and couldn't open a bank account," I answered.

Lane leaned his head back and looked up at the ceiling for a moment.

"I bet he tried to blackmail you into sleeping with him to keep that knowledge a secret from the rest of the family?" he said, returning his gaze to look at me.

"I don't know what he wanted, only that he thought he could intimidate me."

Lane brushed the bruised skin with his fingertips.

"Did he hurt you anywhere else?" he asked, his voice almost a whisper.

"He pulled my hair," I said, lost in his eyes.

"Son of a..." He jerked slightly, dropping his hands.

I reached down and took them in my hands and lifted them to my lips, kissing them until they relaxed.

"I'm okay, really. No broken bones," I assured him. "I've had worse."

His eyes flew back to mine, and his frown told me I'd once again said the wrong thing.

"Your husband?" he asked me.

I nodded. Suddenly, I felt the knot that had been in my stomach from the first time that Elliott had struck me loosen.

I'd never told anyone before. I'd always been afraid of what would happen if I did.

I had been indoctrinated to believe it was his right to punish me as he saw fit. I was, after all, his property. Bought and paid for before I'd even reached puberty. Before I had even known that women bleed each month.

"Did he do that often? Beat you?" Lane asked, his voice

just a whisper. I nodded again, avoiding his eyes. "How old were you?" he asked. This time, my eyes flew to his.

I knew what he was asking. Knew what he would think if I answered truthfully. Did I even care to protect myself any longer? Why did this hurt so much?

"How old were you, Chloe, when you were forced to marry?" he asked again, his hands turning slightly until our fingers tangled.

I looked at them, his large, tan fingers intertwined with my smaller pale ones. The feeling of his skin on mine was like nothing I'd ever felt before.

Just being around Lane made me feel as I did when I'd had too much wine, which I'd only done twice in my life.

He released my left hand and placed his fingertips under my chin, lifting it until our eyes met. "How old?" he asked again. "Sixteen?"

I shook my head and he frowned. "Fifteen?" I shook my head again. I could see the anger grow behind his eyes. "Tell me," he practically begged.

"Twelve," I said finally as tears streamed down my cheeks.

"Damn it," he growled out. He pulled me to his chest and wrapped his arms around me. "I wish I could hunt down..." He stopped and I felt his chest rise and fall as he took a couple of deep breaths. "Later," he said after a sob escaped me. "Later," he said again, and I felt him kiss the top of my head.

The funny thing was, I wasn't crying because of what I'd gone through in my past. There was nothing I could do to change it. I'd survived it. I was here. In a much better place.

No, I was crying because of what Lane probably thought of me. I didn't want his pity. I hated when others looked at me as if I were a victim. I didn't want the way he looked at me to change.

Unlike his cousins, I wanted Lane to look at me with desire. I wanted to feel his needs for me. For the first time in my life, I wanted a man to want me. To take me. To make me his.

I wanted to have sex. Real sex. Hot. Steamy. Sweaty sex. I wanted to feel something I'd never felt before.

And I wanted it with Lane.

Now, with the tears blocking my vision, I knew he wouldn't look at me the same.

He brushed his fingers over my face, wiping the tears away. I held still as he dipped his head and licked them away, shocking me. I held my breath, not wanting him to stop.

My tears dried up as a soft moan vibrated deep in my chest.

"Chloe," he said softly as his mouth moved to the spot just below my left ear. "This is a bad idea." His breath caused bumps to rise all over my skin.

My fingers moved up into his hair, nudging, pushing, keeping him where I wanted.

"No, please don't stop," I sighed as his mouth moved lower. "Please," I begged.

His hands slipped under my shirt, lifting it until he cupped my breasts. I arched, not sure what I was feeling. I was pretty confident I would be unable to stand on my own if he released me.

His mouth feathered over my skin and then suddenly disappeared. I made some sort of sound, causing him to chuckle. With his eyes locked on mine, he slowly lifted my shirt over my head.

Then his eyes ran over me, over my skin and the simple

white cotton bra I'd purchased at the store in town. His smile and the heat in his eyes assured me that he liked what he saw.

Then he was back, only this time his mouth ran over places no man had kissed before.

I arched for him. Into him.

His fingers nudged the straps of my bra down until it joined my shirt on the floor.

When he took my nipple into his mouth, I cried out as I felt my entire body pulsate.

"My god," he growled with my nipple still in his mouth. "More," he said as he unclasped my shorts and nudged them down. "More," he growled, his fingers dipping into my underwear.

I'd never felt anything like it. When his fingertips brushed gently over me, I actually saw stars explode behind my closed eyelids. I cried out, screaming his name as my body convulsed for him.

I felt my slickness as he slid his finger into me just a little.

"My god, you're so wet," he moaned as he continued to suck on my breast. "I have to..." He dropped off and then his finger disappeared.

His hands moved to hold my hips as he knelt in front of me, his head directly in front of my white cotton underwear.

I gasped as he pulled the light material until it ripped away easily. Then his mouth covered me. His tongue darted out, lapping at me, in me, around me.

If he hadn't been holding my hips, I would have sunk to the ground. That or I would have fled. I'd never done anything like this. Had never known it was possible.

He was kissing me. Down there.

His tongue entered me, exited me, then entered again, much like he'd done with his finger.

Why did this feel so... good?

Was this normal? Did others do this?

Oh god. Why hadn't I known this was possible?

I buried my fingers into his hair as he continued. Then he slipped his finger into me again as his tongue ran over me, and once more those fireworks exploded.

In that moment, I knew. For my entire life, I'd been cheated out of sex.

CHAPTER THIRTEEN

"Veil after veil of thin dusky gauze is lifted, and by degrees the forms and colours of things are restored to them, and we watch the dawn remaking the world in its antique pattern."
- Oscar Wilde

Lane

I was no longer Lane Nathaniel Robinson. I was a beast. The kind of animal that would consume a young almost virgin in my grandfather's study, no less.

Feeling Chloe soaking my fingers, convulsing around them, had awoken something buried in me. Something dangerous. Something that wasn't easily sated.

Tasting her was another big mistake. She was the sweetest nectar. The forbidden fruit men were warned away from.

There was no stopping me now. When I felt her knees buckle, I stood up and carried her now naked body to the leather sofa.

I was still fully dressed as I stood over her, looking at what I'd just consumed. More, I thought instantly.

Her long hair was fanned out over the rich leather. Her cheeks glowed with soft hues of pink. Her eyes watched me cautiously.

"Was that your first time coming?" I asked, wanting, no, needing her to say yes.

She sucked that luscious bottom lip of hers into her mouth and bit down on it, and I felt my dick jump in response. How would that mouth feel wrapped around my cock?

When she nodded her head, I growled.

I saw her tense, then she lifted her hands towards me.

"Please," she said softly.

No power on earth could have stopped me from taking her now.

Without thinking, I stepped out of my shoes and yanked my pants off. She sat up, her eyes wide as she reached to help me pull my shirt off.

When I stood in front of her, as naked as she was, her eyes ran over me as if this was the first time that she'd seen a man's bare form.

I didn't want to think about what she'd gone through in her past. Didn't want to know at this moment.

It was very obvious that she was cautious, almost afraid of what I'd do.

One of my ex-girlfriends had confided in me after about a month of dating that she'd been raped back in high school. I'd learned early what she could handle and what she couldn't. I'd like to think I'd helped her heal by showing her that not all men were animals. In the end, Crissy had assured me that I'd handled things perfectly between us.

Now, however, with Chloe looking at me as if she'd

never seen a dick before, I questioned how I was going to handle the situation.

"Do I scare you?" I asked softly. Her eyes remained on my dick as she shook her head from side to side. "Have you... seen a dick before?" I asked. She shook her head again.

"I... never wanted to look," she said, her eyes slowly going up my stomach and chest until they locked with my eyes. "You're so pretty."

I smiled. "So are you," I said. Then I remembered the rubber in my wallet and retrieved it. She frowned as she watched me open the foil.

"What's that?" she asked.

"It's a rubber." I showed it to her. "It will prevent a baby."

She frowned. "Isn't that a sin?" Her cheeks grew pink.

I stilled. "You... you were married"—I didn't want to calculate just how long— "and you never had children?"

She shook her head. "Elliott believed it was because I wasn't godly enough." She bit her bottom lip again.

I cursed the fool once more in my head. I wanted to hunt down her ex-husband, her family, and skin them alive.

I figured the best way to help her relax was to talk to her. So, as I slid the rubber on, I told her what I was doing, what I wanted to do to her.

When I nudged her back onto the sofa and covered her, settling between her legs, she wrapped her arms around me.

I kissed her and told her what I wanted, how she made me feel, until I felt her completely relax.

When I slid into her, I knew her desires had built up as much as mine had. Her legs wrapped around my hips, holding me to her, swaying with each move I made.

Her nails scraped my skin. Her moans mixed with my own.

I was feeling so much I doubted that I could last much longer. I wanted to feel her convulse around me. I needed it.

I deepened the kiss, and the moment I felt her release, I followed, pouring everything that had been locked up deep inside me into her. Giving her more than I had given anyone else before.

I knew that whatever she did with it, I would be okay just having felt this much once in my life.

I collapsed, breathing heavily against her skin. Her arms wrapped around me, holding me, as our hearts synced and slowed, cooling our bodies until I felt her shiver.

"You're cold." I leaned up so that I could look down at her.

I realized that it mattered to me that she didn't feel awkward now.

Smiling, I kissed her until I felt her sigh. At that moment, my stomach let out a very loud growl, reminding me that I had skipped dinner and that was the main reason she'd come into the office in the first place.

"Your dinner is probably cold," she said with a chuckle. "I can heat it up for you?"

I nodded and stood up, letting her get up and quickly put on her clothes as I pulled my own on.

When she reached to take the tray, I touched her arm, only then remembering the bruises my cousin had given her.

"I've got this," I told her. She nodded and allowed me to carry the tray back into the kitchen.

While she heated the food up again, I watched her and could tell she was feeling uneasy around me.

Did she expect me to want sex all the time now? Did she believe we should marry? I frowned at that thought.

I knew she'd grown up with religion embedded into every aspect of her life. From what I could tell, she wasn't religious any longer.

"What now?" she asked me when she set the plate of hot food in front of me.

"Now?" I asked, feeling my gut twist.

"I mean, what will you do to Phillip?" she asked, leaning on the counter.

I instantly relaxed. Okay, so maybe she wasn't expecting a proposal. At least not now.

"Now," I said, taking a bite of the meal, "I kill my cousin."

She frowned and straightened. "No, you can't."

"I'm only joking," I said with a sigh. "What I can do is have my grandfather bar him from his home and from being alone with you again."

She leaned on the counter again and nodded. "I think that's for the best."

I nodded in agreement. "He's an ass. They both are. I don't really remember when I realized that myself. Hell, I was probably an ass most of my youth too." I took another bite of the food. My gut twisted when I remembered just when that had all changed. When Sherry had died.

"You loved your sister," Chloe said, touching my hand. "She loved you."

"Did you have siblings?" I asked.

She sighed and placed her chin in her hands. "A dozen or more."

"Right," I sighed. "Were you close to any of them?"

Her eyes locked with mine. "Up until I married. Then,

after..." She shook her head. "I had other duties to fill my time instead."

"Right," I said again.

"Does it bother you?" she asked, shocking me a little.

"What?" I frowned.

"Knowing. I've never told anyone else before." She watched me closely.

"It doesn't bother me that you've told me. There are a handful of people on this planet I want to kill now, but no." I took her hand in mine. "I don't think differently of you, if that's what you were getting at." She nodded slowly. "It wasn't you. You did nothing wrong." I said it slowly.

Her lower lip quivered, and I reached out and tugged her until she was in my arms.

Instead of crying, she sighed and relaxed.

"Thank you," she said against my chest.

"For?" I asked.

"Showing me what sex could be." She leaned back and looked into my eyes. "I saw the worry in your eyes." She smiled. "I'm not going to force you to marry me."

I chuckled. "That's good. I'm not ready to make that leap, just yet."

She nodded. "I like things the way they are." She looked down at my lips. "I don't know if I'll ever want to marry again."

I nodded, understanding.

"For the first time in my life, I'm in charge," she said with a smile. "I feel as if I'm not only finally in charge of my sexuality, but my entire life."

"You're the boss." I brushed my lips over hers. "If I do something you don't like, feel free to tell me," I said between kisses.

"Lane?" she said softly.

"Hm?" I asked.

"How about we take your food up to my room so you can finish it there," she said next to my lips. "After."

As an answer, I quickly gathered her up in my arms, her legs wrapped around my hips. I tried to take my plate but ended up having to have her hold it while I rushed through the light rain to the garage staircase and into her room.

Once more, we pulled our clothes off, only this time we made it to the bed, and I forced myself to slow down. I wanted to show her everything she'd missed over the years. Everything she hadn't experienced.

By the time we sat in bed, munching on the cold dinner, I was pretty confident I had shown her a few more new things. I was also a little surprised that she'd managed to show me a few things as well.

I'd never experienced the sort of connection we had before. There had been a few women in my past that I'd thought I'd had a deep bond with. But as I fell asleep with Chloe wrapped around me, the soft subtle smell of her filling my senses, I realized I'd been wrong.

I woke to the distant sound of a dog howling and, for a split second, was confused about where I was. Then Chloe's soft body rubbed up against mine, and the memories flooded back.

"It's Byron," she said. She shifted away from me before I could pull her back. I leaned up and watched her quickly pull on her shorts and a shirt. "Your grandfather is probably sleeping, and Byron needs out," she said over her shoulder. Then she smiled. "Stay in bed. I'll be just a moment."

I nodded, knowing exactly what I wanted to do to her when she returned. But she didn't return for such a long time that I grew worried. I pulled on my own clothes and stepped out and saw the back door to the house wide open.

I glanced towards the beach pathway and listened. Maybe she'd taken Byron to the beach?

Then I heard Byron barking from inside the house. I followed the sounds, rushing down the stairs and through the back door.

Chloe and my grandfather stood in the hallway, just outside of Sherry's room. When they heard me, Chloe glanced over at me, her hands covering her mouth.

"Lane, I..." she said, shaking her head.

I stopped next to them and was shocked at the destruction I saw inside. My sister's clothes lay in piles on the floor, cut into pieces. All of her trinkets and pictures were sliced or destroyed.

"What the hell?" I asked, feeling my heart sink.

"Byron was trapped in the pantry somehow," Chloe said softly. "When I let him out, he led me here."

"I didn't hear a thing," my grandfather said. "You know I sleep like the devil, boy." He touched my shoulder. "Even if Byron was barking at whoever did this, I didn't hear a thing."

"He was locked in the pantry downstairs," Chloe said again. "Someone locked him in there."

"Who?" I felt my anger grow. "Why?"

"The back door was unlocked," Chloe said, meeting my eyes. "Whoever did this last night must have used it to get in."

Suddenly, I understood. When I'd carried her out last night, I hadn't locked it. I'd been too preoccupied.

I stepped inside the room, glancing around. All of the furniture was there, but it was shoved aside.

"George, why don't I take you downstairs?" Chloe said suddenly. "Get you something to eat?"

I turned and realized how pale my grandfather's face was.

Leaving the destruction behind, I took my grandfather's arm and helped him downstairs.

"Should we call the police?" Chloe whispered as she made my grandfather a cup of coffee. He was sitting on the sofa with Byron lying beside him.

I thought about it and then glanced around the rest of the house. Nothing looked out of place. Still, I wanted some time to check for myself.

"Give me a while. I'll look around and see if anything else was disturbed. If not..." I shook my head.

"You think this was someone in your family?" she asked softly.

I shrugged. "If nothing else was taken, then yes."

"Why?" she asked, shaking her head.

"That's the question." I sighed and took the cup of coffee she offered me.

An hour later, my family arrived. At this point, there was no doubt in my mind that one of them had destroyed Sherry's things. Not a single thing in the rest of the house had been disturbed.

The only question still in my mind was why.

I'd convinced my grandfather to allow me to toss them all out for the rest of the week. After all, in two days they were all heading back to the city until Monday anyway. Or so they claimed.

"Chloe, why don't you help my grandfather back upstairs so he can rest?" I suggested when I saw their car pull up outside.

The group strolled in as if they owned the place, no doubt expecting breakfast and hot coffee. I stopped them from heading back to the kitchen.

"Grandfather has requested an empty house until Monday," I said, standing my ground. "Why don't you spend some of your time at the house you rented instead of here."

My aunts and uncles laughed at me, then waved me off and tried to pass by. I held out my arms.

"Okay, so we'll do this the not so nice way. Out. Now. And don't come back until Monday." I pointed towards the door.

"Really, Lane," My uncle laughed as my cousins once more tried to move past me.

I made a sound and caught their attention.

"Someone broke in last night," I said, watching everyone for any reaction.

My aunt Kate gasped. "Oh, no. Was anything valuable taken?"

"Until we can determine that, we need everyone out," I lied.

"We can help," Phil suggested.

"No. Grandfather is resting, and we don't need the noise. Go." I waved them towards the door again. "We've got this."

"It was probably that girl," Reba said under her breath as she turned to go.

I wanted to argue, to tell them that I was with Chloe all night, but they didn't even deserve the breath. Instead, I locked the front door behind them, thankful that they hadn't put up too much of a fight.

I had heard my cousin complain about what they were going to do for breakfast, which made me smile.

"Lane?" Chloe said from the stairs.

"They're gone." I stopped at the base of the stairs and waited until she stood next to me.

"I... I think I know what they were looking for," she said, glancing at the shut front door.

"What?" I asked with a frown.

She glanced once more upstairs, then took my hand. I followed her through the house, outside, and back up the stairs to her room.

"Here," she said, opening the drawer of her nightstand.

I stood there in complete shock as she produced a small red leather book. I'd seen Sherry writing in others just like it, years ago.

"Where did you get this?" I asked, taking it from her hands.

"I found it the other day, hidden under the floorboards of her closet." Chloe bit her bottom lip.

My first inclination was to be pissed. My second was more rational. I was thankful. Thankful I now had it in my hands and that it was safe. My third thought had my stomach twisting.

I sat on the edge of the bed that we'd shared last night and just stared at the book. For her entire life, the one thing Sherry had stood against was me getting my hands on her diary.

How would my sister feel if she knew I had it now? My stomach turned at the thought, but I had to know what was in there.

"I didn't mean to disrespect..." Chloe started, but I jerked my gaze up to her.

"You didn't. I mean, Sherry's gone." I held out the book. Chloe frowned and shook her head. "Take it. Please."

"Why?" she asked, sitting beside me.

I set the book down between us, not wanting it in my hands to temp me any further.

Of course, I wanted to read it. But my respect for my sister was greater than that desire.

"Sherry would hate to know that I'd read her private moments," I said, not looking at Chloe. "You read it. Keep it safe." I looked into her eyes. "Let me know if there's anything in there... I should know." I swallowed the guilt and the worry that my sister knew ahead of time what was going to happen to her. That she'd been afraid. For some reason, it seemed better that she'd been blindsided. "Please. I... don't think I could stand to read it myself."

Chloe searched my eyes and then gently picked up the book and set it in her lap.

CHAPTER FOURTEEN

"The breeze at dawn has secrets to tell you. Don't go back to sleep."
\- Rumi

Chloe

I held onto the book as sadness flooded Lane's eyes.

"I've only read a few pages," I told him.

He nodded, then stood up suddenly. "I'd better get in." He glanced at his watch and sighed heavily. "I have a meeting in five minutes."

I nodded again, not wanting to move. When he turned to go, however, I jumped in.

"Do you think there's something in here they wanted?" I asked.

He stopped in the doorway and glanced back at me. "Until we find out, hide it better than in the nightstand." He turned and left.

I sat there for a while, unsure of why he'd allowed me to keep the thing. Was he upset I took it in the first place? I shouldn't have, I knew that now.

Still, had the person who'd broken in last night found Sherry's hiding place? I itched to go look. I also needed to go clean up the mess they'd left behind.

It was strange that Lane and George didn't want to call the police about the break-in. I was thankful, however, since they might question my credentials.

I'd been with Lane all night, and he would back me up on that. But I would probably be on the cops' radar, and also his family's, when my past was exposed.

I looked around the room, trying to find the best hiding spot. When I walked into the bathroom, I thought of the one place often used in prison to keep things out of the guard's view.

I pulled out my tampon box and shoved the book down to the bottom, then put the box in the back of the cupboard.

That hiding spot would have to do for now.

Since I'd left in such a hurry, I took a moment to comb my hair, wash my face, and change into some more appropriate clothes.

Taking some trash bags with me, I headed up to Sherry's room and started cleaning the mess.

The first thing I noticed was that whoever had broken in hadn't found the diary's initial hiding spot. Should I put the book back? Would it be safer there with the rest of her trinkets?

I wondered about that the entire time I cleaned.

All of the clothes I'd borrowed were now destroyed, torn to shreds by a box cutter I'd found in the rubble and had almost cut myself on.

By the time George walked in a couple hours later, the

room was put back to normal, minus everything that had once belonged to Sherry.

"This looks better," he said, leaning just outside the door with his arms crossed over his chest. Byron sat at his feet, as if still on guard.

"How are you feeling?" I asked, worried.

"Better." He ran his eyes over the missing pictures in the room. "I didn't have the heart to get rid of anything in here," he admitted.

"I'm sorry the choice was taken from you," I said, touching his arm. There were four large black trash bags full of Sherry's things sitting in the hallway. "Would you like some lunch?" I asked, looking at the clock in the bedroom.

George nodded and Byron did a few happy circles.

I started to pick up the trash bags, but George waved them away. "Lane can take those out later. You've done enough heavy lifting for the day." He smiled at me.

As we walked down the stairs together slowly, he said, "I bet it will be nice, not having my family around for the next few days."

I smiled. "It is a nice break."

When we got to the bottom of the stairs, he glanced towards the closed office door.

"I happened to notice my grandson didn't come from his own room this morning," he said, winking at me. "Don't worry." He patted my hand. "I won't hold it against you that you've fallen for his charms. After all, he takes after me."

I laughed and then hugged him.

"Should I worry that you're moving in on my catch?" Lane said from the office door that he'd just opened.

George laughed and then kissed my cheek. "If only I could get someone like Chloe to look at me the way she looks at you, boy." He and Byron disappeared into the kitchen.

Lane's smile slipped and he glanced up the stairs. "How's it looking up there?"

"All clean. There are some trash bags that your grandfather volunteered you to cart out." I walked into his arms and placed a kiss on his lips. "They didn't find your sister's hiding spot. The shoe box with her treasures is still there."

Lane frowned. "There was more than just her diary?"

I nodded. "Do you want to go see?"

He shook his head. "Maybe later. For now, I'll take the trash out, then we can have lunch." He kissed me again and then headed up the stairs.

Since the rain had stopped earlier that morning, we ate lunch out on the back patio like we used to before the family had arrived. Just the three of us. Four, if you counted Byron, which I did. Especially since he ate half of my sandwich and chips.

After lunch, Lane headed back inside for another call while George, Byron, and I took a short walk on the beach.

We were halfway back to the house when George slumped slightly. His weight doubled as he leaned on me.

"Oh, girl," he said softly, "I think I need a quick sit down."

Worry flooded me and after sitting in the sand with him for a few moments, I sent Byron to the house in hopes he would get Lane.

Less than two minutes later, Lane rushed down the pathway with Byron barking at his heels.

"What is it?" he asked, kneeling by his grandfather.

"I'm just tired," George said, but I could hear the weariness in his voice. It was more than that. His coloring was off, and his eyes were unfocused.

"Lane," I said, searching his eyes.

He nodded quickly and pulled out his cell phone, then handed it to me. "Call 911. I'll carry him to the road."

As I dialed, Lane lifted his grandfather easily into his arms and started back down the pathway towards the house and the road.

It took the ambulance a little over ten minutes to get there. By then, I'd locked up the house with Byron inside and had grabbed my purse, just in case I needed it. I had time to lock up the house and my room above the garage.

"Will you ride with him? I'll drive right behind the ambulance," Lane said.

I nodded and was loaded into the back of the ambulance with George. I held his hand while a paramedic took his blood pressure.

It surprised me how quiet George was during the process. They put oxygen on him and even gave him an IV drip.

The entire time, I talked softly to him. I didn't think he could hear me, but when I stopped, his eyes would search around as if he were looking for me, so I kept talking. After running out of things to say, I started talking about books. I went through some of my favorite lines or poems, not really caring what the paramedics thought of me.

When the ambulance stopped, I stood back and watched them wheel him into the hospital. I didn't know how long we'd traveled or if we were even still on the island or not.

Lane was there, and he took my hand as we followed them inside.

"Sit," Lane said, motioning to a row of chairs. "I'll check in with the nurses."

I sat, my hands in my lap and tears threatening to fall

down my cheeks as I counted the minutes. Lane returned and we sat in silence, waiting for some word from the doctors or nurses.

His phone rang in my pocket, where I'd shoved it after making the 911 call, and I handed it back to him.

"Yes?" he asked into the phone. "Right now, I can't. We're at the hospital with Grandpa." He was quiet for a moment. "The one in Coupeville." He glanced at me. "Yeah, we'll be here." He hung up. "My family is on their way." He sighed and leaned back.

I took his hand in mine. "They were bound to find out sooner or later."

He nodded. "I'd hoped it would be after we'd heard something."

Just then, the doors opened, and a doctor stepped out. Since we were the only ones in the waiting room, he moved over to us.

"Evening. You're the Robinson family?" he asked.

"Yes." Lane jumped up. "How is he?"

"Resting. Your grandfather was seriously low on potassium. We're running a drip now. I don't like his blood pressure and want to keep him for a few days, if possible."

"Can we see him?" I asked.

Lane took my hand again, and we followed the doctor back through the doors into a private room.

George was lying in a hospital bed with tubes in his arms and an oxygen mask covering his face. He looked so small. So frail. I finally lost control of my tears and had to wipe my face with my sleeve as Lane spoke to him.

I didn't know why I was crying. Was it fear about losing my stability there or had George come to mean more to me than almost anyone else in my entire life?

When the tears became too much, I stepped out of the room, searching desperately for a bathroom.

"Right here, honey," I heard a nurse say. She took my arm and led me to the bathroom.

I locked myself inside, sat on the floor with my back to the door, and cried until I finally got myself under control.

Had it really been just two months since I'd started working for George? How had the man wiggled his way into my heart so quickly? I never let anyone in. Never. Just the thought of losing him brought on a panic attack.

George and Byron meant more to me than anything else ever had. It wasn't because my entire livelihood rested on his kindness. I didn't care if I went back to living on the beach or the streets.

It wasn't as if I'd ever had material things before. Nothing had ever been mine until that day Lane had taken me shopping.

Growing up, before my marriage, everything I had belonged to everyone. My clothes, my bed, my toys—it had all been communal. Much like it was in prison. After marriage, everything had belonged to my husband. He had never let me forget that fact.

When a soft knock sounded on the door, I jumped up, washed my face, and pulled myself together. Then I stepped out and realized it was Lane waiting for me outside.

"Are you okay?" he asked, his eyes running over my face.

I nodded and swallowed the pain and worry before I asked, "How is he?"

"He's asking for you," Lane answered. Then he pulled me into his arms, and I almost lost it again right there.

He pulled back, took my hand, and led me back to the private room.

George was now sitting up, sipping some water.

"There you are, girl," he said with a smile.

I dropped Lane's hand and rushed to George's side and gently hugged him.

"You scared me," I said softly as more tears rolled down my cheeks.

"There, there." George patted my hair as he handed Lane the water cup so he could wrap both arms around me. "I'm okay. Feeling much better since they poked me and are shoving some potassium in me. I guess you'll have to add bananas to the shopping list," he joked.

I sat on the side of the bed and ran my eyes over him. His coloring was getting better. Not back to normal, but better.

When he noticed the tears on my cheeks, he lifted a shaky hand and brushed them away.

"What's all this? For me?"

"No, never," I joked.

George smiled. "When can I go home?" he asked Lane.

Before he could answer, the door flew open and the rest of the family rushed in. Several of them glared at me sitting next to George, so I stood up and moved to the back of the room while he visited with them.

A minute later, I snuck out of the room. I wasn't wanted, that was obvious. More than one of them had accused me of poisoning George or forcing him to exercise too much.

Thankfully, Lane jumped to my defense, but I didn't want to listen to another fight, so I walked out to the lobby area.

There was a soda and candy machine. I'd never experienced anything like it, so I decided it was a good time to try.

Besides, I'd always wanted to have a soda and a candy bar from a large vending machine.

I'd had plenty of sweets growing up, but nothing mass produced. Sodas were a sin, I'd been told repeatedly growing up. I'd had canned teas or bottled water, but never a soda.

I took some change from my purse and followed the instructions on the machine. I was pleased when my selections dropped into the bin. I took them to the waiting area and sat and enjoyed the treats.

I was disappointed in the candy bar I'd selected, though. It had a strong chemical taste. I could make a better dessert with my eyes closed.

I thought about all the ingredients and how I'd put them together to fill my time while I waited.

By the time Lane stepped out and found me, it was dark outside.

"Hungry?" he asked, looking at the wrappers.

"Yes. You?"

He nodded. "Let's head out. They're going to kick the rest of the family out in less than an hour. There's no use sticking around and arguing with them. I'm too hungry and tired for it."

I followed him out, tossing my trash in the can as we went. He helped me into his car, and we sat in silence as he drove.

It was too dark outside to see much as we traveled back towards the house. The first thing that looked familiar to me was the little gas station that I had walked to my first week on the island. That day felt so long ago. Lane pulled in and parked the car.

"I figured we could grab a burger here instead of trying

to make something at the house," Lane said, opening my car door for me.

"Thanks," I said, feeling uneasy about returning to a place that held bad memories.

We walked right in, past the spot I'd dropped the bread while being accosted by the large man.

The place was fairly packed, but we found a table near the back wall and sat down.

Looking over the menu, I was slightly shocked at how expensive the food was. Since I'd been in charge of ordering the food in the house, I knew pretty well what things cost to purchase.

The service George used had a program on the computer screen on his refrigerator. All I had to do was scroll through the items, add it to a cart, and hit the order button. The items would be added to the next delivery. Simple.

I spent so much time scrolling through everything, I probably had the entire menu memorized.

When the waitress came, Lane ordered a cheeseburger, fries, and a chocolate milkshake. I set the menu down and ordered the same thing.

I leaned forward after the waitress left and whispered, "This is my first time at a restaurant." It sounded so foolish.

"Really?" Lane frowned, then everything about him shifted. The tired look he'd had moments before was gone, replaced by something I'd never seen before. "You should have told me." He leaned closer and lowered his voice. "We could have done so much better than here. This is a gas station diner, not a real restaurant. When we get to Seattle tomorrow, I'll take you to a real restaurant."

I smiled. "I'd like that." Then I remembered George. "Will George be, okay?" I asked.

He nodded. "Yes, they want to keep him for a few nights. He made me promise that we wouldn't cancel our plans. I told him that we'd take Byron with us."

"What about your family?" I asked.

Lane shrugged. "They're heading back to the city in the morning as well."

"Are you sure he's going to be all right?" I asked.

Lane reached across the table and took my hand in his. "He'll have round-the-clock care. It's funny, when my grandmother was going through cancer, she hated being in the hospital. But whenever my grandfather has ended up there, he acts as if it's his spa time. He actually told me tonight that he likes hospital food." He chuckled. "I think he likes flirting with all the nurses and female doctors they have on staff there."

I smiled and relaxed a little. "He did look like he was enjoying himself when I saw him."

"Trust me, you don't have to worry about him. We'll go back, get some sleep, then head into the city with Byron in the morning." He relaxed back, still holding my hand.

"What the hell are you still doing on the island?" a deep voice said behind me.

I froze. I remembered that voice. How the man had assaulted me and taken the last sliver of my dignity.

CHAPTER FIFTEEN

"No eternal reward will forgive us now for wasting the dawn."
\- Jim Morrison

Lane
    I noticed the moment Rod entered the diner. I silently hoped he wouldn't see us in the back corner, but when he strolled over, I held in a groan and figured that my shitty day had just gotten worse.

I wasn't in the mood to deal with him. Hell, I was never in the mood.

"What are you still doing here?" I replied, and annoyance crossed his eyes. Then he ran his eyes over Chloe and zoned in our linked hands.

"Who's this?" Rod asked, and it sickened me the way he was looking at her.

"Why don't you crawl back into the hole you came out

of. We're busy." I turned to ignore him, but he stepped forward and stared at Chloe.

"I know you," he said, pointing at her.

"Leave," I warned, fearing he was remembering Chloe from past news reports about her case. After all, her case had made state news. Though I hadn't recognized her. She'd looked so different in the news reports that I'd gone back and watched. So lost. So... strange.

She'd been wearing long oversized dresses. Her hair had been slightly longer and always up in one of those intricate buns FLDS women were forced to wear.

"You're the woman that ran." He pulled a chair up and turned it to face backwards before sitting on it, leaning on the back. "So, you're with him?"

Chloe looked between the two of us, a look of mortification on her face.

"Rod," I warned, starting to stand up.

"I didn't mean to spook ya," he said, ignoring me, his demeanor suddenly going soft.

Chloe took a deep breath, then nodded.

"I know it may not seem like it, but Lane and I go way back." He motioned between them. "It's kind of our thing to piss one another off."

Somehow, Rod's entire attitude had changed. He was talking to Chloe as if she were a wounded bird. Calm. His voice filled with kindness. It was so unlike him that I sat back and listened to him for a moment.

"I'm really sorry about scaring you. If I did," he said to Chloe.

"Thanks," she replied softly.

I was too shocked to say anything. What had caused Rod to do a one-eighty from last month?

Suddenly, Rod stood up. "To make things right, I'll pick

up your check tonight. Since I caused you to drop your bread last time." He smiled at Chloe, then turned to me. "I found something of your family's," he said, tilting his head, his eyes narrowing. Then he turned and walked up to the counter and asked to pay for our meal.

Once he was done, he nodded at Chloe and then left the diner.

"That was..." Chloe started.

"So out of character," I finished. Then again, the last time I'd seen Rod before that incident last month had been years ago.

It hadn't dawned on me that it was Chloe that day when I'd stepped in. It hadn't mattered who it was. I'd seen Rod forcing himself on someone and felt as if it was my duty to step in.

Our waitress stepped back over with a huge smile on her face.

"I'm working on him," she said with a shrug. "When I noticed it was you"—she motioned to Chloe— "I messaged him. He's been wanting to make it up to you since that day."

"Thanks," Chloe said softly. "Are you two married?"

"Not yet," the woman said. "Not until he finishes healing and growing." She leaned closer and lowered her voice. "Anger management. Course, it was me he was angry at that day. We'd had a fight that morning. I think he hit on you just to piss me off." She turned to me. "I'm Lindsey, by the way. Rod has told me so much about you. How he used to torment you and your cousins every summer." She chuckled. "He says it was his only form of entertainment while school was out."

I nodded. "I'm a little shocked after what just happened."

She laughed again. "He'll get there. If not, he'll miss out

on this." She motioned to herself. "So, yeah, he's working on it." A bell rang and she said, "That'll be your food." Then she turned around and left.

She dropped off our burgers, and we ate in silence for a while. We were so hungry that we devoured the greasy food.

After we finished, I left Lindsey a big tip and then drove us home.

Byron was happy to see us and a little confused that we took him up to the apartment instead of back into the house to sleep.

I fell fast asleep, holding Chloe in my arms. Byron slept at our feet in his bed, but halfway through the night, he snuck up and wedged himself between our bodies, almost dislodging both of us from the bed.

When we woke, it was to a foggy gray morning. We were both still so tired. While I went inside to gather my things, Chloe packed a small bag for herself along with Byron's things, such as food and his bed.

As we drove away from the house with Byron excitedly rushing between the back windows to see where we were going, I could tell Chloe was deep in thought.

"Are you okay?" I asked her once we hit the road that would take us to the ferry.

"Yes, it's just..." She turned to me, then chuckled when Byron shoved his face between ours. "I'm worried. Scared, really."

"Of?" I asked, focusing on driving.

"That the magic of this place will have disappeared when we return," she said with a sigh.

I glanced over and saw her look out the window as Byron settled down. I understood. I was afraid of the same thing. Things had been going well, except for our run-ins with my family. I was enjoying my time with her and didn't want it to end just yet.

I had grown to trust her. Actually, the more I thought about it, the more I realized I trusted Chloe around my grandfather more than I trusted any member of my family. That didn't mean I was going to leave her to fend off the vultures that were my blood relatives.

"My entire life, I've never thought about the future," she said, turning to me.

I was silent for a moment, unsure what to say. From an early age I'd never had to worry about where my next meal was or if I could afford to go to school so I could get the career I wanted. If I'd wanted anything, I simply got it.

With what I knew of Chloe's past, her family had provided for her up until her marriage. Then that had fallen on her husband's shoulders. Everything in her life had been decided for her.

"You're free," I said suddenly. "What do you want to do?"

She was quiet for a moment. "I like where I'm at now. But yesterday made me start thinking about what would happen if George passed."

Before answering, I pulled into the parking area for the ferry. We were early, so I parked and we watched the boat heading across the waterway towards us through the thick fog.

Byron had fallen asleep in the back seat and was snoring loudly. I took Chloe's hands in mine and told her the truth.

"When George passes, no matter what happens, I'll help you find another position. If that's what you want." Sadness flooded her eyes, so I continued. "You're really good at what you do. I know it probably sucks, having done it your entire life. Taking care of others. Cooking. Cleaning."

"No." She shook her head. "That's just the thing. I love it. All of it." She smiled. "I agree, I'm good at it."

I smiled. "Okay, so then we build off that. If you want some sort of career, there are things you can do to increase your desirability in the workplace. Classes, such as..." I thought quickly. "CPR, basic medical training for older clients, computer classes to help with financial planning. Those type of things."

She was frowning again. "Where? How would I do that?"

"Well, most classes you can take online. They also teach some of them in town at the schools or the community centers. We can look at signing you up when we get back."

The ferry was docked now, and cars were exiting. We'd load up in a few moments, so I turned the car back on.

"Thank you," Chloe said. She laughed when Byron woke up and shoved his face between us. "I don't know what I would have done if he hadn't found me on the beach."

I didn't like thinking about that either.

During the drive to the city we chatted about a bunch of other things, but in the back of my mind was that troubling thought.

I worked for the law. For the justice system. Yet that system had allowed a woman with no shelter, no money, and no family to walk away from a year's incarceration with nothing.

Chloe had told me that she'd lied to her parole officer and how she'd only had to check in once. I knew for less serious cases like hers that was true. Still, she should have had a social worker assigned to her, considering her past.

We stopped for coffee and donuts shortly after getting off the ferry.

When I pulled up to my townhouse and parked, it was almost lunch time, thanks to the traffic that the dense fog had caused to pile up on the city streets.

"What do you say we get Byron settled, then head out for some lunch and shopping?" I asked.

Chloe nodded, looking at the townhouse building in front of us.

The brick building housed more than a dozen units and there were at least six other buildings scattered around the complex. There was also a clubhouse, a gym, a swimming pool, tennis courts, and several parks and walking paths.

It was as close to a community that you could get without purchasing a real home. The buildings and grounds were maintained by the homeowners' association.

Most of the owners had some small plants or decorations outside on the steps to make their units unique. I had a doormat that said Welcome.

"This is nice," Chloe said as I carried her bag and Byron's bed up my outer stairs.

"It beats a small apartment downtown." I shrugged. "The law firm I work for is just down the street." I motioned towards the office. "There's a grocery store that way about a block." I waved then unlocked the door.

Chloe was letting Byron pee on the bushes at the foot of the four stairs. Once the door was opened, he rushed in, pulling Chloe along with him.

"He's okay to roam," I said, unhooking his leash after setting his bed down inside my home study.

My style of decoration for the house was simple. I liked neutral colors, straight lines, and nature, so a lot of wood and blues filled the space.

The leather sofas I had bought my first year out on my own were worn and comfortable.

I didn't have people over often. When I dated, I had never brought any of them here unless we'd been going out for months. In the past two years, that had only happened once.

My space was mine.

Chloe looked around the study. "I like the painting." She motioned to the sailboat over the fireplace.

"I bought that at one of the galleries I represented." It was one of the only pieces in the house that I truly loved. It reminded me of the island and all the summers I'd spent there, watching the sailboats and seagulls. "The artist is Allison Jordan."

Chloe ran her eyes over it slowly.

"It's stunning," she said softly. "I've always wanted to learn how to paint." She turned towards me. "I'm pretty good at drawing." She shook her head and then turned away. "Show me around?"

I took her hand and walked through the first floor. Opposite of my study was the living room, which was twice the size of the study. There was a bathroom between the study and the dining room that sat at the back of the house. There was a kitchen and eating space, and off the back was a small deck and private fenced area that Byron explored while I walked her around the rest of the house. Up the stairs were three bedrooms. The main one sat at the back of the house.

It wasn't anything special. Honestly, the building wasn't new and could have used a lot of updates, but it was mine and it suited my needs.

The fact that it was really close to my work was the most important thing. I hated the Seattle commute and traffic. If I didn't live close to my work, I probably would have moved out of the city years ago.

"Ready for lunch?" I asked once I was done showing her the basement laundry room and home gym I had down there.

She glanced at her clothes and shrugged. "Am I dressed okay?"

Since I was wearing a pair of jeans and a button-up shirt, her jeans and blouse were perfect for what I had planned.

I wrapped my arms around her and assured her she was perfect.

I hadn't planned on letting myself get deeper into the relationship, but the next couple hours were the best I'd had in years.

We ate lunch at a chain restaurant a few blocks away, then went shopping. Just seeing how excited Chloe was stepping into the mall was one of the top moments of my year.

She informed me she had a thousand dollars to spend. I expected her to buy a handbag or some shoes with the money. After all, most of the women I'd dated in the past wouldn't have been able to purchase more than one item with that amount of money.

However, Chloe surprised me. She bought six full bags of items—clothing of all types, hair products, makeup, and even a few dog treats for Byron.

What really shocked me was that she purchased a small gift for my grandfather. That made me feel guilty, so I ended up buying him something as well.

While she'd been trying on some clothes, I'd called and made reservations at one of my favorite fancy restaurants for later that night.

After leaving the mall, we headed back to the house and took Byron on a long walk. Since we still had an hour before dinner, I suggested a shower and a change of clothes.

I'd never felt that my shower was too small before, but I'd never shared it with anyone. Now, standing with my back against the wall, I realized just how small the space was.

"Okay, so maybe I need to do some remodeling," I joked, pulling Chloe against my chest.

"I've never showered with anyone before," she said with a chuckle. "I kind of like the closeness."

She rubbed her body against mine, and I forgot why I'd been complaining as I ran my hands over her wet body. I could see each of her ribs and thought she could easily gain a dozen more pounds.

"You're too skinny," I mumbled against her neck as my fingers brushed her nipples. I heard her gasp and arch into my hands.

"I finally feel like I have access to food," she said with a sigh. "Lane?"

"Hm?" I said, running my tongue over her skin, enjoying the taste of her.

"I think we need to get out of the shower." She laughed when I turned off the water and lifted her into my arms.

We made it to the countertop, and I set her on the edge of it and slipped inside her.

I couldn't remember ever feeling so much for someone so quickly before. The more I looked into her eyes, kissed her, was inside her, the more I wanted her.

When I felt her convulse around me, I let go of everything that had building for the past few days.

Hearing her chuckle brought me back to reality.

"Is that what people call a quickie?" she asked next to

my ear.

I frowned, realizing just how inexperienced she was. Damn. I should have been more careful with her, shown her things that she deserved. Not taken her on the bathroom countertop like some sort of... animal.

"I liked it," she said next to my ear, and I felt my dick grow harder. And I was still inside her.

"Okay," I said, shifting away. "If we don't finish showering and dressing, we're going to be late for our dinner."

She was smiling at me as if she knew how much control she had over my body.

"Go, get dressed," I warned and turned towards my closet.

When I came out in one of my suits, she was standing in front of the bathroom mirror in a pretty blue dress with low cream-colored sandals that she'd purchased that day. She was drying her hair and had already applied some makeup.

She looked so different. So... beautiful. If I had met her on the street like this, I definitely would have hit on her. Of course, I probably would have just hooked up with her. I felt my stomach roll at the kind of person I'd become in the past few years.

"You look amazing," I said, when she shut off the blow dryer.

"Thanks." She smiled and then motioned to her curling iron. "I'm almost done here."

"No rush." I leaned on the counter and watched her finish with her hair.

"Tell me about the place we're going," she said as she curled her long hair.

"Six Seven. That's the name of it," I added when she frowned over at me.

"That's a strange name."

"It sits on the water. I reserved a table out on the patio so we can watch the boats and marine life." I told her everything I knew about the place, and then she asked me about my work. I filled her in as we headed out.

The drive was short, and the roads were pretty clear heading into the city.

When we pulled up, the valet helped her out and I checked in my car. I took her hand in mine, and we walked inside and were seated. It was about half an hour before sunset. The fog from earlier had cleared up, leaving perfect conditions for a beautiful sunset.

"This is amazing," Chloe said, her eyes trying to take it all in. Then she was handed a menu, and I saw fear cross her face. "What do you like?" she asked me.

"Wine first." I glanced over the menu, then ordered a bottle I'd enjoyed before. When we were alone, she leaned over and whispered, "I've never been to a place this fancy before. What should I order?"

I ran over a few options, and we both decided to try one of their specials. I went with the salmon, and she ordered the steak. That way, we could try each other's meals.

After ordering, we chatted about how much she enjoyed shopping. Suddenly she stilled, her glass of wine frozen halfway to her lips. A look crossed her face that I'd never seen before.

"What is it?" I asked, following her gaze. There were three tables behind us, each occupied by couples. The indoor dining area was filled with people. I had no idea what had spooked her, but it was obvious that something or someone had scared her. I turned back to her. "Chloe?" I touched her hand, which seemed to get her moving again.

"Lane, I just saw my ex-husband." She blinked a few times as all the color left her cheeks.

CHAPTER SIXTEEN

"Every sunset brings the promise of a new dawn."
- Ralph Waldo Emerson

Chloe
I had never expected to see Elliott again, though I don't know why. I knew it was unlikely he would leave the Seattle area.

When the police had asked me to tell them where he was, I'd told them the truth. I had no clue.

It had been days since I'd seen him last. That hadn't been odd. After we moved to Washington, he'd often disappeared for days at a time.

I was left to fend for myself and to tend to any other families that were visiting or staying in the massive home. But most of the time we had the house all to ourselves.

I had never known who owned the home, nor had I thought to ask.

Most of the rooms had sat empty. We only used four of the rooms ourselves—the one where all of the computers were, a bedroom, a bathroom, and the kitchen.

Everything else sat empty. When there were more families there, they slept in other rooms in sleeping bags.

Of course, the police hadn't believed me when I'd told them I didn't know where my husband was or where he went all the time. They also didn't believe that I had been unaware of the scams he'd been pulling. The millions and millions of dollars he'd stolen from banks, businesses, and people.

It was hard to explain just how ignorant I was to it all. How I wasn't allowed to leave the bedroom if he wasn't there, or how I spent most of my time in the kitchen, making meals or washing clothes in the sink, since there hadn't been a washing machine or dryer.

"Okay," Lane said, pulling out his phone.

"What are you doing?" I asked, suddenly feeling better as the shock wore off.

"Calling the police," he said, glancing around. "Which one is he?"

"He..." I looked, but he was gone. "He's gone," I said, relaxing back.

Lane set his phone down. "Want me to go after him?"

"No!" I practically shouted it. "No," I said again, taking his hand.

I knew what I'd seen. Knew it had been Elliott. He'd been dressed in a business suit, much like he'd always worn. He was heavier, older looking. And he'd been with a woman half his age.

I knew what he could do to women. Knew how he liked to use his fists, his words, his control to get what he wanted.

No doubt he was living a good life with all the money he'd stolen.

I didn't want any part of my past to ruin what I had with Lane. To spoil our night. To spoil any part of us.

"No," I said again with a sigh. "I... I could have been mistaken," I said, even though I knew I wasn't.

The thought of ending our dinner to talk to the police didn't sit well with me.

At that moment, the waiter showed up with our dinner.

We ate, but the conversation had dried up. I felt awkward and unsure what to say to Lane. Did he think I was trying to cover for Elliott? Keep him hidden so he wouldn't pay for his crimes?

I felt like I owed him an explanation, only I couldn't decide what to say. The fact was, Elliott had ruined something else of mine.

"Are you okay?" Lane asked as we left the restaurant.

"Yes. I'm sorry about tonight," I said as we waited for the car.

Lane pulled me into his arms and kissed me. "You have nothing to be sorry for," he said softly. "I'll call in a favor with someone I know at the police department and have them check the security cameras and pull the receipts from tonight. If he was here, the police will know about it."

"Thanks," I said, not fully understanding if this would affect me but wanting more than anything for Elliott to pay for what he'd done. Not only to me, but to everyone else he'd destroyed.

I sat in silence as Lane called in his favor. He put the phone on speaker. It surprised me to hear the woman he'd called answer, "Lane, baby, I knew you'd come crawling back to me. What's it been? Five years?"

Lane chuckled. "Malory, you know you're the only

woman for me." He glanced over and winked at me. "How are the husband, kids, and grandkids?"

"Doing great," Malory answered. "The youngest, Levi, is going to be one next week. But I know you didn't call at this time of night to check up on my family. What's up?" Malory said, suddenly sounding serious.

"I might have some information for you," Lane told her.

By the time we parked at his townhouse, Lane had filled the woman in on how we had seen Elliott at the restaurant. Malory agreed to have her people look into the matter and update Lane on what they found when possible.

"Feel better?" he asked me. I nodded, finally relaxed for the first time since seeing Elliott.

"Much," I answered. "Thank you for tonight. I hope I didn't spoil it too much."

He took my hand in his. "You didn't spoil anything." He tugged me until he could wrap his arms around me.

"He does that. Sucks all the good out of the air," I said into Lane's chest.

"Not any longer." He kissed my forehead. "Come, I think I might still have some ice cream in the freezer." He pulled back, smiling down at me.

While I let Byron out in the small back area to relieve himself, Lane hunted down some ice cream and cookies. We sat in the kitchen area, eating our dessert and going over a bunch of what-if scenarios.

"They can't come after me again for not telling the police where he is. I mean, where he was tonight. Can they?" I asked, a new worry flooding my mind.

"No," Lane said quickly. "Besides, I told Malory I was with you and that you're the one who spotted your ex. Technically, you assisted in helping find him."

"Right." I relaxed. "What if they don't find him?"

Lane thought for a moment. "They will," he said, but I could tell he wasn't all that sure himself.

I was weary of talking about Elliott. Of thinking about my past. I wanted to move forward. The thought of going to school, real school, for the first time excited me.

I had just gone on my first real shopping trip, buying whatever I wanted. And I still had over a hundred dollars left. I had gotten some really nice clothes, and some items that had always been forbidden to me—makeup, a blow dryer, a curling iron, sexy underwear. Those I was currently wearing. I had bought them in hopes of surprising Lane that night. All he'd seen me in so far was boring cotton underwear.

When Lane stood up to take our dishes to the sink, I stopped him.

"We can deal with those in the morning," I said, taking his hand. I laid his hand over my breast as I hiked up the skirt of my dress and straddled him in the chair. "For now, let's enjoy ourselves." I kissed him.

God, I loved the feel and taste of him. His hands moved up to my hips, his fingertips digging into my butt as he slowly rocked me. I felt him grow hard against me and my entire body responded. I wanted him inside me.

I took the kiss deeper as his hands moved under my skirt. Then he hoisted me up to sit on the table in front of him, breaking the kiss.

I wanted to complain, but then he spread my legs and, with his eyes on mine, hiked my skirt all the way up.

His eyes traveled to between my legs, and he smiled. "I like your style," he said as he brushed his fingertip over the red lace covering me.

"I've discovered I like wearing sexy things under my clothes," I said proudly.

Lane made a soft groaning sound and then gently nudged the material aside so that I was exposed to him.

When he bent down and ran his tongue over me, I cried out and held onto him. I was getting used to Lane's needs, and mine matched his pace.

I'd spent my entire life being controlled by others. Now, however, knowing what Lane wanted, I easily allowed my body to give in. I cried out his name as the convulsions came, then my entire body went lax against him.

He carried me until I lay on his bed upstairs. Only when he started gently pulling my clothes off did I stir. When his fingers brushed against a sensitive spot, I smiled and started tugging his clothes off. I needed to see his skin and feel it against mine.

I had never believed I would like sex. I'd avoided even thinking about it. I'd hidden from it, mentally and physically, when I could.

Now, I sought it out. Thought about it often and even dreamed about it. Lane was the reason I was healed. He was the reason I desired a man for the first time in my life. He gave me motive to dream of a future I could mold on my own.

"Please," I begged him when he slid into me. "Don't stop."

I knew that he didn't understand that I wasn't just talking about what he was doing to me at the moment. In my mind, it went far beyond these minutes of intimacy.

I held onto him as if willing the rest of the world away. When we both fell together, he covered us with the blanket and held me until I drifted off to sleep, sated physically and mentally.

I should have known the dreams would come to me that night. I should have guessed after seeing Elliott.

My body jerked, remembering the first time he'd undressed me and told me that my duties were to obey him. To do things to him that literally made me gag and vomit. I would be punished until I learned to keep the disgust to myself.

In sleep, I felt the sting of his slaps. The tearing of my body as he used it. He'd always been so much bigger than me. So much stronger. He'd used his superior strength and knowledge to berate me, belittle me, abuse me.

I had never stood a chance.

I'd been a child. Only a child.

Later, I'd gotten knowledge from books I read when I was left alone, stolen and hidden from my husband. The large house we'd moved into had been empty with the exception of a box of classic books in the attic.

How was I supposed to fight back?

I could feel the sting of his hands on me still as Lane shifted and pulled me against him.

"Chloe, it's a dream," he said softly next to my ear.

Then I felt Byron jump on the bed and lay across me as the dream slowly disappeared.

"He's worried too," Lane said in the dark. "Are you okay?"

"Yes," I said, burying my face in Byron's fur. "I should have known seeing him again would cause memories to surface."

"Want to talk about it?" Lane asked, his hands slowly moving over my hip.

"No, sleep. We can talk on the way home." I hugged Byron to my chest after the dog settled next to me.

It wasn't hard for me to slip back into sleep, spooned by the two men I'd fallen so fast for.

When I woke, the bed was empty, and sunlight was streaming in the windows.

I could hear Byron barking outside the window and Lane talking to him in response. I smiled, then showered quickly and dressed, pulling on a new pair of jeans and one of my new tops and ankle boots.

After applying some makeup and packing all my new things in my new suitcase and bags, I went downstairs to find Lane and Byron in the kitchen making breakfast.

"You look wonderful," Lane said as I stepped closer and kissed him. "Like I said, I like your style."

"Thank you. Can I help?"

"Nope. This morning, I've got everything handled. You sit, I'll get you some coffee." He motioned to the table.

I sat down, and Byron came up and dropped an apple in my lap. I smiled.

"Where did he get this?" I asked.

Lane glanced over and then laughed. "When I opened the fridge, he took it from the drawer. I was surprised it was still good. I haven't been home for weeks."

I stood up, washed the apple off, then grabbed a knife and cut it in half, giving one part to Byron. He carried it to the back door and laid in the sunlight to enjoy his treat.

"I've never known a dog to like apples so much," Lane said with a chuckle.

"I've never known any dogs." I shrugged and bit into the other half of the apple as I watched Lane make pancakes and bacon.

"We're a little limited on the food, but since we're heading out in about an hour, I figured this would do."

"When are they going to release George?" I asked while I ate.

"Later today," Lane answered. "I had planned on

spending a few days here, but now I just want to get back and make sure he's okay."

I nodded. "I feel the same." I took his hand in mine. "I'm already packed."

Lane smiled. "Let's clean this up, then I'll go up and pack and we can head out."

"I like that idea."

The drive back to the island took half the time it had taken us to get into the city the morning before.

"How do people do it?" I asked, once we were on the ferry back to the island.

"What?" Lane asked, leaning his head back on the headrest and closing his eyes.

"Deal with the traffic?" I looked around and noticed there were only a handful of cars on the ferry this time. Yesterday, the ferry had been full.

"It's a necessity. You drive to work to make the money to pay for a house that sits empty ninety percent of the time and the cars you sit in traffic in." He shrugged and looked over at me.

"Do you like city life?" I asked, wondering which he preferred. It was obvious he liked being on the island. I just couldn't see him being happy going back and forth to work every day, only to return to his place alone.

"It pays the bills." He glanced over at me. "We all can't afford to live where we want."

"Where would you want to live?" I asked, curious.

He turned back to the window and sighed. "I used to know the answer to that."

"Now?"

He reached over and took my hand, then lifted it and placed a kiss on my knuckles. "Now I'm not so sure."

Just then, his phone rang. "It's Malory," he said before

answering. "Good morning," he said easily. Seconds later he was frowning and jerking his gaze towards me. "No, we're in the car heading back up to the island." He listened again, nodding several times. "Sure, let's say..." He paused as if thinking. "Tomorrow afternoon? We need to get my grandfather out of the hospital and settled, then we'll head back." He was quiet again. "Okay, thanks." He hung up.

"Well?" I asked when he remained quiet.

"They've got your ex in custody," he answered and for the first time since seeing Elliott the night before, I relaxed.

"Where did they find him?" I asked.

"He was staying with that woman he was with last night and her husband. She paid for the drinks on her credit card. The police would like to talk to you."

I tensed again and started to sweat. "Why?"

Lane took my hand again. "It's just a formality. I'll be right there with you. They just want to ensure that you've had no contact with him."

I nodded but felt my stomach twist in knots. "Tomorrow?" I asked. Lane nodded. "You'll come with me?" He nodded again. "I'll act as both your lawyer and your alibi."

Just then the ferry docked, and I remained quiet as we drove to the hospital to get George.

When we got off the elevator on the floor for George's room, we heard shouting. Lane took off running towards his grandfather's room.

He rushed into the room seconds before me. By the time I got there, Lane had his uncle Robert pinned up against the wall. The look in his eyes was pure hellfire.

"Want to tell me just what the hell you're doing?" Lane growled out.

Since Robert was the only other person in the room besides George, I rushed over to stand next to the bed.

George looked terribly upset and angry, something I hadn't seen before.

Two nurses rushed into the room shortly after we arrived. Both of them looked scared, but seeing the situation was now under Lane's control, they moved over to check on George, so I stood back.

"Dawn was breaking, like the light from another world."
- Alfred Jarry

L ane

I don't think I had ever been as angry as I was seeing my uncle standing over my grandfather's hospital bed, yelling at him at the top of his lungs.

I wanted to bust his face in. I wanted to shout at him. Toss him through the wall instead of holding him until I felt all the fight go out of him.

"This is none of your concern, boy," my uncle said, lacing the last word with disdain.

When my grandfather called me boy, it was with endearment. When the rest of my family used it, their intention was clearly to belittle me.

"You made it everyone's concern when you yelled so loud we could hear you down the hallway," I said in a low tone, shoving him a little more before releasing him. If I didn't drop my hold and take a step back, I'd punch him.

"Later," my uncle hissed, then he walked out without another word.

"I should call the cops on him," I said under my breath.

"Don't," my grandfather said, waving the nurses off. "I'm fine. My grandson will sign my release papers now," he told one of the nurses.

She looked up at me and I nodded. "I'll go get them," she said, and both nurses disappeared.

"Are you okay?" I asked my grandfather. He was already dressed to go home but was sitting on the hospital bed as if he didn't have the energy to stand.

"Just want to go home and sleep in my own bed," he answered. Then he turned to Chloe. "How was your trip into the city?"

"Fine." She sat next to him and laid her hand on his arm. "Are you okay?"

My grandfather patted her hand. "Fine. My son can't ruffle my feathers and it pisses him off," he said with a smile. "Let's go home."

Half an hour later, we drove away from the hospital with my grandfather sitting in the passenger seat and Chloe and Byron in the back. The entire time, Chloe filled my grandfather in on our time in the city, leaving out the part about seeing her ex.

When we pulled into the driveway, I had to park beside several cars. My family was already there.

What shocked me was that they were inside. We'd locked up and, to my knowledge, no one else had the keys. We stepped inside to find everyone had made themselves at home.

"I thought that everyone was going back to the city until Monday?" I asked. "It's only Friday."

"We canceled our trip. We were just too worried about George," my aunt Reba said, muting the television.

"So worried that no one wanted to go visit him or drive him home?" I asked dryly, earning several glares from around the room. "How'd you get inside?" I asked.

Everyone looked around at one another as if they had a great secret.

"I'm calling a locksmith and changing the locks," I said, pulling out my phone.

"Good, you're back. You can make lunch," Phil said, motioning to Chloe. Then he returned his attention to his phone.

"No," I jumped in before Chloe could disappear into the kitchen. "Out. Everyone," I barked, shoving my phone back in my pocket. I'd call the locksmith after they were all gone. "I've had enough. Grandfather needs his rest, not to play host." I motioned to the door. "Go find your lunch elsewhere and don't come back until Monday as you agreed." When no one moved to go, I yelled. "Now!" They slowly got up and left.

"You've got a spine," my grandfather said, patting my arm. "I think I'm going to go up and shower off the hospital smell."

"I'll make us some lunch," Chloe said, heading into the kitchen.

I stood in the living room and realized that my family must have been at the house a lot longer than I'd expected. The place was a mess. There were beer and soda cans and food wrappers everywhere.

Feeling disgusted, I called the locksmith, agreeing to

pay extra for a rush visit that day. Then I walked around with a trash bag and cleaned up after them.

"I can do that," Chloe said from the kitchen.

"I've got it," I said, growing even more frustrated. "Who in the hell do they think they are?" I mumbled as I straightened the pillows on the sofa.

Thankfully, Chloe didn't answer me.

By the time my grandfather came down, I had the house back to normal. The locksmith had rekeyed every door, including Chloe's and the garage door. The three of us were the only ones that had copies now.

Thankfully, I noticed the coloring had come back to my grandfather's cheeks.

As we ate, I grew very curious and asked my grandfather, "What was Robert yelling at you for in the hospital?"

My grandfather sighed and took a sip of his tea before answering me.

"He's gotten wind of the last will update. I wanted an answer from him on something." His eyes moved between Chloe and me. "Enough business. The two of you seem to be getting along."

Chloe's cheeks heated, and she avoided his eyes.

"We have to go back into the city tomorrow. Just for a few hours," I said.

"Oh?" My grandfather turned his attention back to me.

"Yeah." I glanced at Chloe. "It's a personal matter we have to deal with."

My grandfather's eyes narrowed, but he nodded quickly. "I'll be fine here on my own," he said, finishing his tuna sandwich.

"Are you sure?" Chloe asked.

"Don't worry about me, dear. I've got Byron to look after

me," he said with a wink. "Now, tell me what else you purchased on your shopping trip."

I knew it was my grandfather's way of changing the subject. He didn't like shopping. He'd always complained when my grandmother had forced him to go with her. Still, he listened to every word Chloe said, as if he found it all so fascinating.

After lunch, I disappeared into the office and tried to get some work done. Before we'd left town, I had made a quick run to my office and gathered the documents I'd needed for a couple of cases I was working, but now I had to cram the rest of my work in so that I could take tomorrow off to drive back into the city.

I had believed that I would miss being in court and meeting with clients. The truth was, since returning to the island, I'd realized that the majority of my work was better handled in solitude.

When I worked in the office, there were so many distractions. Phone calls, coworkers stopping to chat, employee meetings. Most of it was just time-filler.

Being locked in a room without any distractions, aside from my own family, had been helpful to my career. I was getting more work done in five hours than I had in two days in the office.

By the time dinner rolled around, I had finished everything I needed to do and figured I could spend the rest of the evening with my grandfather and Chloe.

I was growing accustomed to sitting on the back porch and chatting after dinner. Even though it was currently raining, we sat around the small firepit under the patio and listened to my grandfather tell stories about the things he and my grandmother did before settling down and having children.

I could hear in his tone as he talked about his kids that he'd loved them as children, but then they'd turned into money- and power-hungry adults.

"Of course, I'm to blame for it," he said as he sipped his wine. "While they were growing up, I was too busy trying to get ahead in my career. I became senator shortly after Robert turned five. From then on, I put my career ahead of everything else." He set his glass down and sighed. "Don't make the same mistake," he said, looking directly at me.

"I have no intention of going into the public eye. I'm happy where I am," I told him.

But, later, when Chloe lay in my arms fast asleep, her legs wrapped around mine and her head resting on my chest, I questioned that statement.

Was I happy where I was?

Was I contented living in the city as Chloe had asked?

I really did like being on the island again. The slower life. Not always rushing. Or feeling the need to keep up with others.

Then again, if not for my job, I doubted I could afford to live on the island. I did have some money saved away. If I sold my townhouse, I could probably afford a small place on the island. But loan payments would eventually require some sort of job.

There were a handful of lawyers on the island. Could the small community support one more?

I guess it wouldn't hurt to look into it. Then I could make the decision. Jumping into things wasn't the Robinson way.

The following morning, after helping Chloe clean up after breakfast, we headed back to the city.

The drive went more quickly this time since it was past rush hour.

When we arrived at the police station where Chloe was going to be questioned, Malory was standing outside smoking a cigarette.

"She's waiting for us." I motioned across the parking lot.

"Is that Malory?" Chloe asked, following my gaze.

"Yes. She's been a detective at the S.P.D. for over ten years."

"She's... different than I expected." Chloe turned to me. "The way you were flirting with her, I expected... someone younger." She chuckled.

I looked over at Malory and smiled. The woman was easily twice my age. She was probably in better shape than I was, and I'd seen her take down a man double her size. She could intimidate anyone she interviewed and usually got what she needed from a perpetrator or witness.

The woman was hands down the best detective on the force.

"I'd still snag her up if she wasn't helplessly in love with her husband," I joked. "Come on, we don't want to keep her waiting." I jumped out and opened Chloe's car door.

The next few hours would probably be hell on her. I knew that Malory would do anything to get the full truth.

I'd thought of warning Chloe, but I knew better as a lawyer. What Malory got out of Chloe had to be raw and truthful.

I felt sick to my stomach as we were shown into an interview room. Less than a minute later, the interview started, and I did my best to represent Chloe. I was surprised at how well she handled herself.

For the entire inquiry, she sat rod straight in the chair, only taking a couple sips of water as she relayed the events of the other night when she had spotted her ex-husband.

I listened to every detail, hung on her every word as she

told Malory of the last time that she'd seen Elliott Meyers prior to that day.

"It was a Tuesday," she started, but Malory jumped in.

"How do you know that?"

"Every Tuesday, I changed the bedding on our bed so I could wash them. Elliott liked his house run like clockwork. He liked things to happen on the same days of the week. Even to eat the same meals weekly."

At first, I'd been impressed that she could remember such a detail. Now I understood why. Fear. I could see it clearly as she continued to talk.

"Oh yeah? What did you make for breakfast that morning?" Malory asked.

"I made the standard Tuesday morning breakfast: scrambled eggs, runny, like he liked them, with four slices of pork bacon. He didn't like the turkey kind." She rubbed her wrist at this point, as if remembering an old injury. She shook her head as if breaking herself out of a spell. Her chin rose as she continued. "He had two cups of coffee, no cream, two spoons of sugar. He was wearing his black suit with the blue tie and his fancy shoes that I'd shined the night before. He had told me he had a big meeting that day and he had to look his best."

"What time did he leave?" Malory asked.

"I don't know. Elliott didn't allow me to know what time it was," Chloe answered.

Malory frowned and looked down at a large file. She flipped a page. "There were no clocks in the house?"

"No. The ones on the stove and microwave were set to zero. Elliott deemed time to be something men should worry about. Not women." She glanced at me momentarily.

Malory mumbled something but then asked, "Go on. What happened after he left?"

"I went about my day. After cleaning up the breakfast mess, I headed upstairs to strip the bed. Once everything was washed, I cleaned the bathrooms. Tuesdays were bathroom scrub days too. I bleached the shower, the tub, the toilets. All of them in the house."

"How many were there?" Malory asked.

"Ten in the house. Not that we used all of them, but once..." She stopped and slumped her shoulders.

"Go on," Malory said.

Chloe lifted her chin again. "Once, I skipped one of the bathrooms. Elliott knew instantly. I never skipped any after that." She looked down at her hands.

"Okay," Malory said after a moment of silence. "So, the last you saw him was that day, on..." She glanced at the paperwork. "February tenth of last year?"

Chloe nodded. "Until the other night."

"Do you know if Elliott has frequented Six Seven Restaurant before?" Malory asked.

"I didn't know anything my husband did outside of the home." She looked directly into Malory's eyes. "I wasn't allowed to leave."

Malory's eyebrows shot up. "You... weren't allowed? I'm sorry." She leaned forward. "Are you telling me you never left the home?"

Chloe nodded.

"For how long?" Malory asked.

"Since I first arrived there," Chloe answered.

Malory glanced down at the file and after a moment of scanning the pages, she shook her head.

"You moved into the home at twenty-two Canary Lane ten years ago," Malory said.

Chloe nodded. "Yes, that's about right. I'm not positive on the dates, but I spent about ten summers in that home."

"And in that entire time, you never left the house?" Malory asked.

"No, I wasn't permitted," Chloe answered.

"Why is none of this in the file?" Malory asked suddenly, her voice raising slightly.

"I..." Chloe looked worried.

"Not you, honey, I'm talking to Detective Delph." Malory pointed at the mirror. "Get your skinny butt in here," Malory said, standing up.

I looked at Chloe, but she was suddenly looking pale as a tall, skinny blonde woman stepped into the room.

Instantly, I understood that Chloe knew the woman.

"Why the hell isn't any of this in her file?" Malory barked at the other woman.

"It never came up." Detective Delph answered.

"Didn't it?" Malory waved her hands. "Within the first fifteen minutes of talking to her, she hints of not only abuse, but imprisonment. But it never came up?" Malory's voice rose again.

"No, detective. It didn't. Sarah Meyers was—" Detective Delph started.

"Chloe," Chloe broke in. "My name is Chloe Dawn."

Detective Delph narrowed her eyes. "She refused to even look at me." The woman pointed at Chloe.

"I wasn't permitted to speak to anyone my husband didn't authorize. The last time I'd spoken to anyone other than him was a year prior to the police busting down the door and waking me up in the middle of the night," Chloe said softly. "I'd been told that if that ever happened, that you all would try to entrap me into speaking ill of my husband, which was a sin in god's eyes."

Detective Delph tilted her head slightly and looked at Chloe as if seeing her for the first time. "You've changed."

Chloe nodded. "I had to."

Detective Delph sighed heavily and then nodded. "Okay."

"This is shoddy work," Malory said. "Really shoddy."

Detective Delph moved over and sat down. "What else can you tell us about your husband?"

"Ex. Ex-husband," Chloe corrected, not missing a beat.

Detective Delph smiled. "Ex-husband."

"Not much. I wasn't allowed into his computer room, except to give him food. Wesley Allen would know more about everything. Have you asked him?"

"Who?" both Detective Delph and Malory asked at the same time.

But I saw a hint in both of their eyes that they knew exactly who Chloe was talking about.

Chloe frowned. "Wesley Allen. Elliott brought him over several times. They worked together."

Malory glanced at the file again. "It says here that Elliott was having drinks with a Lisa Allen the other night at the restaurant." She glanced up at Chloe, who shrugged. "Lisa paid for their drinks on her credit card."

"I don't know her. I only knew that Wesley and Elliott were working together, and that they would go away on business trips, which is where I assumed he was for those days before the raid," Chloe answered.

From there, things grew loud and busy. Everyone seemed to talk over one another, and Detective Delph rushed from the room yelling.

"What?" Chloe asked, turning to me.

I reached over and took her hand just as Malory asked, "Who else do you know who your ex-husband worked with?"

"No one. Just..." She thought for a moment. "There was

a DJ. I never knew his last name. That's it. I never met or saw DJ. Elliott would talk about him as if he was the boss," Chloe said.

"DJ?" Malory asked, writing something down in the file.

"Yes. Every time he talked about the man, he grew nervous. I always assumed that he was the one with the money since Elliott and I came to Washington with only the clothes on our back. Elliott had grown up in Seattle before coming to Utah. We were lucky the local FLDS took us in and let us move into the house that their trust owned." Chloe shrugged. "Members of the church had donated their million-dollar home to the trust run by some of the FLDS members when they signed up to join the religion."

Malory was writing everything down. "You didn't mention any of this last year?"

Chloe shook her head and looked down at her fingers. "No, I don't remember saying a word. I was..." She looked towards the closed door. "I was afraid."

Malory glanced towards the door. "Detective Delph can be a little intimidating. I assure you, she's good at her job. Most of the time," she added under her breath. "Now, I hate to do this, but we need to go over everything once more. From the top."

CHAPTER EIGHTEEN

"Morning without you is a dwindled dawn."
- Emily Dickinson

Chloe
There was little I believed could faze me after the past year. Seeing Detective Delph walk into the room somehow shook me more than seeing Elliott the other night.

That woman had yelled at me more than anyone ever had in my entire life. She hadn't believed what few words I said to her that day over a year ago. She'd looked at me as if I was lying and covering for Elliott.

I had never feared a woman, until I'd met Detective Delph.

Feeling Lane's hand in mine, I tried to relax but couldn't until the woman finally left the room.

By the end of the interview with Detective Malory, I was even more relaxed. The woman had an easy attitude with me, maybe because she had guessed what I'd gone through. Whatever the case, I was thankful Lane had called her instead of the other woman. Something told me that if it had gone the other way, I might be in trouble again instead of heading back to the island.

We'd spent more than seven hours in the interview room going over my past, including any names my husband had ever mentioned or anyone who had visited us.

I'd talked more than I had in my entire life. My throat felt raw. This time, instead of feeling guilt after talking to the police, I felt a giant sense of relief, like a weight had been lifted from my body. I knew what I was doing was right. Elliott no longer had a hold over my conscience.

The lie he'd made me believe about everything being my fault could no longer control me.

"Well?" Lane glanced over at me.

We stopped at a little Italian fast-food drive-through for meatball sandwiches. I didn't want to go inside and be around people and, thankfully, Lane agreed to eat in the car. It was hard to do with the messy sandwiches.

"I guess we should have gone in," I said, wiping my hands.

Lane glanced at me and burst into laughter. He held up a napkin for me.

"I've never had a meatball sandwich before or eaten in a car," I admitted as I took the napkin and wiped my mouth.

"Really?" He turned to me, then I watched his entire attitude sober. "I'm glad your ex is behind bars. From what Malory has said, he's going to be there a very long time."

I nodded, feeling a weight lift from my shoulders. "I remember being so shocked when I finally understood what Elliott had done. I knew he was a bad man from the moment I met him on our wedding day, but..." I dropped off.

"What?" Lane asked, shifted slightly.

"I didn't know he was a thief. I'd foolishly believed, up until my first night in prison, that no one of faith could possibly be bad. That everything I'd gone through, up to that point, was my fault. I hadn't been godly enough. I was a woman and therefore full of sin." I thought about how many times I'd been told that.

I'd been blamed for things that weren't my fault simply because I was born a woman.

"Tell me you don't believe that any longer," Lane said softly.

"No, of course not. Though it is hard. I'd been conditioned well," I admitted. "Guilt still weighs me down daily. I think your family easily spotted my weakness and exploited it."

"Yeah." Lane started the car again. "I'm sick about it. Which is why I'm trying to keep them away."

"Having time away from them is great. I know that George needed the reprieve as well."

"I haven't been around my family this much since before Sherry's death," Lane said as he pulled onto the highway.

I thought for a moment about losing someone close to me, about the possibility of never knowing who had killed them. Of them not getting justice like I knew Elliott's victims would be getting in the coming days.

Malory had assured us that first thing the next morning, she was having a press conference to update the world about the case. Which meant I would likely be in the spotlight once more.

I hadn't realized how big the case had been in the media last year. Or how much everyone hated me for what my husband had done. When I'd been locked up about two months, a newcomer to the block had approached me.

Her name was Beth Hudson. She was serving two months for what everyone called a white-collar crime. She'd written two hundred thousand dollars' worth of bad checks. When she entered the dining room on the first day of her sentence, her hair and nails were perfect.

She marched in as if she was the queen instead of one of us. When her breakfast was served, she demanded a healthier choice, then threw her tray down and demanded to speak with someone in charge when she was denied anything different.

Shortly before lunch, she spotted me sitting in what was called the entertainment room. Basically, it was a library, television room, and a game room. I was reading a book when she marched over and jerked the book from my hands, glaring at me.

"You're her, aren't you?" she demanded, crossing her arms over her chest.

"Who?" I had asked, confused.

"That bitch that helped steal all my money. Sarah Myers. You're the reason I'm in here." She glared at me. "You played all innocent, like you were a victim, but everyone saw right through that act." She tossed my book down and then leaned closer to me. "I'm going to make your life a living hell for the next two months." She straightened and turned on her heels and stormed away.

For the entire time she was there, she interrupted any reading time I had. She dumped my tray of food more than a dozen times.

The petty games barely registered since I was dealing with Foxy and her gang threatening to cut off my fingers or stab me in the showers.

Whenever I would run into Beth Hudson, she would remind me of how many other people were suffering because of me and my husband. I never once stood up for myself. Never corrected her. Or even enlightened her as to my own suffering at my husband's hands.

After all, I deserved everything I got because I was an unholy woman made for the sole purpose of pleasing my husband and having babies.

"You got quiet over there," Lane said, breaking into my memories.

We were almost to the ferry. All the city lights had disappeared, leaving nothing but darkness outside the windows.

"How big of a deal will this be that this is going to be in the news again?" I asked.

Lane took a moment before answering. "Well, I don't think we'll be able to keep your identity from my family after tomorrow."

"Right," I agreed.

"I was impressed at how well you handled yourself," Lane said as he pulled into the ferry parking lot. The ferry was gone, which meant we would have to wait a while.

"Thank you. Last time, I barely said two words."

Lane shut off the car and turned to me. "You've changed so much just in the short time since I first saw you. I can only imagine how much you've grown in the past year."

Smiling, I leaned over and accepted the kiss Lane gave me.

The sound of the ferry horn made me jump, and I laughed.

"I don't know if I'll ever not jump at loud noises," I admitted.

"You hinted at abuse in your past. I hope someday you'll feel comfortable opening up to me about it," Lane said, and I instantly felt bad for not already doing so.

At this point, I was quite sure I was in love with him. Just like I loved George and Byron.

I'd never imagined feeling the way I did towards the three of them. Never in my wildest dreams had I believed any man or beast would treat me with such kindness. They acted as if I was important to them as well. At times I had to pinch myself to believe that it was real. All of this was real.

"We have about half an hour before we're back home." I relaxed back as he started the car to pull into line for the ferry. "Where do you want me to start?"

He glanced at me, then took my hand and lifted it to brush his lips across my knuckles.

"Wherever you want to start. I'm all ears."

I waited until we were parked on the ferry to begin.

"We can sit in here," I suggested.

He unhooked his seatbelt and turned towards me. I did the same, taking a moment to get comfortable.

Taking a deep breath, I started at the beginning.

"My first memories are learning just what would be expected of me in my life. Learning how to dress properly and cover myself. Keep sweet and obey, that was the main rule. I learned the five approved ways of braiding or bunning my hair, when it was finally long enough. Who I could speak to and who I couldn't. To keep away from any apostates, basically. How to tend babies, to cook, clean, and most importantly, to pray each and every hour. For the first eight years of my life, these things were all I was given."

"What about reading? Writing?" Lane asked.

"School was especially important for the younger children. When we got older, we might learn more if there was time after all the chores that we had. I was a fast reader, which helped. Some of my sisters weren't. Most girls married before they could even read or write since they were too busy learning how to be a perfect wife. Which I had to learn as well."

"You were taught about sex when you were a kid?" he asked, frowning.

"God, no, not sex," I answered quickly. "How to be a wife and submit to my husband and remain sweet. Looking back, I doubt most of the women teaching me even knew what sex was. Real sex, I mean." I reached over and took his hand. "I was told that it was a sin for me, for any woman, to get pleasure from what her husband did to her. Women did not deserve pleasure. It wasn't what we were created for. We were created to give men pleasure and to obey them." I took a deep breath.

"Tell me you don't still believe that bullshit?" Lane asked in a deep tone.

"No, I don't." I smiled. "But I can assure you that what went on between me and my husband never once gave me pleasure."

Lane was quiet, then said, "Go on."

"Most of my sisters were married off, and all of my brothers disappeared over the years. We were told they left the FLDS and were apostates now. As I mentioned, shortly after my twelfth birthday, once I had, become a woman"—I shifted in the seat, feeling slightly uncomfortable admitting this to Lane— "it was arranged that I was to be married. There had been some debate about this. Several of the elders wanted me," I said, leaning back in the seat and closing my eyes. "Even three men that I thought could possibly be my father put their names into the hat." I opened my eyes and glanced at Lane. It was too dark in the car to see his expression, but by the way he was holding himself, I could tell he was upset at what I was saying. Still, I continued. "There was a large meeting two days before my marriage. Two more girls, my sisters, had come of age as well. Yet, no one wanted them as much as they wanted me for some reason. I believed at the time that it meant I was the daughter of our leader, Joseph Jessup."

Lane leaned forward. "The man currently rotting in jail for sexual abuse of children?"

"The very same," I agreed. "I'm an apostate now. An outcast. Like all of my brothers. The night we left, the night of that first raid, I became an apostate, even though it was Elliott who broke me out that night in Utah."

"The compound you were living in was raided?" Lane asked.

"Yes. I found out when I was in jail that the raid was not as large as Elliott had led on. Six men living there had been taken in on charges of property tax fraud with the trust. Two are in jail now for sexual abuse of children, including Joseph Jessup, my father. Or so I still believe."

"You don't know for sure who your parents are?"

"No. I had more than thirty mothers, or women I called mother. I had a few favorites. Some I steered clear of. There was only a handful of men I believed could be my father, since Joseph kicked most of the men off the compound shortly after he took over. Any young boy who dares asked for a wife or came of age was kicked out as well. Joseph deemed himself our next leader and snatched up the other men's wives for himself. He married anyone over twelve not already married the week after taking over."

"Sick. He deserves to rot in jail," Lane said.

"Yes," I agreed. "When Elliott was brought in, I was thankful I'd get to marry an outsider instead of one of the men I'd been calling father all my life. Joseph claimed he owed Elliott a favor. I believed this was my chance to follow a truly godly man."

"You didn't deem the others as godly?" he asked.

"They were squabbling over marrying me, the girl they had all called daughter, days before I bled for the first time." My voice was laced with anger, an emotion I had never been allowed to show before. "Hell, yes, they were all ungodly."

"But Elliott ended up being more so?" he asked.

"Yes." I leaned back and waited as the ferry docked and we started driving again. "I wasn't Elliott's first wife. I was his third or fourth. Even I was unclear on how many he already had before me and after me. But that night, the night of the raid, it was my room he came to. Me that he pulled down the hallway, into the secret passage. We carried three large bags filled with money through secret panels in the house and out a back exit more than a quarter of a mile away from the compound. Then we ran through the dessert in the middle of the night. There was a small house just outside of town where he had a car. We loaded up, then drove." I was feeling tired suddenly.

"This was ten years ago?"

"Almost eleven now. I had just turned sixteen when we were forced to move, and I lost what family I had. Now I was to become Elliott's slave. I was secluded from anyone except those he wanted around. Even then, I wasn't permitted to have conversations with anyone without him in the room. I couldn't go out and pick up the mail from the mailbox at the end of the drive. He didn't trust me to deliver the mail to him. He said I would lose it along the way. Even if he was watching me, he didn't trust me with anything other than what he fed to me. I didn't watch television without his approving the programs ahead of time. I didn't go to the store or leave the house. The one good thing that changed after moving to Washington was that I no longer had to pray as much. Religion wasn't really on top of Elliott's mind. I was thankful he didn't take any more wives after we moved, which was his right. When we'd lived in the compound, his other wives, the ones before me and the ones he took after we wed, were vicious and conniving, all trying to claw their way into his favor. Since I had borne no children, I was bottom of the pile. The last to eat. The last to fall asleep and the first to wake. My chore lists were always twice as long as the others, since their first duty was as mothers, even though none of the children were Elliott's. Most of the women had been married to apostates and gifted to Elliott at different times."

I kept talking as the car sped across the empty country streets. When we passed the gas station, I was surprised that it was dark. Then I glanced at the clock and realized it was almost eight at night.

For years I'd gone without paying attention to the time. Some sort of internal clock allowed me to stay on schedule, a new sense I'd honed to keep me out of trouble with my husband.

Now I realized it was just one more way to control me. Elliott had even taken time away from me.

I was twenty-six years old and had nothing to show for all those years. Most of the sisters I had grown up with were still on the compound in Utah.

When we pulled into the driveway, the house was dark. Lane shut off the car and leaned back, looking at the house.

"It appears my grandfather has already called it a night. Let's head up to your room and not disturb him." He took my hand in his.

I wanted that. Wanted him. More than I'd wanted anything in a long time.

We climbed out of the car but as we passed the yard, Byron came rushing up to us. He was soaking wet and covered in sand and mud.

"What are you doing out?" Lane asked, glancing towards the house. "Stay here." Lane rushed towards the back door, which was sitting wide open.

My heart skipped and my knees turned to liquid. I slid down to the wet grass and hugged Byron.

Looking at the dark house with Byron's nose pressed into my shoulder, somehow, deep in my heart, I knew that George was gone.

CHAPTER NINETEEN

"Night never had the last word. The dawn is always invincible."
- Hugh B. Brown

Lane
    My heart pounded as I rushed through the open glass doors. The entire house was bathed in darkness.

I flipped on the dining room light, and it illuminated the madness within. My mind could barely register what I was seeing. It refused to believe the scene in front of me.

I took a giant step backwards, back outside, where the summer mist was slowly blowing around me. My mouth opened and closed several times, as if I was trying to say something. Anything.

How?

Why?

Who?

There had been so much blood. Too much.

Why?

"Lane?" I heard Chloe. "Byron's bleeding," she said from somewhere behind me.

I turned to see her sitting in the grass in the light from the dining room, tears rolling down her cheeks. She held up her hands and showed me the rust-colored blood covering her hands and Byron's fur.

I shook my head as her eyes locked with mine.

"No!" she cried out, seeing the answers in my eyes. "No!" she said again, her face buried in Byron's face. "No." She continued to cry.

Hearing her anguish, I pulled out my cell phone and dialed 911.

Four hours later we were sitting on the sofa in the front room sipping coffee that Chloe had made. The first to arrive was officer Oliver Whitlock and a younger officer I didn't know.

They took one look in the house, and the younger man turned and rushed to the bushes outside the kitchen window and threw up. Officer Whitlock shook his head and removed his hat. Then his eyes fell on Chloe, who was sitting under the porch, still holding Byron. Both still covered in blood.

"Who's this?" Officer Whitlock had said, laying his hand on the weapon on his belt.

"She was with me all day, in the city," I said firmly.

Still, Officer Whitlock didn't relax. "I said, who is this?" He turned to me.

"Chloe Dawn, a family friend, and my father's caregiver. As I said, we were in the city all day. We left around nine. Returned moments before finding my grandfather." I saw Chloe tense at my tone. "The dog was covered in blood.

Some of it transferred to Chloe while she was holding him to keep him from going inside."

"What were you doing in the city?" Officer Whitlock asked.

"Later. We'll answer questions later. For now, call S.P.D. Detective Malory. She'll vouch that we were with her all day. Do your job," I growled out. I turned around. "We're going to head up and get cleaned up first, then we'll talk."

"Hang on." The younger cop rushed over to us. "Let me snap some pictures. Just... in case. For the file." He held up his phone.

I looked at Chloe and then back to Officer Whitlock, who nodded.

"It might help. You never know," he said.

I nodded and then stood by while the younger officer photographed both Chloe and Byron. They both sat stone still and stared at the back door while the officer moved around taking more than a dozen photos.

When he was done, I took Chloe's blood-soaked hand in mine and led her up the stairs with Byron following us.

While more officers arrived, including Alex Everette, Chloe showered and changed into some dry clothes while I tried my best to give Byron a bath. Since the dog was wet and would get under foot, we left him upstairs and headed back down.

We were interviewed by detective Langford, a man roughly my parents' age. We sat in the front room, answering each of his questions more than three times.

Chloe, being herself, made several pots of coffee for the officers coming and going. She even pulled out a pan of cinnamon rolls she had made and had sitting in the freezer.

It was in her nature to feed others. To serve them. I

wanted to break her of it, to tell her that she no longer had to wait on anyone. That she was free from the horrors of her past. But in truth, she appeared to enjoy the tasks.

Keeping busy seemed to keep her mind off the fact that the coroner was taking my grandfather's body away.

My mind, however, was stuck on the scene just inside the back door. On what someone had done to the only man I had ever looked up to. The only man I trusted. The only one I'd ever loved and the only one who had ever loved me.

The house was photographed, and flashes from the camera mixed with the lightning outside while the rain continued to fall.

Once the storm had passed and both the coroner and the detective had disappeared, Chloe asked Officer Whit-lock if we could clean up.

It was strange, thinking about cleaning my grandfather's blood from the floors. I had never really thought of what happened after someone was killed. I'd watched a bunch of CSI type shows with one of my ex-girlfriends, but none of them had mentioned what happened to the scene of the crime after the police left.

When the last of the police were gone, leaving us all alone, we stood there in silence for a long time.

"Do they really think it was a robber who did this?" Chloe asked in a sober tone.

I put my arm around her shoulder, looking down at the now-clean floor.

"No," I answered. "But they're labeling it as a home invasion for now."

Looking outside and seeing the sun coming up, I pulled her into my arms.

"Let's head up and shut down for a while," I suggested.

"What about your family? Shouldn't we call them and tell them?" Chloe suggested.

"No, the detective said he was doing that. H wanted to be the one to tell them. He's going to interview everyone in my family and anyone else who might be willing to kill my grandfather." Just thinking about the possibilities had my stomach rolling. Then the realization that the man was gone hit me again.

I was thankful I didn't have to do the job. Talking to my family members was daunting already. The thought of telling them someone had murdered another family member made me sick.

I took Chloe's hand in mine and locked up the house again, and we headed up the stairs.

Byron greeted us happily, turning several circles, a sure sign he had to go down to the yard to do his business.

"I'll wait for him. You go clean up and change," I suggested.

"Thanks," Chloe said, lifting on her toes and placing a kiss on my lips.

While I watched Byron sniffing around the yard as if he hadn't witnessed the murder of his master a few hours ago, I thought about what came next.

What was going to happen to Chloe? Would she want to come back to the city with me? Did I want her to? What about Byron? A dog wouldn't fit into my current life.

There were days I was away from the home from sunup to sundown. Byron had to go out at least three times a day.

When Byron was done doing his business and sniffing around, he went to the back door to the house. I called him and he rushed up the stairs and inside.

He sat at my feet, making a whining noise.

I knelt and wrapped my arms around him.

"I know, buddy. He's gone," I said softly.

When we finally climbed into bed, Chloe crawled into my arms.

"What now? Where am I going to go?" she said softly. "Who is going to love me now?"

Her words were slurred, and I could tell she was too exhausted to realize what she was saying.

My arms tightened around her.

"We'll figure that out tomorrow. For now, just know that whatever happens, I'm here." I kissed her forehead, brushing her blonde hair slowly. "I'm not going anywhere."

It was the truth. As I felt her drift off to sleep, my mind ran over the possibilities.

The fact was, I wasn't ready to head back to the city. I'd arranged with work to stay remote until the end of summer, so I wasn't due back into the office until August. That gave me another month and a half.

No matter what happened with my grandfather's estate, I was going to make sure that Chloe was taken care of. She wasn't family, but she was better than anyone I was related to.

She loved my grandfather more than any of my relatives had.

It wasn't until I finally settled in my mind that I was going to ensure Chloe was not only safe but happy that I finally fell asleep.

We slept until just after noon, when my phone rang and woke us up.

I knew it was my parents without even looking.

I tried to sound awake, but I was still groggy when I answered the call.

"We're on our way up there," my mother said quickly. "We're meeting with the detective."

"Okay," I said, sitting up and wiping my hands over my face. I really wanted a cup of coffee and something sugary to help wake me up.

"Did they interview that girl? The one that is staying there?"

"Yes." I closed my eyes. "Chloe was with me all day in Seattle."

My mother was quiet for a moment. "We'll be there in half an hour. You can fill us in on everything."

My mother didn't even wait for a goodbye before hanging up.

"Your family?" Chloe asked beside me.

"Yeah, they'll be here in half an hour." I glanced at my watch and groaned. "No doubt expecting lunch."

Chloe tossed off the covers and got up. "I'll shower and make something." She disappeared into the bathroom before I could tell her it wasn't needed. My family could go hungry for all I cared right now. But I realized Chloe was just doing what she thought was best.

By the time my family stepped through the front door, there was a feast waiting for them.

Seeing my parents stroll in made me realize that I was still in denial. I was still under the illusion that my grandfather's murder had been random.

Yet, watching my family act as if this was just another day opened my eyes.

My cousin Tiffany was there. It was the first time I'd seen her in almost a year, and I was both grateful and a little surprised. I had thought that her relationship with her husband Mark was going well. After all, they'd only been married a few years. But I changed my mind as her husband strolled in with empty arms as he talked on the phone while Tiffany struggled with holding their young son, Johnny, in one arm and a huge baby bag in the other. Mark appeared annoyed at the fussy kid.

Tiffany was the only member of the group that took the time to hug me. I took the fussy boy and held him on my hip while I introduced Tiffany to Chloe, who immediately took the baby bag from Tiffany. No one else in my family had even offered.

"Here, we can put your things in the upstairs room," Chloe said. "Does he need food? A nap?" she asked eagerly.

I watched how easily Chloe helped with the baby and thought of what she'd told me about her not being able to have kids.

Did she want any? She'd mentioned how thankful she was that she and Elliott hadn't had any. But seeing the way she was with my cousin and the baby made me wonder.

The rest of my family went about eating lunch as if they were enjoying a buffet, chatting about everything other than the fact that I'd discovered my grandfather's murdered body feet from where they ate.

Maybe they were all numb. Did they know any of the facts of the case? How my grandfather had been killed? Had the detective told them at least the basic details?

We'd been asked not to reveal anything to them until each of them could be questioned. The detective was on his way over now.

Somehow, my family had convinced the police to interview them here instead of down at the police station.

I wasn't sure how they had achieved it, but I guessed that it was thanks to my family's pull.

I tried to eat something, but my stomach tightened at the thought of eating so close to where I'd found my grandfather.

Instead, I used that time to watch each member of my

family. They all appeared to be heartless. As if they were invincible themselves. Death wouldn't dare touch them.

Was I as heartless as the rest of my family? Instead of feeling sad and mourning my grandfather, I was angry and desperately searching for clues as to who had done this to him. Was this normal?

When Sherry had been murdered, I'd felt pretty much the same way. The police, when they'd held and questioned me, had seen my anger as an admission of guilt. After that, I'd stayed angry for years to come. I'd never really gotten over her death or the betrayal of my family for not sticking up for me. I had never really been able to mourn my sister properly.

Maybe my family felt the same way I did and were only hiding it. Robinsons were very good at hiding their emotions, after all.

The more I watched them, the more I realized that hardly anyone spoke to one another.

It wasn't until after the detective and Officer Whitlock had arrived at the house to question everyone that I finally saw several of my family members show emotion.

But was it just for show? They were all watching one another and feeding off each other's energy.

There was an air of tension, something I'd never felt before. Not even when we'd found Sherry's body or after her funeral.

Everyone was questioning whether the others had had anything to do with the murder. When Sherry had been discovered, there hadn't been any question. Most everyone in my family blamed me. I'd seen it in their eyes.

Now, however, they weren't just looking at me. They were scanning everyone else's faces as well.

I ran my gaze over every one of my family members, assessing. Questioning.

Looking for any clue that one of them had betrayed the family.

One by one, the detective met with each of them in my grandfather's study. He started with my parents, who apparently had been home alone for the entire evening.

While the others waited their turn, the house remained silent.

Chloe busied herself by cleaning up after lunch and refilling drinks or setting out snacks.

Finally, after almost two hours, I pulled her into a chair and poured a glass of wine for her. Byron jumped up next to her and laid his head on her lap. The pair looked comfortable with one another. The dog would have never done that to anyone else. Especially not anyone in my family.

My uncle was playing that damned video game on the television, with the sound off, thankfully. The rest of my family members were on their phones or other devices.

So far, the detective had interviewed both of my parents and my aunt Kate and her husband Donnie. Currently in the room with him were Robert and Reba.

It was slow going since each interview took roughly an hour. I made a mental note of how each of my family members looked going into the room with the detective and how they looked coming out.

Chloe made sandwiches for lunch, which everyone ate without even thanking her. I'd never realized how privileged my family was before.

"We've made the news," my cousin Derrick said suddenly after they had all returned to the living room.

I was helping Chloe clean up after lunch and still

snacking on some crackers and cheese, since my stomach had yet to settle down.

"What do you mean?" my mother asked him.

"Here," Derrick said, getting up and changing the television from the video game to the news.

He flipped the channel between several stations until a picture of my grandfather filled the screen.

"Ex-senator George Robinson was murdered in his home late last night. He was found by his grandson Lane Robinson. George Robinson was an acting senator for the state of Washington for more than three decades until he retired last year after suffering a minor stroke. The police are describing his death as a home invasion gone wrong. At this time, they are interviewing suspects."

From there, the report continued to highlight several of my grandfather's career moves.

"Does that mean we're suspects?" Tiffany asked.

"Yes," I said easily when everyone turned to me. "Until each of us are ruled out."

From that moment on, the mood in the house changed. The television remained on mute on the news channels. Each time a report came on, everyone listened intently.

I watched as worry washed over each of them.

Chloe and I sat at the table while everyone crowded around the television as if it held all the answers.

Chloe had a notepad, but I hadn't been paying attention to what she was doing at first. I'd been too preoccupied with watching my family.

When my cousin Derrick was in being interviewed, she finally nudged me and motioned to the tablet.

On it was each of my family members' names. Beside each one a question mark with the word *motive* at the top.

Without a word to me, she handed me the pencil and motioned to the notepad.

Clearly she was thinking the same thing I was. I took the pad and thought about each one.

Moments later, I wrote the word *money* across all of it.

Chloe sighed and nodded before shutting the tablet.

"I'm going to take a walk," she said. "Byron? Walk?" The dog jumped up from his spot in the sunlight and rushed to the back door. "Do you want to come?" she asked me.

I shook my head and motioned to my family. I was too busy assessing them. I needed answers. I needed to watch them.

Chloe nodded before heading out.

The instant the back door shut, several of my family members turned to me.

"Why is she still here?" Phillip asked.

I narrowed my eyes at him.

"Really, Lane, you shouldn't let her continue to be here," Reba said. "After all, her employment here is over."

"I'm sure once George's will is read tomorrow and his estate is in order, she'll understand she needs to move on," my mother chimed in.

"She's not going anywhere," I said firmly, angry that they assumed my grandfather's estate could be so easily obtained.

"Besides, probate can take months even years," my father said.

The rest of my family gasped.

"But you know what his will says, right?" my uncle asked.

"No." I shook my head and frowned. "I don't. Why would I?"

"You... he hired you as his lawyer," my cousin said.

"His estate lawyer, yes. I handled things like moving his legal obligations around. Opening trust accounts. Dealing with his retirement and investments. Lee Steinbeck has handled his will for the past two decades."

My entire family went quiet. For a moment, I wondered if any of them believed me.

They continued to sit in silence until every last one of them was interviewed.

Chloe and Byron returned just as the detective and Officer Whitlock asked to speak with me privately.

"Well?" I asked once I shut the study door. "Anything?"

"Not yet. We'll need to check a few of your family members alibies," Whitlock said.

"For now, I've ruled out a simple break-in, since you confirmed last night that nothing was taken," the detective said.

Even though there was a lot of blood last night, I hadn't really seen how my grandfather had died.

"Can you..." I swallowed the distaste I had just thinking about asking the question. "Can you tell me how he died?" I finished.

Whitlock glanced at the detective, who nodded quickly.

"Since you and Chloe Dawn are no longer suspects after my conversation with Detective Malory earlier, I'm free to share that information." The detective sighed. "Your grandfather was hit over the head with something."

"He was attacked from behind," Whitlock added.

"We think he knew his attacker and let them in. We believe that he was killed when he went to let the dog out."

"What time?" I asked, needing more information.

"Between seven thirty and eight. You and Miss Dawn

must have arrived half an hour to fifteen minutes later," the detective said.

I sank into one of the chairs and put my head in my hands.

"If we hadn't stopped for dinner," I groaned. "Or if we'd eaten on the road."

"It wouldn't have mattered unless you could have caught the ferry an hour earlier," the detective pointed out.

Somehow, that didn't make me feel any better.

When I stepped out of the study and walked the detective and Officer Whitlock to the front door, my family remained where they were.

"Well?" everyone asked when I stepped into the living room.

I had no proof. Not yet. But I was positive that someone in the family had done this. I knew it in my heart.

For years I'd fooled myself into believing that Sherry's murder was nothing more than some pervert hunting down my sister, kidnapping her for a sick twisted game. Now, after seeing what someone had done to my grandfather, I was suddenly having doubts about Sherry's murder.

I wasn't basing this on evidence or clues. No, this was purely a gut feeling. The more I watched how my family acted upon hearing the details I could now share with them, the more I was sure of it.

Someone in my family was a murderer. And until they got what they wanted, they wouldn't stop at killing twice.

CHAPTER TWENTY

Chloe

The dynamics of Lane's family was beyond my comprehension. There was no set hierarchy since George's death.

The days after his murder, I was busier than I'd ever been.

Lane refused to allow anyone to move into the house, thankfully. So each night after dinner, the entire gang shuffled out the door and headed to the other home. Unfortunately, they would shuffle right back in before breakfast.

George's will wasn't read until a week after his murder.

His body had been released and cremated according to his wishes before Lane could tell the rest of the family.

He had hinted that if they had known ahead of time, that they would have buried him instead.

The urn sat in a box in the study until we could spread his ashes in the garden and beach area.

I knew Lane was waiting for a perfect time to do this. Sometime after we were done dealing with his family.

The entire family was requested to meet with Lee Steinbeck, George's lawyer. It shocked me when Lane told me that I was requested to be there as well.

I was quite sure it was due to the fact that George owed me my last paycheck. After which, I was sure I would be told to get off the property.

Lane had tried to assure me that whatever happened, he would see to it that I was safe. But he had yet to ask me to move into his townhouse in Seattle.

If I was honest with myself, I didn't even know if I wanted to.

There was no doubt I'd fallen in love and wanted to try and spend the rest of my life with him, though I had yet to tell him. It was scary, telling someone how you felt. I'd never done it before.

Did he feel the same?

We spent every night up in our little apartment above the garage, wrapped around one another. I was still shocked that I had come to enjoy sex so much. He was still showing me things I hadn't known were possible.

He was also patient with me when I wanted to try things for the first time. Even though he said I turned him on when I fumbled, I still doubted my sexiness.

As our relationship grew, the bond he had with his family faded. I was sure it was because he believed one of them had murdered George. I thought that as well.

He was certain the motive was money. I had my doubts. After all, his family wasn't poor.

All of them wore expensive clothes and drove luxury cars. If they didn't already have money, then how could they afford those things?

I just knew there had to be something else behind George's death.

Since Lee Steinbeck was due to arrive shortly before lunch, I had made a bunch of finger foods for the family instead of sandwiches or a full meal.

I'd seen a video on Lane's iPad, which he'd let me borrow, about charcuterie boards. I spent most of my morning slicing meats, cheeses, carrots, celery, and a variety of fruits. I arranged everything nicely on a massive wood platter that I found in the back of the pantry and laid out the feast on the kitchen island. Then I added crackers, olives, pickles, and those little cookies that George always enjoyed.

It was a work of art. I was incredibly happy with how it all turned out, but when the family saw the spread, they all complained.

Feeling defeated, I stepped outside and took a walk to the beach with Byron without eating anything myself.

I was sitting in the sand when Lane sat next to me.

"Have I mentioned that my family members are all asses?" he said, taking my hand in his.

I smiled and shrugged. "It's okay. I won't be serving them for much longer."

"No, you won't. They're all heading home tomorrow. They've even canceled the rental early." Byron dropped a ball at his feet. He took a moment to toss the ball into the water, and Byron raced after it.

"What about you?" I asked, holding my breath.

"Me?" He glanced over at me. "What do you want to do?"

I glanced away, feeling my heart jump and then fall quickly. No one had ever asked me that before. What I wanted I knew could never be.

I wanted more than anything to stay put. To live where I was. To spend my days and nights with Lane and Byron. To take long daily walks on the beach, this beach.

I wanted George to be here. I missed the advice that he'd give me. The jokes he told when silence fell between us. The way he always managed to make me smile, even when I knew he was hurting.

"Hey," Lane said, nudging my shoulder until I looked at him.

He surprised me by reaching up and wiping a tear from my cheek. I hadn't even realized I'd been crying.

"I miss him," I said with a sob.

Lane's arms wrapped around me. "I do too," he said into my hair. "But I can't afford to be sad now. I'm too pissed off. Angry that someone did this and might get away again."

"Again?" I tensed and then leaned back, running my eyes over his face. "You think that whoever killed George also killed Sherry?"

It was the first time I'd thought of it. I didn't know all the details of Lane's sister's death. I should have asked earlier.

Lane nodded, then leaned his elbows on his knees. "There aren't any similarities in their deaths. Other than the fact that they were Robinsons." He glanced sideways at me. "My sister was sexually abused," he said. "Some people, even some in my family, assumed... that I could do something like that."

I shook my head quickly. "I didn't," I said truthfully. Then I remembered the journal entry. But before I could mention it to him, he stood up and walked to the edge of the water.

I got up and stood beside him, taking his hand in mine.

"She was beaten to death, like she was a fucking piñata," he said. "Then she was dumped in a pond not far from here." He looked out over the water. "The police believed I had something to do with her murder, since I was the last one to see her. We had walked to the corner store together to get snacks. I returned home without her. They found her the following day. The pond they found her in was in the opposite direction of home. From the gas station, she had to head into town." He turned towards me. "She would have never gone that way by herself."

"Maybe she was going to meet someone?" I suggested.

Lane frowned. "No."

"What about Eric?" I asked, remembering the few entries I'd read in Sherry's diary. I hadn't gotten much further than a few pages since I'd been so busy lately.

"What?" Lane tensed. "Where did you hear that name?"

"It was in Sherry's diary. She wrote that she and Eric were in love. She also mentioned something about..." I hated telling him this detail, but maybe it was important. "About being abused."

Lane dropped his arms to his side, spun on his heels, and marched back to the house. I had to jog to keep up with him.

Instead of going to the main house, he climbed the stairs to our apartment and walked over to my hiding spot for the diary.

"Show me," he said, handing me the book. "Read the entry to me."

I sat down on the sofa and scanned the pages. Then I read him the line where she'd talked about being abused.

"Especially after all the sex that has been forced on me already."

So far, it was the only mention of it. Lane grew angrier than I'd ever seen him before.

"What else?" he asked.

I turned the page and read him the entry about Eric.

"There is no one on this planet that I hate more than my family. They actually think that they can tell me who I can fall in love with. I don't care what they say, Eric and I are in love. But since they have an ongoing feud with Eric's family, they are all saying that I can't see him. I'm fourteen, or at least will be next month. I can see whoever I want. I hate them all. My family sucks balls"

When I was done reading, I looked up to see Lane pacing in front of me.

"Eric?" He turned to me. "Who the fuck is Eric?"

"I assumed you'd know, since she mentioned a feud with his family."

"The only feud we had was with Rodney," Lane answered. "Does she say that he's the one forcing her?"

"I don't know. Maybe Eric was a nickname for him?" I suggested.

Lane shook his head, then snapped his fingers. "Eric Rodney Clarkson," he said softly. "Son of a bitch. I remember his mother yelling at him one summer when he'd broken his new baseball bat. I'm going to kill him." Just then, we heard a car pull up outside. "I can't process this right now." He shook his head. "That will be Lee. You need to finish reading that soon." He pointed to the diary.

I nodded and put the book back in the hiding spot. Then I followed him downstairs for the meeting.

Lee Steinbeck was a frail-looking older gentlemen with a voice and demeanor that demanded respect. I was surprised when Lane's family fell into line when asked to gather and all take a seat quickly.

"I want to head back to the city before dark," Lee said, unlocking his briefcase.

The entire family, including me, sat or stood in the living room. I stood along the back, fearing what was to come.

"Since George didn't want any of his assets sitting in probate, he and Lane spent the last year shifted everything he owned into a trust. Which means the assets can be distributed immediately.," Lee said.

Everyone in the room relaxed. I saw several people's smiles grow.

"With that said, George has named Lane Robinson as sole executor of that trust."

At this point, several people complained. Lee held up his hand to stop them from fighting.

"I'm here to read this." He held up the paper. "The matter is not up for debate," he said firmly. Instantly, everyone quieted down. "Continuing. Each of you will receive copies of the will after I finish reading it." He shifted and read, *"I'm naming my grandson Lane Nathaniel Robinson as sole trustee and executor in charge of my trust and all of my assets and cash funds."*

"What?" Robert, Kate, and Lane's father all cried out at the same time.

"Like hell. There's no way we're going to allow Lane to have control—" Robert started, but he stopped when Lee held up his hand.

"Once again, this isn't up for debate. George moved all of his assets into a trust. What's done is done. If you care to challenge, do so later. Be warned, there is a no-contest clause, which means, if you contest the will and lose, you won't receive anything. But, if you still feel so inclined, I suggest you have your lawyers get in touch. For now, I'm going to do my job and finish." He motioned to the will and started reading again.

"*Initially, I wasn't going to put Lane in charge, but in light of some information I found out from my own children last year, Lane is the only one in my family that I trust. With that said, the following items are my only bequeaths. First and foremost, I leave my beloved dog Byron to Chloe Dawn. She loves him almost as much as I did. May he be a comfort and true companion just like you were to me.*"

Tears streamed down my cheeks. I bent down to hug the dog, who was sitting at my feet.

"You're mine," I said to Byron, burying my face in his fur.

"Get on with it," someone barked when the room grew silent.

I didn't look up from Byron, but I assumed everyone was watching me. I didn't care. I was so happy that no one could ever take Byron away from me.

The fact that George had cared this much about me and Byron being together touched me so deeply. Whatever happened to me in the future, I knew that I could handle it with Byron by my side.

"*Second,*" Lee continued. "*I leave my home at 20 Beachwood Lane, Whidbey Island, to my grandson Lane. Boy, I hope you have many years of joy in it, as I did.*"

"This is bullshit," Robert said, tossing up his hands and standing up.

Lee glared at him until he sat down again.

"*Lastly, I leave the following items to the following people.*" At this point, Lee handed out a slip of paper to everyone in the room, including me. "I'll let you read the list yourselves."

On it was a list of items with names beside them.

I scanned the list, surprised that I found my name. Beside it said, Silver Ford Truck, furnishings in the apartment above the garage, all of Byron's belongings, the contents of my safety deposit box at Regionals Bank on Whidbey Island.

I had to read this three times before it sank in. I owned a truck. I'd never even driven before. Now, I had a truck.

"This is bullshit," Robert said. Several other people agreed. "He was my father and all I'm getting is a dumb grandfather clock?"

"What the hell am I going to do with an old radio?" Donnie asked.

"You're lucky he mentioned you. Phillip and I aren't even on this." Derrick tossed the paper down.

"Let me finish," Lee said, getting everyone's attention. When the room grew silent, Lee continued. "*As to the reason I have left my two grandsons out of my will, they know the reason. They are not to receive a dime of mine nor any property. As far as I'm concerned, the Robinson name would have been far better off if they had never been born. If I could, I would strip them of even my name.*" Lee glanced up as Phillip jumped up and kicked the side table, knocking over the lamp and sending glass shards scattering everywhere.

I jumped and cried out, then jerked back as he stormed towards me.

"You little slut," Phillip said, charging me.

Byron let out a low growl, then Lane was there, blocking Phil from getting near me.

"You slither your way into my grandfather's bed and steal everything out from under those who deserve it," Phillip growled. Then he reached over and toppled over a bar stool before leaving out the back door.

Derrick stood up and followed him without a word.

"There's more," Lee said with a sigh. Everyone turned back to the lawyer. *"The cash and funds from assets I have that can be sold should be split in the following way. Seventy percent of any funds should be split down the middle between Lane Robinson and Chloe Dawn. Ten percent to Tiffany Wallace. Ten percent should go into a trust fund for Johnny Wallace until he's eighteen, to ensure not a dime is touched by his father, Mark Wallace. The remaining ten percent I would like to donate to the animal shelter on the island where I found Byron."*

"What?" This time it was from everyone in the room except for Lane, me, and the lawyer. The entire room burst into shouts and chaos.

Then we heard someone's car alarm going off outside.

"Shit," Lane said, rushing out the back door. Several people followed him, including me and Byron, who was barking and howling at the loud noise.

I was shocked to see every window on George's truck shattered while the siren blared loudly. When I got closer, I realized that all four tires were slashed as well.

Then it dawned on me. This was my truck. The one that George had just willed to me.

"Where the fuck are Phillip and Derrick?" Lane growled, looking around just as a car sped out of the drive-way. "Son of a bitch," Lane said, pulling out his phone. "I'm calling the police," he told everyone standing around.

"Are we done here?" Robert asked, glaring at Lee and Lane. Lane was busy on the phone relaying what had happened and the details and descriptions of his cousin's car.

"The rest you can read in your copies of the will. If you'll step back inside, I'll supply each of you with a copy," Lee answered.

I stood outside with the truck's security system going off, listening to Lane talk to the police. When he hung up the phone, he turned and took my hand.

"Let's go find the keys to turn off the alarm. The police will be here soon."

I followed him inside and handed him the truck keys from where George had always kept them. He disappeared outside, and I heard the alarm turn off. The rest of his family had left, most likely going through the front door.

When Lane came back in, he shook Lee's hand.

"Sorry you had to deal with my family," Lane said.

Lee shook his head. "George warned me. I'll expect a few calls from your family's lawyers before the end of the week."

Lane nodded. "Yeah, they weren't happy."

"For now," Lee said, looking between the two of us, "everything you need to know is here." He handed Lane a large folder. "I'd suggest you move forward with the rest of George's wishes, quickly."

"Thanks," Lane said, shaking the man's hand.

Just then the police pulled up outside.

"Want me to stick around?" Lee asked.

"No, you wanted to get back to the city before dark." Lane motioned towards the front door.

"What now?" I asked Lane.

"Now we head out and report the destruction to your truck. And the lamp."

I glanced at the glass on the floor. "I should clean that up."

"No, not until after the police see the mess." Lane took my hand and pulled me out the door.

While Lane talked to the officers, I zoned out, running over everything that had just happened. Every detail. How I now had a dog, a truck, and furniture. Possessions. I had possessions. I'd never owned anything before. Well, except my copy of *Don Juan*. And I had to fight to keep that tattered book. I supposed I would have to do the same for the truck. It was obvious that Lane's cousins didn't like that George had given it to me and not them. Why? They both owned luxury cars.

I didn't know which one was driving the vehicle that we had seen speeding out of the drive.

While the officer was taking pictures of the truck, I asked Lane.

"Which one did this? Derrick or Phillip?"

"My guess? Both of them," Lane answered. "There's too much destruction for just one of them. The moment the glass broke, the alarm would have gone off. I think they did the tires first, then threw the rocks through the windows." He motioned to the large stones that lined the drive. There were three of them sitting in the front seat of the truck.

"Whose car was that pulling out?" I asked as he wrapped his arms around me.

"I don't know who was driving. But it was a rental they used to get up here," Lane answered. "They don't own cars themselves, I don't think. Derrick has been staying in Vegas, and I don't know if he has a car out here." He shrugged.

"Phillip normally drives one of his parents' cars when he needs to go somewhere or bums a ride from them."

"They don't own cars?" I asked, suddenly realizing why they would be hurt that their grandfather had given me his truck instead of them. I didn't even have a driver's license.

Lane shrugged again and then had to go answer a few more questions. When the police officer left, we headed inside.

I started cleaning up while Lane called a tow company to take the truck to the local repair shop for new tires and windows.

"Will you teach me how to drive?" I asked as we sat on the back porch sipping a glass of wine while Byron played in the yard.

Lane glanced over at me, then suddenly burst into laughter.

"My grandfather left you a truck, and you don't even know how to drive. God! What a slap in the face to my cousins." He continued to laugh, and I couldn't help but smile too. "Yes," he said, wrapping his arm around my shoulders and pulling me closer. "I'll teach you to drive."

"What are you going to do with this place?" I asked, motioning to the house. The kitchen and living room lights were on and in the darkness of the night, the place looked like a beacon of safety. Every time I looked at it like this, I felt warm and happy.

Lane sighed as he followed my gaze. His silence had my stomach jumping around.

"I'm not sure yet," he answered after a few moments.

Would he sell the house? George had hinted that he wanted Lane to live there. But Lane lived in the city and had his townhouse. He'd mentioned that he loved visiting the island but that didn't mean he could move there. After all, his job and life were in Seattle.

I didn't know exactly what he did at the law firm, but I doubted there was enough demand for lawyers on the island that he could move here full time.

The truth was slowly sinking in. Soon, I'd have to find a new job and somewhere else to live.

CHAPTER TWENTY-ONE

*"The dawn is a wild, fair woman, with sunrise in her hair;
look where she stands, with pleading hands, to lure me
there."*
- Robert Loveman

Lane

I had shifted all my case files for the week so that I could handle my grandfather's estate, so I wasn't expected back in the city for a while. As an added bonus, I now had enough time to teach Chloe how to drive.

We enrolled her in a driving course at the local high school that started in a few weeks. To get ready, every day we went out on the back roads, and I taught her what I could.

She was a quick learner. Her only issue was fear. Whenever she saw a car heading towards us, she pulled off onto the side of the road. I figured the more she drove, the more relaxed she'd get.

We spent an hour each day weaving through the back streets of the island.

I'd received a call from the detective with an update on my grandfather's case.

During that call, I was shocked to find out that there was a missing person file on Rod Clarkson. His girlfriend claimed that he'd gone missing the same night of my grandfather's murder. She'd found his truck in the garage with a pool of blood under the hood.

The police were looking into the possibility that the two cases were connected since they had been seen entering the bank together hours before my grandfather's death.

That in itself was odd, as Grandpa had just been released from the hospital the day before.

The detective was still trying to confirm alibis for four of my family members.

Since I'd kicked everyone out of my grandfather's place the day before, everyone said they had returned to the city until Monday.

My uncle Robert had claimed he was at home with my aunt Reba. However, it was confirmed that my aunt was at a book club meeting with more than a dozen of her friends.

My uncle Donnie had said he was home alone, but during the interview, my aunt Kate told the detective Donnie had gone out and hadn't gotten home until after ten thirty. The timing was right for him to have driven back from the island.

Phillip and Derrick were each other's alibies, and they claimed they had been hanging out together in a bar in downtown Seattle. Unfortunately, the bar they claimed they'd been hanging out at had been closed that night due to a rodent infestation.

Anyone of them could have been responsible. The least likely person, in my mind, was my uncle Robert. He was, after all, a current member of Congress. Even if my grandfather had refused to back him in his next run, I doubt that my uncle would kill him for it. It just didn't add up.

As for Donnie, I had some questions. He was the second lowest on my list. It was more likely the man was having an affair, and that's why he had been away from home. Plus, there just wasn't any reason for him to kill my grandfather. Donnie was a man boy. He liked his video games, and he ate like a teenager. He didn't give a shit about the finer things in life and certainly didn't want anything from George that he couldn't just take from his very busy wife.

So could my cousins have killed him. My gut response was hell yeah. They had a dozen reasons each. But would they stoop to killing? That question I didn't know the answer to.

I wanted to think they wouldn't, but the fact was, they used to torture the hell out of me when we were kids.

The one thing that didn't make sense to me was them working together on anything. They were constantly at each other's throats and couldn't even work together on tying a knot.

Did they often hang out at bars together? Yes. Of that I had no doubt. And they were just dumb enough to mix up the bar names. That I could easily see them doing.

After I'd gotten off the call with the detective, I got Lee on the phone. "Did you receive any contests to my grandfather's will?" I asked him.

"Several of them. Each of your uncles and your aunt, along with both your cousins. They are also suing you and Chloe Dawn."

"For?" I asked, rubbing my forehead. I'd spent the entire morning on the phone or looking at my computer screen. What I needed was a long walk on the beach with Byron and Chloe. Instead, I knew I'd be stuck in the study for a few more hours.

"Executor displayed favoritism toward estate beneficiaries. I'm sure this is in regard to Chloe Dawn's insertion into your grandfather's estate," Lee answered. "They want it on record that they believe you manipulated your grandfather into changing his will." Lee sighed heavily. "Which is bullshit," he added with a chuckle. "I've been working with your grandfather for the past twenty years. Not once have your two cousins been included in his will. Actually, when he first came to me, his first goal was to exclude both Derrick and Phillip from ever seeing a dime of his."

"When did my grandfather add Chloe to his will?" I asked, curious. I hadn't thought about it at the time, but she'd only worked for him for three months. It was a little strange for her to be included.

I understood Grandpa giving her Byron and the truck. But I was to split the money with her fifty-fifty once my cousin and the animal shelter got their shares. That was a large chunk of money. Not that I didn't think she deserved it. And it was, after all, my grandfather's money to do with what he wanted.

"A little over three weeks ago," Lee answered. "He called me, and I came up to visit him. We met at that little gas station diner he likes."

"Right," I said, remembering the day my grandfather had driven himself into town without Chloe or myself. I'd been flooded with work and dealing with my family. Chloe had been busy baking or tending to my family's needs.

"He mentioned that the conversation he'd had with Chloe was behind his reasoning for splitting things down the center with you. He told me a little about her past. I would never have thought she'd been through that hell after meeting her last week," Lee said with a sigh.

"Right," I said. Just then I got a text from Malory to call her as soon as I could.

"I also heard from the local PD on the island that your cousins are in trouble for that little stunt they pulled when I was there. How's the truck?" he asked.

"Fixed and sitting in the garage now."

"Idiots. Sorry, I know they're family, but if they didn't want to get caught, they should have done the damage under the cover of night."

"Right?" I chuckled as I rolled my eyes. "Neither of them have ever learned how to control themselves." Which was another reason they were high up on my list of suspects.

"Well, for now, I've filed their complaints," Lee said. "You know the drill from here."

"Yes," I groaned. "Thanks." I hung up the call.

I figured Chloe would want to be a part of the call to Malory. When I stepped out of the study, Chloe was sitting on the sofa with a very familiar red book in her hands. She was so engrossed in the pages that when I sat beside her, she jumped a little.

"Sorry," I said, trying to avoid looking at my sister's diary. "Find anything useful in there?" I asked.

"No, not yet." She closed the book. "It's entertaining, though. Your sister was a very talented writer."

"She was?" I frowned. There was so much I didn't remember or even know about her. There were also so many things that I missed about her. Her laughter, which, oddly enough, I heard in my dreams often. Her smile, which I saw in my mother's smile when she allowed herself to relax and let go of the control she desired so much. But the one thing I missed dearly about Sherry was that she loved me. Unconditionally. Just like I'd loved her.

"Yes," Chloe said, holding the book to her chest as her eyes closed. "She's grown so much since the first pages. At the beginning of the summer, when she started this journal, she despised every member of your family for some reason and the farther I get into this, now it sounds like she just hates a few of them." She smiled over at me. "She changed her mind about you too. I think it was the strawberries."

"Strawberries?" I frowned, then smiled when I remembered the first weeks of that last summer with my sister. My grandmother was allergic to strawberries and therefore had never planted them in her garden. Sherry loved strawberries and always complained that we couldn't have them. So, I'd bought a few strawberries from the store and buried them just outside the yard the week we got here. When the first berries appeared, Sherry was so excited.

"You planted them for her," Chloe said.

"I did," I answered. "Well, I buried a bunch of strawberries, hoping they would grow. I had no idea if they would."

"My garden is going crazy," Chloe said, glancing out the window. "We'll have a wonderful harvest this fall. Already, I've used some of the tomatoes and onions. The rest still needs time." She sighed. "I eventually want to plant a lot more. I only did a few things, since I wasn't sure what George would like."

"Plant as much as you want," I said, meaning it. I missed the days when I could walk outside and pluck a carrot from the ground and eat it. "Maybe I should plant a few apple trees. Byron really likes apples. That way, he could enjoy the ones that drop."

I wasn't sure what I'd said to make Chloe cry, but her

eyes grew damp, and she jumped up and rushed from the room.

I followed her and knocked on the bathroom door when she shut it.

"Are you okay?" I asked through the door.

"Yes," she called back. "I... I just..." The door flew open and she hugged me. "The fact that you'd plant strawberries for your sister and an apple for a dog makes you the best kind of human, in my opinion," she said, holding onto me. "Lane, I don't know all the rules of a relationship, but I don't think I can wait any longer." She pulled back and smiled up at me. "I'm in love with you."

Okay. I thought.

Sure.

Yes.

Hell yes.

This was great.

I loved her too.

Right?

I guess all those thoughts took a little longer to process in my head than Chloe believed they should have, because now instead of smiling up at me, she was frowning as more tears pooled in her eyes.

"Hey, I'm sorry, yes, of course," I said, taking her back into my arms. "I love you too. Gosh, I'm such a fool. I love you. I have for a while. I should have said it first."

"You..." She sniffled. "You're not just saying that because..."

"No." I pulled back and looked down at her again. "I'm not just saying that. I love you." I kissed her.

Since my grandfather's death, the only place we'd allowed ourselves to show each other affection had been up in the apartment. The house still felt too much like my grandfathers to relax in.

Now, however, neither of us were thinking.

We'd just admitted that we loved each other.

Chloe took the kiss deeper, pressing her body up against mine until my needs for her were uncontrollable. I pinned her against the wall, pulling, yanking, tearing off clothing until we were skin against skin.

I slid into her with an urgency that I'd never felt before. I swore under my breath when I bumped my elbow against the doorway.

I had to have more of her. Needed everything she would give me.

"More," I growled against her ear as her nails left red streaks down my arms. "More."

"Lane," she cried out as I hoisted her up. She wrapped her legs around my hips as I walked her to the bathroom sink and set her down so that I could plunge harder, deeper into her heat.

There were no words. None needed. Her soft moans mixed with my grunts as I continued to take, to give her everything.

Once I felt her convulse around me and tighten, I knew that I would never be the same. I wasn't just in love with Chloe, I was completely and wholly in love with Chloe. It was something I had never felt before.

"I love you," I said again when my own release consumed me.

Chloe's fingers were buried in my hair, her legs still wrapped tightly around my hips.

"What now?" she asked with a sigh.

"Now?" I thought for a moment. "I don't know, but whatever it is, we'll figure it out together. Agreed?"

"Agreed," she said with a sigh, and I felt her relax. "How about I start dinner?"

Then I remembered the phone call I'd come in here to talk to her about.

"Sure, but we've got a phone call to make first. Malory wanted to update us," I said as we pulled on our clothes.

"Is it bad?" she asked.

I shrugged. "She just sent me a text telling me to call her." Seeing the worry on her face, I stopped what I was doing and pulled her into my arms. "Whatever it is, we're in this together. Remember?"

She took a deep breath and nodded. "Okay, let's call her in the other room though."

I smiled and then pulled back to finish getting dressed.

We sat at the kitchen table and waited until Malory answered the phone on the fourth ring. She sounded a little breathless and angry.

"Yeah?" she barked out.

"Is this a bad time?" I asked.

The phone was silent and then we heard a loud bang as a door shut. "No," Malory said with a sigh. "I'm just going to come out and say it. Your SOB of a father let Elliott Meyers out on a million-dollar bail, and he's jumped ship."

"What?" We both sat forward.

"We warned him, but your father decided Meyers wasn't that big of a skip threat. He didn't believe he could scrounge up a cold mil for bail and, even if he did, he wasn't a flight risk."

"What does that mean?" Chloe asked me.

"That means he can get out of jail until his hearing date," I answered, taking her hand.

"Which he did. Now, we can't find him. The worse

news is"—she took a deep breath— "he knows right where you are."

"What?" This time I stood up and pounded the table.

"Which is why I'm running around like a chicken with no head. I'm trying to get approval to head your way," Malory added quickly.

"When did he disappear?" I asked, glancing around the house. Both the front and back doors were unlocked. Hell, half the windows in the house were wide open to let the summer breeze in.

"He walked out of the jail around six yesterday morning and wasn't at his hearing this morning. He hasn't checked in either," Malory answered.

I shut and locked the back door.

"Son of a..." I started.

"In this case, it's more like, father of a... I did mention it was your father on the bench this time, right?" Malory said. "Listen, if I can swing it, there will be a couple patrol cars heading your way. If I can't, I may just need to take a few days of vacation. Either way, you'll see me before nightfall."

"The guest room is always ready," I said before hanging up. Then I walked to the front door and locked it. I spent a few moments shutting and locking all the windows.

When I returned to the kitchen, Chloe was still sitting at the table, looking at her hands.

"You..." she started. She took a deep breath before continuing. "You don't think he's going to come after me, do you?"

"No," I lied. Her eyes jerked up to mine, and I knew she could tell I was lying. "Shit. Yeah. Yeah, I do. Which is why..." I looked around and quickly thought. "Why don't we head out? Take a few days at this little bed and breakfast

I know down the coast?" I suggested. "They have the cutest cabins…" I dropped off.

Chloe shook her head. "I won't run." She looked back at her hands. "Not from him. He's taken too much from me already. He doesn't deserve anything more."

"Okay," I said slowly. "Then let's head up to the apartment and gather a few things so we can stay in the main house with Malory tonight."

Chloe slowly nodded. "She's a good friend."

I smiled. "The best."

"How did the two of you meet?"

I felt my heart skip. "She was the detective on my sister's case," I said softly.

Chloe's eyes met mine. "Oh."

"Yeah." I smiled. "She was convinced right away that I had nothing to do with Sherry's murder. Unfortunately, she was a rookie back then. Sherry is the reason she's such a hard-ass sometimes. She feels as if she let her and me down." I looked down at my hands.

I remembered how cold the handcuffs felt that first time they'd been slapped on my wrists. The feeling of helplessness as they hauled me away in the back of the patrol car, with all of my family watching. Judging me.

Then I looked at Chloe and realized that she'd had it a lot worse. Not only had she gone through hell, but then she'd spent a year in prison.

We had talked some about the trials she'd been through, the friends she'd made, the enemies that had tortured her. She claimed it was all behind her.

Whatever happened now, I knew in my heart that I would do anything to keep Chloe safe. Safe from my family and from her past.

CHAPTER TWENTY-TWO

"Hope is brightest when it dawns from fears."
- Walter Scott

Chloe
I just couldn't get my heartrate to steady or slow down.

I'd spent months on the outside and not once had I feared that Elliott would hunt me down and harm me in any way. Or worse, drag me back under his control.

But hearing the worry in both Malory's and Lane's voices, suddenly that fear consumed me.

After we'd gathered our things and put them in Lane's room, I tried to busy myself by making dinner and dessert while Lane worked on his laptop at the kitchen counter. Every now and then I'd look up to see him watching me or looking at the closed windows. He'd shut all the curtains and blinds in the house, so we'd turned on the lights earlier than usual.

I remembered the first trip that I'd made from my

hiding spot in that tall grass to the house. How Byron had led me to George.

Just thinking about the old man had my eyes burning, so I shook those thoughts from my head and focused on rolling the dough for the sourdough bread I was making to go along with beef stroganoff. I'd found a slow cooker in a cupboard and wished I'd had one all those years ago.

The house was filled with mouthwatering smells by the time I took the bread out of the oven.

When Malory arrived, she parked her vehicle in the garage to hide the fact that she was there.

While I finished dinner, the pair of them sat at the table talking quietly.

Malory informed us that she hadn't gotten official approval to be there, so she'd had to take a week's vacation.

"I'd wager that it won't be a week before he tries something," she said to me as I set the food on the table. "If it takes longer, I suggest the two of you take a little vacation until he messes up," she added with a wink.

I liked the idea of Lane and I taking a vacation. I'd never been anywhere. A drive down the coast to visit some of the places I wanted to see in California sounded wonderful. Or to stay at the little bed and breakfast he'd mentioned.

I'd read an article on Napa Valley and then had dreamed about visiting ever since.

I wished that Malory would tell us why she was so sure that Elliott would be coming here, but when I asked, she would glance at Lane, who quickly changed the subject.

I tried listening in on their conversation while I was cooking, but they were talking too low and with their heads bent close together.

Now as we sat around the table eating, I finally demanded.

"Why do you think Elliott will come after me?"

I glared at Malory until the woman sighed heavily and put her fork down.

"It's a hunch. Really," she said. When I narrowed my eyes further, she threw up her hands. "We found a shrine in the house where he had been hiding. The one that belonged to the Allens. There was a walk-in closet full of your items, pictures of you, and newspaper clippings from your case. There were so many photographs of you, some from before the police raid. They appeared to be from a home security system." Malory paused.

I remembered Elliott having a security system installed in the massive place. He'd told me it was because he didn't trust me and needed to watch my every movement so that I wouldn't screw anything up. It had been one more reason there had been no escape from him.

"Then there were images of you in court, and in jail," Malory said as she glanced at Lane, who nodded. "And some of you here."

"Here?" I practically squealed it. "Here, here?" I asked looking around. "Did you know about this?" I asked Lane, who nodded.

"I asked him not to tell you. I knew you'd worry. He was locked up. There were images of you and Lane walking on the beach. Playing with Byron in the yard. The two of you kissing. My gut tells me he was at the restaurant that night not to have dinner, but to spy on you. Or worse."

"How can that be? They were leaving the restaurant. Him and that woman. We had just arrived there and..." I broke off, not fully understanding the timing.

"They had walked in moments after you and had only ordered one drink at the bar. Lisa Allen claims that she'd met him to discuss some business since her husband, Tim, had gone MIA. We are still looking for him, by the way," Malory added. "Lisa claims that Elliott agreed to meet her outside of Lane's townhouse building. She'd assumed Elliott was staying there but when she arrived, Elliott suggested that they head out for a drink. We believe they followed you to the restaurant." She took a sip of her iced tea and waited as I refilled it. "I believe Elliott wanted you to see him. To be afraid of him. I don't think he believed for a moment that you'd call the police," Malory said. "I think he's known right where you were from the moment you stepped out of prison." She pulled out her phone and handed it to me.

On the screen were several photos of what looked like a large closet with a mix of papers and photographs.

I took the phone and scanned more than three dozen photos and other items related to me. Malory was correct—there were images of me and Lane, me and George, and ones of me walking alongside the road in the outfit I'd been in when I'd been released from prison. Images of me and Byron sitting in the wet sand sharing that first apple. There was even an image of me sleeping in the tall grass in my little makeshift home.

I felt a shiver run down my spine and my stomach tightened. He'd been stalking me from the moment I'd gotten away from him. The moment I'd been freed from him.

Jumping up, I raced to the bathroom and lost the few bites of dinner I'd taken.

Lane was suddenly there, pulling back my hair, rubbing my back.

"Easy," he said softly. "Breathe."

I closed my eyes as tears fell, streaming down my cheeks. My hands shook, and I felt light-headed.

Why?

I kept asking this over and over.

"Why me?" I managed to say.

Lane handed me a glass of water. I kept my eyes closed as I swished the cool water and spit several times.

I leaned back and closed my eyes, resting my head against the wall.

"He likes control," Malory said from the doorway. "It ate at him that a woman turned him in. That it was you. That you'd gone against him. Also, I knew instantly that he hated that I'm the lead detective." She smiled at me. "And that you got away."

"I didn't get away. I was taken away," I pointed out. "If not for that, I probably would have never left. Never thought to leave. Until that day, the day the police came over a year ago, I believed every word, every lie, that man told me." I felt sick again but swallowed it down and took another sip of water. "I would have remained his meek dutiful wife for the rest of time."

"Then you're luckier than most," Malory said, leaning against the door and crossing her arms over her chest. "How many other women are in the same position that you were in and won't get that chance?"

I thought about it and, suddenly, the self-pity that had consumed me moments earlier was replaced with hatred. Hatred for the man, the men, who used religion and fear to control people.

I'd been a child when I'd first been told that if I didn't keep sweet and obey something bad would happen to me. That I'd go to hell or, worse, that I'd become an apostate.

How many others believed these lies? How many girls or women had no means of escape?

"I can see you're thinking about that. Good. I don't like protecting weak people," Malory said with a nod. "And I can tell by the anger in your eyes that you're not weak. So clean yourself up and get your skinny butt back in there so we can enjoy one of the only homecooked meals I've had in over a year," she added with a smile.

"I like you," I said. I laughed when I realized I'd said it out loud.

Malory laughed too. "I like you too," she said, then she turned and disappeared.

"Well?" Lane held out his hand and helped me up.

"I'm going to head up and brush my teeth. Go eat. I'll be right back down." I hugged him, then headed upstairs to clean up.

It took me longer than I'd expected. I'd soiled my shirt and wanted to change. When I made it back downstairs, the dining room was empty.

The meal that I'd made sat cold on the table, untouched. Lane and Malory were nowhere to be found.

"Hello?" I called out, thinking that they'd disappeared into the study for some reason. I looked into the dark room and realized instantly that it was empty. "Hello? Lane? Malory?" I called as I walked quickly from room to room.

Then I realized that even Byron was gone. He'd been by my side in the bathroom, until I'd headed up the stairs. Then he'd opted to stay by Lane's side where the food was.

By the time I returned to the kitchen, I was in full panic mode. Then I noticed that the back sliding door was open, and my heart jumped.

Of course, they were just outside. I stepped out and knew instantly that something was wrong. The yard was empty. The night silent.

Here I'd been so worried that Elliott would get to me. Not once had I imagined that he would try to hurt me by getting to Lane.

Not thinking clearly, I raced through the yard and

headed towards the beach, screaming their names over and over.

My heart was beating so fast that I couldn't hear anything above the sound of it pounding in my ears. Whenever I yelled for them, I would stop and listen for a reply. The only sounds I could hear were the waves softly hitting the beach and the low hum of crickets.

When I finally came to the clearing, the sliver of moon in the sky provided just enough light to see the empty beach on either side of me. The soft rays bounced off the dark water as I scanned for any sign of Lane or Malory.

I called out again, this time screaming at the top of my lungs. I thought I heard a muffled voice and started running towards the sound.

Then a shot rang out and echoed in the night. For a moment, I was confused as to which direction the sound had come from. Then I heard Byron bark, so I raced towards the sound, not caring about my own safety.

I should have known where Elliott would go. I raced towards my first hiding spot, remembering the image he'd taken of me asleep in the tall grass. Cursing under my breath for not calling the police before racing headfirst into danger, I stumbled a few times in the sand and grass.

Byron's barking grew louder. The tone changed from aggressive to happy and excited so quickly that I stopped in my tracks.

"Lane?" I called out.

"Over here," he replied. "It's okay. Malory to the rescue." I heard him chuckle.

When I saw Lane's dark silhouette in the night, I raced to him and didn't stop until his arms were around me, holding me tight.

Byron was jumping up on my side, so I reached down and wrapped an arm around him too.

"We're okay," Lane said with a sigh. "Everyone's all right."

"What happened?" I asked, pulling back. Only then did I see that Malory was shining a light on Elliot. He was face-down in the tall grass, grunting loudly with his hands hand-cuffed behind his back.

I was surprised to see another man lying beside him, unconscious.

"We got the SOBs," Malory said happily, her knee still in Elliott's back, holding him to the ground. "Damned if I didn't even get to enjoy one night of my vacation. Hell, I didn't even get one goddamn home-cooked meal."

"Did you shoot him?" I asked, motioning to the other man. When her light flashed on him, I realized I'd seen him before. It was Wesley Allen.

"No, Lane and I managed to get them down. The shot was a warning shot when Elliott tried to run after Lane knocked Allen out," Malory said.

"Head on back to the house," Lane said, reaching over and yanking up Wesley Allen, who groaned and stumbled.

"What about..." I motioned to Malory and Elliott.

"She's got this. Don't you?" he asked Malory. She quickly nodded and started hauling Elliott up off the ground.

"I can handle him." She pulled Elliott up next to her and when he tried to jerk free from her hold, she yanked on his arm until he fell in line. "No, you don't," Malory said, yanking his arms even harder. Elliott groaned and then fell into step with her as they marched down the path towards the house. "You guys coming?" she called over her shoulder.

"What happened?" I asked as we made our way back to the house.

Lane was dragging Wesley along. The man was awake now but groaning and dragging his feet.

"I went to let Byron out, and Elliott was waiting for me across the yard. Then I felt a gun between my shoulder blades. It was this guy. He snuck up behind me. The two of them forced me out here," Lane said with a sigh. "I don't even think they knew that Malory was here. We hadn't even made it to the spot when Byron rushed us, barking and taking their attention off me. I felt them hesitate and move the gun away from me. I could hear Malory following us and knew she was right there if I needed her. So I fought like hell," Lane said with a shrug.

"Stupid," Malory called back.

"Yeah, it was," Lane admitted. "I knew they had a gun, but he was distracted by Byron. When they both turned on the dog... something snapped in me. I would have done anything to keep that dog safe."

I stopped and gave Byron some attention.

"Luckily, I was here," Malory said as we stepped off the pathway into the lit backyard. "Seeing as you were having a difficult time fighting off two of them."

The light from the patio shone on Lane's face, and I saw blood coming from his nose. He had a split lip that was bleeding as well.

"Oh!" I said, reaching up and touching his face. "You're bleeding."

"Not as bad as him. I broke his nose," Lane said with a smile, motioning to Elliott. Wesley also had blood trickling down his face.

Suddenly, there were several police officers rushing towards us.

"I called the cops," Malory said with a smile. She started barking orders at the officers, and my ex-husband and Wesley were hauled away into the night in the back of a patrol car.

Thankfully, Elliott was once more out of my life. Our lives.

"Are you okay?" Lane asked me, his arms still wrapped around me tightly.

"Yes. You?" I asked back, looking up at the dried blood on his nose and the bruises forming on his cheek.

"Never better." He smiled and then kissed me, wincing slightly with pain.

"With the new charges, there's no chance in hell he'll get out this time," Malory said as she sat down at the table and leaned back, looking tired. "Any chance you can reheat this?" She motioned to the food. "I refuse to fill out my report on an empty stomach."

I raced over and hugged her, then kissed her cheek.

"Thank you for being here," I said before rushing off to reheat the meal. I even added another scoop of food on top for good measure.

I was thankful that I'd made extra food that night so we could share with a few of the officers. I even packed a couple to-go containers for some of them.

When I handed out slices of my raspberry cream pie, there were only two officers left, Officer Oliver Whitlock and Officer Alex Everette.

"You should open a restaurant. This island could use food this good," Alex said.

"We have to drive almost an hour to get pie this good," Oliver added.

I blushed. Besides Lane, no one had ever complimented me on my cooking.

"That's not a half bad idea," Lane said with a smile.

"I do love cooking and baking," I admitted.

"There's no doubt that your stroganoff and pie could win a few blue ribbons," Malory said.

The officers left and Lane locked up the house. I had just finished the dishes, and we all sat around the table.

"Now that the excitement is over, and I'm done filling out all this paperwork, I'm going to use that guest room for the night and head back home in the morning," Malory said with a yawn.

"Go. And in case I haven't said it a million times already, thank you." Lane walked over and hugged her.

"You got it, kid." She hugged him back. "Glad I was here to help this time."

I walked over and engulfed both of them in my arms. "Say the word, and I'll send you a pie, a cake, or any home-made meal you want." They both laughed.

It was a little strange to lie in bed in Lane's arms with Malory sleeping just down the hallway. Not to mention, the bed in this room was a lot smaller than the one in my apartment.

When Byron jumped up and tried to snuggle between us on the bed, we both almost fell off. Byron wasn't happy that he had to lie at our feet instead. Several times during the night, he tried to sneak up between us, and we'd have to force him down.

Neither of us got a lot of rest. I still managed to wake early, determined to give Malory another homemade meal before she headed home.

It had been a while since I'd made my coffee cake, so I jumped to the task and added a side of scrambled eggs, bacon, and cut fresh fruit.

Okay, so I might have gone a little overboard.

The looks on Malory's and Lane's faces assured me that I had made enough food for a dozen people.

After we finished eating, I packed up the rest of my coffee cake for Malory to take with her.

Watching her pull out of the driveway was hard. I'd felt safe with her there. In that short time, I'd gotten to know her, and she felt like family. Like George had.

I'd never bonded with people so quickly before in my life. It had only taken a few days for George to win my heart over. It took a little longer for Lane. I had been untrusting and so scared to open up to him.

I'd changed so much in the past year and the last few months. I actually trusted people now, something I had never done before.

Even though I knew that Elliott was locked up with no chance of escape this time, I couldn't help the sinking feeling that there was something or someone else lurking in the darkness. I guess I still doubted that I deserved a happy ever after.

CHAPTER TWENTY-THREE

"The dawn is not distant, nor is the night starless; love is eternal."
- Henry Wadsworth Longfellow

Lane

After that crazy night, when I'd been held at gunpoint and had to fight off Chloe's ex, things settled down and fell into a good pattern. A very good pattern.

We'd made a couple of necessary moves to ensure that my family would leave us alone. Possibly even stay out of our way forever. We didn't take filing the two lawsuits lightly, but they were both well deserved.

The day after Elliott's attack, we filed the first lawsuit in Chloe's name against my father for failure to follow the Code of Conduct of a Judge. He'd been the judge who had allowed the crazed man out on bail, knowing he was both a flight risk and a danger to Chloe, someone he not only knew but had current lawsuits against.

The second lawsuit was against everyone in my family for emotional abuse. I hated doing it, but if they were willing to go all the way with their own lawsuits, it was necessary.

After filing that paperwork, Chloe, Byron, and I settled into life together.

I didn't want to move back out to the apartment above the garage, so I moved furniture instead. After a week of fighting with Byron for bed real estate, it was necessary.

Even if my family was contesting my grandfather's will, it didn't negate the fact that he'd left me this place. Because all of his property had been moved into a trust, I could instantly have everything shifted over to my name as trustee.

I knew my grandfather would have wanted me to make the home mine. Correction—ours.

When my family and I had stayed here every summer, my parents had used the guest room, leaving Sherry and I to our own rooms.

Since the break-in, Sherry's room had sat empty, void of everything that had been hers except one of her spare comforters, which Chloe had found in the linen closet.

My room was still filled with my childhood things. They had seen better days and had no place in a grown man's room. Especially one I was trying to get romantic in.

Since I had time, I spent an entire day boxing up toys, sports gear, and some very old porn magazines that I'd found under my mattress.

When I was done, I thought of hauling my bed out to the garage, but then realized that the room was far too small for a king-sized bed.

I'd never really spent a lot of time in my grandparents' room. I hadn't even gone in there since I was a teenager. So, it surprised me when I opened the doors to find a modern room lacking any clutter.

Actually, the only private items in there were a picture of my grandparents that sat on a newer-looking dresser and a sleep apnea machine on the nightstand.

The walk-in closet was full of my grandfather's clothes, but I was shocked to see all of my grandmother's clothes still in there as well.

I touched one of the shirts I remembered my grandmother wearing all the time. Leaning in, I smelled it and was flooded with memories of her.

It was like being hit over the head. The emotions were so strong that I swayed. Love flooded every ounce of my body.

No wonder my grandfather had never thrown away anything of hers. I doubted I'd be able to either.

"There you are," Chloe said from the doorway, making me jump. "Sorry." She smiled. Then her eyes scanned my face and she stepped into the closet. "Are you okay?"

I nodded and held up the shirt sleeve. "It still smells like my grandmother," I said, realizing too late how stupid I sounded.

Chloe's smile was back. "That's a good thing." She touched my arm. "Want some lunch?"

I nodded. As we walked back through the room, I stopped her by taking her hand.

"What do you think of moving in here?" I asked, looking around.

Chloe's eyebrows shot up. "How do you feel about that?"

I looked around for a moment, then shrugged. "I think it's what my grandfather would want. What he expected."

Chloe smiled and then nodded. "Okay."

"Okay?" I asked.

She wrapped her arms around me. "Okay."

Just like that, we were making this place our home.

After lunch, we started to move our things into the main bedroom. Since I didn't have the heart to get rid of any of my grandparents' things just yet, we moved everything of theirs into my old room.

"George told me that he had downsized in the past year. He hated the thought of you having to go through his things, throwing out stupid little trinkets that meant nothing to him any longer," Chloe said as she remade the king-sized bed with clean sheets. "The first week I was here, we hauled more than a dozen boxes of what he called junk to a shelter on the other side of the island. Most of it was your grandmother's makeup or handbags and shoes. Some of it I kept. The rest we got rid of." She finished making the bed. "Now, just one final touch." She left the room and returned with the picture of me and Sherry. "This belongs in here." She set it down next to the picture of my grandparents.

The picture frame had been destroyed during the break-in. Now, it sat in a new silver frame.

"I found this frame in a closet. We're lucky it was the right size," she said, standing back. "It's perfect."

"We need one of the three of us," I suggested, motioning to Byron, who was happily snoring in his dog bed.

Chloe laughed. "I've never had my picture taken. At least not when I wanted it taken," she added with a frown.

It still shocked me any time she mentioned that she hadn't done or experienced simple things that I took for granted.

"Then we'll have to dress up one day this week and head to the beach to take some," I suggested, running my lips over the spot just below her ear.

I felt her melt against me just as my phone rang in my

pocket. Groaning, I pulled it out to see my father's face on the screen.

I'd known this call would come sooner or later. Now was just as good a time to deal with it as any other.

"I'll go get the rest of my things from the bathroom and put them in ours," she said with a smile.

I nodded and answered my father's call.

"What's up?" I asked, sitting on the edge of the bed.

"What's up?" my father screamed into the phone. "What in the hell do you think you're doing?"

"My job," I answered, knowing that he'd finally been served the paperwork. "I am a lawyer."

"Your job?" he screamed. "You're ruining my career. Throwing me under the bus because of what the family decided."

"The family?" I asked, flipping on the television. This was bound to have hit the news by now.

Sure enough, the first news channel I found had a picture of my father on half the screen and one of Elliot Meyer on the other. The words, "Local judge being sued for failure to follow the Code of Conduct for allowing dangerous felon out on bail" scrolled underneath their faces.

"My decision was well within the law," my father growled out.

"You allowed a dangerous man out on bail, one who was not only a flight risk but proven to be stalking Chloe, a woman you knew and currently had legal proceedings against. The man didn't even waste a single day before coming up here with a gun and trying to get to her," I said in a calm tone. "Did you know he held me at gunpoint?" I asked, knowing that part wasn't on the news.

"What?" My father's tone changed.

"Yes. When I let Byron out, he came at me from behind. He was leading me to the beach so he could kill me to hurt Chloe. He was going to leave my body where she'd spent a few nights sleeping back when she'd been homeless, before saving your father's life." I felt a pit in my gut for the man who had raised me.

My father remained silent for a moment. Then he asked, "Are you okay?"

"I am, no thanks to you. Oh, and Chloe is doing fine too," I added.

"Drop your lawsuit."

"I can't do that."

"What if I could convince the family to drop theirs? To stop contesting my father's will?" my dad asked.

"That would be great. But," I added quickly, "it wouldn't change anything on our end. You put us in danger for your own selfish motives. You knew what you were doing when you let Elliott out on bail. Knew he was Chloe's ex-husband. That you were too close. You should have recused yourself from the case. You had to have known. Which goes against the oath you took when you became a judge. As you used to tell me, you made your bed, now lie in it." I hung up.

When my phone immediately started ringing again, I turned off the ringer and turned to see Chloe standing in the doorway, holding a pile of towels. The look on her face had me rushing to her.

"What's wrong?" I asked, concerned.

"Did Elliott really say those things to you?" she asked me.

Damn. I'd hoped to keep that part from her.

I took the towels from her hands and set them down, then pulled her into my arms.

"Yeah," I said softly into her hair. "Sorry, I should have told you sooner."

Chloe was stiff in my arms and pulled back. "Why don't you start from the top and tell me everything."

"Well, that was pretty much it. They put a gun to my back, told me to walk." I replayed the night in my head. "He said that he was going to get back at you for leaving him. That you were his. You know, the standard stalker lines."

"Like?" she asked, narrowing her eyes at me.

"How you belonged to him. That he'd paid for you, and no other man was going to get away with taking what belonged to him. Then he said he was going to shoot me in the heart and leave me where you'd slept those first nights. He also said that it was Allen who stayed around here taking pictures of us, relaying to Elliott what we were up to. Every move we made."

"He's crazy," Chloe said softly. "They both are. If I was Elliott's, why didn't he pick me up from the prison? Why did he let me sleep in the grass?"

"He laughed and told me he wanted you broken. That you had to learn a lesson about what life would be like without him." I felt hatred for the man all over again. "I want to break his nose all over again when I think about it."

Chloe wrapped her arms around me. "I'm sorry he hurt you."

"He didn't. My cousins and I used to do a whole lot worse to each other. Hell, you've seen it yourself."

"I have," Chloe said with a nod. "I'm surprised they've left us alone this long."

"Yeah," I agreed.

"Lane, I have a gut feeling this isn't over with Elliott. That something more is coming."

I could see the worry in her eyes.

"Whatever it is, we'll handle it together," I assured her.

She glanced around. "We've been avoiding talking about it." She dropped her hold on me and walked over to the bed and sat down. "I think it's time we did."

"Talking about...?" I asked, moving to sit next to her.

"This." She motioned around her. "You're behaving as if you plan on staying." She turned slightly towards me. "Are you?"

I'd been doing a lot of thinking on the subject. I didn't know just yet what I wanted to do. But there was no doubt in my mind that I wanted more time with her. Any time she discovered something new, it was as if I was seeing it for the first time too.

The joy of rediscovery was intoxicating. Almost as much as her kisses were.

"To be honest," I said, taking her hands in mine, "I'm not sure yet."

She nodded. "I can respect that. I want to move forward with a few things. I start drivers' education in a few days. When I get my license, I want to look at renting a building around here. With my portion of what George left me, I'd like to open a restaurant," she said, smiling.

I pulled her into my arms. "That's an amazing idea."

"I don't know much about running a business," she admitted against my chest. "I think one of the first steps is to hire a lawyer to help me out."

I chuckled. "I think I might know a few good ones. I can get you their contact information."

Chloe pinched my side and I laughed.

"Okay." I held up my hands. "I'll do it." I kissed her. "I might know a building that will work. It's in town. Maybe we can swing by later to look at it?"

"I'd like that," she said, then her smile slipped. "I don't

want you to feel that I'm forcing your hand. Making you stick around here, but..." She took my hand in hers.

I chuckled. "You're not. Whatever I decide, I'm one hundred percent sure that I'm not going to sell this place."

"Good," she said with a sigh. "George wanted you to have it. Not just to sell, but to live in it."

I nodded and looked around our new room. Instantly, I thought about bringing some of my furniture from my townhouse up here. Maybe even all of it. Even though most of the stuff in the house was newer, there were a few pieces I liked of my own.

One of the first things I'd done was put the massive house in Seattle where my grandparents had lived up for sale, the one now occupied by my uncle Robert and aunt Reba.

I could just as easily sell the townhouse since I couldn't see myself living there any longer. Everything I wanted was here.

"How about we head into town, and you can show me the place you were thinking about, and we can have dinner at the gas station diner?" Chloe suggested.

"Sure," I said, then I snapped my fingers. "You were given the contents of my grandfather's safety deposit box. I'm dying to know what is inside. We can swing by the bank first."

Chloe smiled. "She looked down at the shorts and T-shirt she'd worn to clean and move stuff around. "Let me change first."

I nodded. "I'll meet you downstairs." I headed down to the study to gather the necessary documents we'd need for the bank.

As we drove into town, I filled Chloe in on the legal steps in opening a business. Most likely she'd need her driver's license first, which wasn't a problem. That would give her enough time to get everything ready to start her business.

But to begin with, we could open the business under the trust's name.

I felt as light as a feather as we walked into the bank. We presented the teller with the legal paperwork that we needed to get into the safety deposit box, and the manager came out and chatted with me for a moment. They tried to complain that Chloe didn't have a driver's license, but I reminded them that the documents she did have were legally acceptable in this case.

Half an hour later, right before the bank closed, we were shown into the vault, and the manager opened the locked box with the key I had been given by Lee.

The manager set the safety deposit box on the table in the middle of the room.

"We close in five minutes," he said, then he left.

"Well?" I said, motioning to the metal box.

"You want me to open it?" Chloe asked.

"Everything inside is yours," I pointed out.

She walked over and lifted the lid, as if expecting a snake to jump out from inside it. Instead, a single envelope with Chloe's name on it sat inside.

Picking it up, she frowned at me.

"Go on," I said.

She opened it and took out the letter. There was a small silver key tucked inside the paper. She looked at it, then handed it to me as she read.

"My dearest Chloe, I know this might seem strange to you, but it was the best I could do on such short notice. I hated dragging you into my messed-up family affairs. But at this point, you're better than family. Last year, I found out

some disturbing information about my family and, outside of Lane, you're the only person I trust. So, here goes. Today I've changed my will so that you and Lane receive pretty much everything of mine. The only other people in my family worthy of anything is Tiffany and her child. I've seen to it that they are both compensated, without allowing her no-good-husband to take any of it. I have my reasons, and I know my family will try to contest my last wishes. If I know Lane, he'll fight them to the very end. It must come as a shock to you to be thrust into such drama. For that I'm truly sorry. The moment I woke to you standing over me in my kitchen, you reminded me of my sweet Florence. You have the gentlest and kindest soul I've ever seen. Too good for the likes of any Robinson. With that said, if by some miracle you and Lane marry, there is one caution I would give you. Someone in the family murdered my granddaughter, Sherry. This is a fact. I was unable to find out who before locking this letter away. Both of my sons know more than they led on all those years ago. The only proof I have of this was a discovery I made a year ago. I buried the discovery in the special place you showed me. I would do anything to keep you safe, but I'm afraid that by sharing this information with you, I've put you and Lane in danger. If I was years younger, I would have known what to do with the proof. I would have had the courage to stick up for what was right. For Sherry. Now, I'm afraid I've signed my death warrant just by writing this. I'll leave you with this last piece of joy. You were as much of a granddaughter to me as Sherry was. There isn't a day that goes by that I don't miss her laugh, her smile. In the short time I knew you, I loved you with all of my heart. May your future be as bright as the dawn. It's very fitting that you chose it for your last name. Love, George."

Halfway through the letter, she was crying so hard that

I took the paper from her and read the rest of my grandfather's message.

When I was done reading it, I tucked it back in the envelope and then hugged Chloe until I felt her settle down.

The manager cleared his throat to get our attention, so we left holding on to one another.

I tucked the envelope and the key into my pocket, and we walked out of the bank together.

"Do you think you can shut this down for now until we get home? So that we can look at the building?" I asked.

"Yes." She smiled. "I need something good right now."

I drove two blocks and parked in front of the empty building. It would be perfect for what she wanted, but I saw that the sign in the window showed that it was for sale, not lease.

"I'm not sure you'd want to make such a big commitment so soon," I said, turning off the car.

"It's perfect," she said, ignoring me and jumping out of the car to look through the windows.

When I glanced inside, I remembered how the place used to be a comic book and candy store back when I was a kid.

"We used to ride our bikes up here and spend all of our allowance on comic books," I admitted.

Chloe smiled over at me. "Good memories. How much do you think they want for it?" She bit her bottom lip. "I guess the first question is, how much do I have?"

I'd looked over my grandfather's finances and had been slightly shocked at how much cash he'd had on hand. The rest of his assets, including the house my uncle and aunt had taken over, rent free, would be liquidating soon. That house alone was worth millions.

"Enough," I assured her. I pulled out my cell phone to arrange a meeting with the realtor, who quickly agreed to meet us at the diner in a little over an hour.

I could tell Chloe was excited and nervous. She kept looking out the windows of the diner and watching the door. We ordered burgers and just as we were done eating dinner, the realtor finally stepped in and glanced around.

I waved at her, instantly recognizing her as one of my sister Sherry's old summer childhood friends.

"I thought that was you on the phone," Melissa said, hugging me. "This must be Chloe?" She pulled back and held out her hand. Chloe shook it immediately.

"Yes," Chloe said with a smile.

"Melissa and Sherry used to be best friends in the summers," I told Chloe.

"Oh, how nice." Chloe smiled.

"Yes." Melissa sat across from us. "I hear you're in the market for a building?"

"I'm thinking of opening a restaurant," Chloe answered, and I could tell she was trying to keep her excitement contained.

"How wonderful. It would be nice to have someplace different to eat in this part of the island."

"Yes, the nearest place to eat, excluding this diner, is ten miles away," Chloe added.

"It is?" I frowned.

Chloe nodded. "In the city that wouldn't be such a big deal, but it's a pizzeria. The closest restaurant like I'm thinking of opening is twenty miles."

"I know that place well. My husband Jacob and I drive there once a month for date night." Melissa smiled. "Well, I suppose we should get down to business." She pulled a folder from her briefcase and slid a paper across the table.

"This is what the owners are asking, though I'll tell you right now, they're motivated. The building's been sitting empty for over two years now."

I glanced at the asking price and was shocked at how low it was. Even for a building that had been sitting empty for two years.

"Are there any issues with the structure?" I asked.

"No. Here is the latest inspection." Melissa shifted another paper towards me. Sure enough, there were a few small things, but nothing major.

"Is this a good price?" Chloe asked. She turned to Melissa. "Sorry, I... I've never owned property before."

Melissa smiled. "I hope you don't think me strange, but I've been following what has been going on between you and your crazy ex." She rolled her head slightly. "Actually, everyone on the island probably knows every single detail of what's happened to you, both of you." She motioned towards me. "I'm so sorry you went through all that. Sorry about your loss. Your grandfather was a kind man. I had an abusive ex myself, before I met Jacob." She looked between us. "Looks like you found the right man now."

I took Chloe's hand and squeezed it softly. "She did."

CHAPTER TWENTY-FOUR

Chloe

While Lane and Melissa talked logistics and price, I scanned the flyer that she'd brought about the building. Looking over all the pretty glossy pictures of the inside, my imagination went wild.

There would need to be some work done to it. The kitchen would have to be extended and updated. Still, the rest of the building was perfect. There was even a large freezer in the back that, according to the paperwork, worked properly.

I would need tables, chairs, maybe some booths for out front. In the summer months, I could set tables and chairs out front like a restaurant in Paris that I'd seen in a movie.

I just knew in my heart that I could turn the place into a very romantic spot.

At this point, I was already running through menu

items, trying to decide which dishes of mine people would enjoy the best.

"Isn't that correct?" Lane said, glancing over at me.

"I'm sorry?" I shook my head.

"I was telling Melissa that you're reading through Sherry's old diary. The last one she wrote that summer."

"Oh, yes." I smiled. Then my eyes grew big. "You're Missy." I pointed at her.

Melissa laughed and nodded. "I am. Sherry used to call me that, and I used to call her Sher-bear." Melissa laughed.

"She goes on and on about you. How the two of you snuck out of the house and used to meet on the beach at night," I said, remembering the entry. I was about three-quarters through the diary. I only was able to read it when I had free time during the day.

"We did." Melissa laughed again. "I introduced her to beer." She rolled her eyes. "Right before..." She took a deep breath. "I haven't had a best friend since Sherry."

I thought of how lucky she'd been to have one. Growing up, I'd had sisters and brothers to play with. None of them I would have considered friends.

"Well, I'm glad someone found her last diary," Melissa said. "I know your family was looking for it. They even asked me if I had it or knew anything about it."

"They did?" Lane asked, frowning. "Who?"

Melissa shrugged. "I think it was your uncle. It might have been your dad?" She shook her head. "I was fourteen and had just lost my best friend."

"I'm so sorry," I said suddenly, thinking of George's letter for a moment. "It must have been so hard on you."

"Not as hard as on others." Melissa motioned to Lane. "At least I wasn't accused of killing her and dumping her body in a pond."

I glanced over at Lane, who was frowning down at his hands. "Right," he said softly. I could tell he too was thinking of George's letter and the key in his pocket. "Well, we'll look this over and let you know."

"If you're done eating, would you like to go take a look at the inside of the building?" Melissa offered.

"Yes," I answered a little too quickly. "If we can?" I asked Lane.

"Sure." He smiled at me. "I'll just go pay up, then we can meet you over there," he said to Melissa.

"See you there." She got up and left.

While Lane paid our bill, I thought about what Melissa had said about Sherry's death. How Lane had been accused of her murder.

He'd hinted that some of his family members had believed he was guilty. How did someone get over that?

Elliott had hurt me in the past, but now he was out of my life forever. Lane still had to deal with his family on a weekly basis.

As we drove back to town in silence, I played over each interaction he'd had with his family in my head. He didn't seem to be ruled by bitterness. Not with his parents, at any rate. Then again, he'd had years to get over their betrayal.

We parked in front of the store again and met Melissa out front. She had unlocked the glass door.

When I stepped inside, something just clicked. I'd never felt surer of anything in my entire life. Except from the moment that I'd seen George's house. Here, I was home, too.

This was the place I'd been looking for all my life.

The warm hardwood floors glistened in the sunlight. The cream-colored walls appeared to be freshly painted.

There was a full wall across the back separating the front dining area from the kitchen.

"I'm sure this wall could be opened up," Melissa said, "if you wanted to create a bar type atmosphere."

I instantly saw that and nodded. "Yes, that would be perfect."

"The kitchen needs some work. We had a bakery in here a few years back. They did most of the upgrades from when it used to be the comic book place." She turned to Lane. "Remember how much time we spent in here?"

"I do," he said with a chuckle.

I continued to walk around while they chatted about the past.

The walk-in freezer was perfect for what I would need. There was a back door that led to an alleyway where all my deliveries could be handled.

There were two smaller bathrooms off the back hallway.

Honestly, I doubted there was any other space in town more perfect for a restaurant than this was.

"It's perfect," I told Lane as we drove home. We'd spent almost an hour in the building, chatting with Melissa. Now, it was full dark outside.

Lane had been letting me drive during the daylight. I was still afraid of oncoming cars and couldn't imagine driving at night with the visibility so low. I'd only ridden in a car at night a handful of times. Even that scared me still.

"I know." He took my hand. "I'll draw up an offer when we get home."

"I'm tired," I said with a sigh. "It's been a rollercoaster day." My emotions had drained me to the point that I had a headache. "What do you think he buried?" I asked, suddenly.

"I guess we'll find out when we get home." He glanced over at me.

Just then we both heard a loud engine roar behind us, and bright lights flooded the car. Then we were both jerked forward as the sound of metal scraping metal split the silence.

I think I screamed as the car jerked forward as we were pushed faster down the road.

Lane jerked the wheel and tried to apply the brakes, but the car was rammed even harder from behind. The tires hit the gravel on the side of the road, tossing rocks and dirt up every which way.

I closed my eyes as my entire world spun several times. I heard glass break, felt it raining over me, tasted blood, heard tires squeal, and smelled fresh grass just before a large splash of water had me holding my breath.

When I opened my eyes, everything was pitch black and there was a loud ringing in my ears. My face was under water, and I gulped in a swallow of pond water. Coughing, I desperately tried to free myself from my seatbelt.

Strong hands covered mine, and suddenly I was released from the restraint and pulled upward until my head was above water. I coughed, spit up, and sucked in a deep breath.

"Lane?" I cried.

"Easy, I've got you," he said, holding me. "Think you can swim to shore?"

I looked around and saw lights from the road. "Is it safe?" I asked.

"Guess we'll find out. My phone is down there. Stay put. I'm going back to grab it." Before I could say anything, he disappeared beneath the dark water.

I didn't know how deep the car was. I could just make

out the headlights under the surface, but everything looked warped. My eyes stung suddenly, and I realized I had a cut on my forehead that was bleeding. The blood was dripping into my eyes.

Leaning my head back, I tried to clear the blood from my forehead and eyes.

"Hello?" someone called out from the road. "Are you okay?" It was a woman's voice. A bright light hit me in the face.

"Help," I called back, coughing.

Just then Lane was back by my side. "Got it."

"Someone's here," I said, "A woman."

"Okay." He held up his phone and punched 911. "Just in case," he said as he relayed the information to the dispatcher while we made our way slowly to shore.

By the time we crawled out of the mud at the edge of the pond, there were three more cars on the side of the road.

Blankets were tossed over our shoulder while we waited for an ambulance and the police.

The woman who had called out to us worked at the gas station diner in the kitchen and was on her way home when she saw a large black truck ram our car. She had immediately called the police.

The paramedics bandaged the cut on my forehead and several on Lane's arms.

Since we both felt fine, they let us go as long as we agreed to head to the hospital if we felt bad in the coming days. To be honest, we were both too tired to be hauled down to the hospital. Nothing was broken. All we had were a few cuts. We were more shaken than anything else.

It wasn't until we were in a patrol car heading home that I started shaking. Lane wrapped his arms around me and softly assured me everything was okay.

The fact of what had just happened hit me. Someone had tried to kill us.

When we pulled up into the drive, Lane's low curse had me jerking my gaze up to the house.

Every single light was on in the house, and the front door stood wide open.

"Stay put," Officer Whitlock said, getting out of the vehicle.

"Alex, let me out," Lane yelled as the other officer got out.

"Can't do it, Lane," Alex said. He locked us in and followed Officer Whitlock inside.

"Damn it." Lane yanked on the door, without budging it. "Damn it."

"Where's Byron?" I asked, leaning closer to the window to get a better look.

"Safe. I'm sure of it," Lane said, hitting the door a few times.

We waited, watching the house for what seemed like an hour. When both officers came back out, I finally relaxed, seeing Byron happily trailing behind them.

Officer Whitlock opened the door and let us out.

"Well, whoever was here is long gone. They left a little mess, as if they were searching for something."

"The diary," I said, getting their attention. I raced inside.

"Diary?" I heard Alex ask as I disappeared inside.

I'd been reading it earlier and had forgotten to put it away. Or had I? I couldn't remember now.

I raced up the stairs and rushed through our new room into the bathroom and saw the box of tampons I used to hide Sherry's journal still sitting on the counter. I opened it and relaxed when I saw the red leather inside.

Then I frowned down at the box, realizing that it had been far over a month since I'd used any tampons. I quickly calculated in my head and was positive I was more than two weeks late.

A baby.

I was going to have a baby.

I was going to have Lane's baby.

I smiled and felt my heart flutter at the possibility.

"What?" Lane said from behind me. "Is it gone?"

"No, it's here. It's just..." I held up the box. "I... I'm late. Two weeks late." I held the box between us.

Lane's eyes moved down to the box, then back up at me.

"Okay," he said slowly. Then he smiled. "Okay." He nodded several times. "This could work."

"It can?" I asked, dumbfounded.

He walked over to me and pulled me into his arms.

Seeing our reflection in the mirror, I almost laughed. We both looked like drowned rats. Our clothes were muddy and wet, our hair and faces caked with blood and dirt.

Yet, the smiles on our faces were the brightest I'd ever seen.

"We both knew we were heading there," he said next to my hair. "I mean, we've been careful, but there were times we weren't."

I nodded, knowing what he was saying. He was right. I hadn't cared for a while if we used protection or not. We were in love and if by some miracle we made life, I was okay with that.

I had dreaded the idea with Elliott, but not with Lane.

"Okay," I said with a chuckle.

"Just to be sure, we'll swing into town tomorrow and get a test." He kissed me.

"Everything okay?" Alex said from the doorway, his eyes going between us and the box of tampons.

"Yes," we both said at the same time.

"Everything's perfect," Lane added with a laugh.

There was only a little mess in Lane's study. It was as if whoever had broken in had only wanted to scare us or had quickly gone through the house but only had enough time to thoroughly search the one room.

Byron had been locked in the backyard, as if someone had let him out and shut the door behind him so they could do whatever they wanted inside.

Which meant that Byron had known whoever it was. Right?

After the officers left, we showered and changed into warm clothes. Then we found a new hiding spot for the diary. I planned to finish reading it the following day, but I wanted to know it was safe for the night.

I helped Lane put fresh bandages on his hands and arms, and he put a new one on my forehead.

We were both cut and bruised, but happier than we'd been in weeks.

Taking a flashlight, we grabbed a shovel out of the garage and headed to the beach with Byron on our heels.

Thankfully, it was a full moon, which helped us along the pathway. I could have found my hiding spot with my eyes closed.

Still, I felt a shiver race down my spine, remembering the last time we'd been here. How close I'd come to losing Lane. To losing everything I loved.

"Here," I said to Lane, who stopped and handed me the flashlight.

I held it while he dug. We had to dig a few holes before finding the small silver lockbox.

We sat side by side in the sand, and Lane pulled out the key and unlocked it.

Inside sat the small locket that I'd given to George shortly after someone had broken into Sherry's room. Lane reached in with shaky hands and picked it up.

"This is Sherry's," he said with a frown. "It was supposedly lost in the pond where she was dumped." He glanced at me. "How did my grandfather get this?"

"I gave it to him. It was in her hiding spot where I found her diary. After someone broke into her room, I gave everything that was still hidden there to George for safe keeping. There's something more in there," I said, shining the light inside. I saw another white envelope with my name on it and something shiny. A glint of gold at the back of the box.

Just then we both jumped as Byron let out a low growl and darted off into the darkness.

"Shit," Lane said softly beside me. Then he took the flashlight from my hands and shut it off.

I heard him take the items out of the box and shove them into my hands.

"Run," he whispered, then he pulled me up off the sand and shoved me towards the trees.

I wanted to argue with him, but he shoved me again. "For our baby. Run," he whispered next to my ear.

Lane took off towards Byron's growls. I stood there for a moment, dumfounded. Then I heard Byron cry out in pain and instantly thought of running towards my dog. To save him. To protect him.

Instead, I did what Lane had told me to. I ran through the tall grass, heading straight for the trees.

What had been a clear night with the moon lighting the way earlier had somehow in the past half hour turned into a darker night. The skies were filled with clouds now, which blocked out the moonlight periodically.

I was running almost completely blind in pitch darkness as I cradled the locket and what I assumed was a ring and another letter from George. With every step I took, I feared that I would drop them both. I tucked them deep in my jean pockets but still feared they would bounce out as I ran.

I heard shouting behind me and picked up my pace. When the shot rang out, I cried out and dropped to the ground.

Lane!

I waited and listened.

There was only silence. Only darkness.

What should I do?

I glanced back, then forward, then back.

I wanted to go to him. Only... I laid a protective hand over my belly. Was there really a baby growing in there?

I couldn't chance it. I promised Lane I would protect the baby. His baby.

I got up on my knees, trying to listen, trying to see, to think.

When I heard movement in the grass near me, I jumped up and ran again.

I was so worried that someone was following me, someone who had murdered Sherry all those years ago, that I kept glancing over my shoulder. I wasn't paying attention to where I was going and ran directly into strong arms.

"There she is." I heard a deep voice. Then he laughed and I knew instantly who it was.

I knew for a fact that family had killed family.

"Let me go," I screamed, trying to break free of his grip.

"I don't think so. Rumor is, you have something that's very valuable to me," Derrick sneered.

I tried to kick him in the shins, to twist out of his hold, but he was far too strong. He started pulling me through the tall grass, back towards the house.

Where was Lane? Was he out there searching for me? Would he find me in time?

I screamed a few more times but this only made Derrick laugh harder. His eyes momentarily moved away from me even though his hands held firm.

I had a second to think before I reacted. I leaned up on my toes and bit him square on the jaw, sinking my teeth into his skin so deep that I tasted blood.

"You bitch," he screamed, trying to dislodge me. He shook me until I was forced to release my bite. I fell backwards, realizing quickly that he'd released me.

Once more, I ran into the darkness, blind to the danger that I was running right into.

CHAPTER TWENTY-FIVE

"I never see the dawn that I don't say to myself perhaps."
- John Dos Passos

Lane

I watched as Chloe disappeared into the darkness. The tall grass swallowed her whole.

Turning, I headed towards Byron's angry barking. I was close when he yelped in pain and grew silent.

"Son of a bitch." I threw myself at the dark figure that hovered over my unconscious dog. Just as I plowed into the shadow, he looked up.

I had a moment of pause before our bodies were thrown into the sand with the force.

A fist rammed into my gut, robbing me of my breath just as my elbow connected with his chin.

I fought like my life depended on it. Unlike all the past times I'd fought with my cousin before.

This time, I knew the winner would be the only one left alive.

All my life I'd never been able to beat him. He was much bigger than I was, so much stronger.

So I did what I'd been training to do at the gym in the boxing ring. I used his own force and strength against him. Every time he swung out, I dodged and he would fall into the sand.

When he kicked out, I connected with the leg holding him up.

When I'd dodged him three times, he lay in the sand, cursing at me. Then he suddenly turned towards me, and I was assaulted with a handful of sand. I was blinded long enough that his fist was able to connect with my jaw so powerfully I started to black out. I didn't see the gun. I did, however, hear it go off right before everything went black.

When I woke, everything was quiet. There were clouds over the moon, blocking out the light.

I could taste blood, feel it oozing out of my side where the bullet had lodged. Every time I took a breath, my ribs hurt.

When I sat up, my head spun. I bit my lip until my eyes focused. I thought I heard a scream. Thought I heard a dog barking.

No, that couldn't be right. Byron was down.

I glanced over to where I'd seen his dark form lying in the sand. The spot was empty.

Crawling to my hands and knees, I cursed as I stood up. Swaying, I took one deep breath and then another.

Chloe. Chloe was pregnant.

I was going to be a dad.

I counted to three.

I pulled out my phone and dialed 911.

When I heard the scream again, I tucked the phone into

my pocket and took off running towards the sound. It appeared it was coming from the house.

Racing back down the pathway, through my grand-mother's garden archway, I saw Chloe standing in the kitchen with my cousin.

Only, standing across from Chloe was Derrick instead of Phillip. It had been Phil who I had just fought with and had been shot by.

What the hell?

I walked closer, stepping into the light of the porch.

They both seemed to see me at the same time.

Chloe jerked her head towards me. Her eyes went wide as she screamed, "Lane!"

Just then, I was hit over the head from behind and, once more, everything went dark.

This time, when I woke, there was a blinding light shining in my eyes.

"There he is," my cousin said, and then he kicked me in the side where I'd been shot.

"We thought you were going to miss all the fun," Derrick said with a chuckle. There was blood trickling from what appeared to be a bite mark on his chin.

"What in the hell," I said, holding my side and sitting up.

Phil was leaning on the kitchen counter, eating an apple from the large bowl Chloe always kept for Byron. His nose was bleeding from where I'd connected to it, but other than that, he appeared very smug.

"I told you I didn't kill him yet," Phillip said to Derrick, who just shrugged.

"What in the hell is going on?" I asked, trying to take control of this situation.

"Don't act dumb. We know you visited the bank today.

If you haven't figured it out by now, then you're even dumber than we thought," Derrick said. "Where's the ring and the diary?" He turned to Chloe.

The ring? Shit. I thought quickly and realized they were talking about one of my cousin's family rings. But why did he believe one of the rings was a clue into Sherry's death? Then I remembered Rod mentioning he'd found something of my cousin's.

The only possibility was that he'd found it at the pond. Which would have put one of my cousins at the sight of my sister's death.

But then, how did they know about the diary?

"I don't know," Chloe said, lifting her chin slightly.

I knew that if she gave them the items, they would kill us. Even me, their cousin. It wasn't as if they hadn't done it before. But why? Why would they kill Sherry?

"Why?" I growled. "Why did you kill my sister?"

Both of my cousins looked at one another, then shrugged.

"We were just trying to have some fun," Derrick answered.

"It's not like we hadn't had fun with her before," Phillip said with a sneer. "She was always flirting with us. Wanting it."

I felt my stomach lurch at their meaning. "You raped her." I moved to get up from my spot on the floor.

Phillip pulled out his gun and pointed it at my head.

"It's not rape if she enjoyed it." Derrick chuckled.

"You're sick," Chloe said.

"But then she went and fell in love with Rod," Phillip said. "The bastard."

"So, you what? Killed Sherry because she liked

someone you didn't?" I asked, hating them more than I had ever hated before.

"Like I said, we didn't mean to kill her," Derrick said again, tossing the apple out the back door.

"We saw her riding her bike home. You'd left her all alone. So, we pulled over to have some fun. Only, she refused to get into the truck with us," Phil said.

"We knew she'd liked it plenty before. Even begged us for it by wearing all those short skirts and tiny bathing suits." Derrick chuckled. "Remember that pink one she'd wear?" he said to Phil.

"You could see right through it when it was wet." Phil chuckled.

"How?" I asked. My stomach turned, but I needed to know. "How did you do it?"

"Derrick finally convinced her to get into the truck," Phillip said, looking down at his hands as if he was trying to decide whether he needed to clip his fingernails or not. "He held her down while I had my fun, then I did the same for him."

"Only, somewhere in between, she stopped moving," Derrick said with a shrug. "So we dumped her in the pond, weighing her down with some rocks in her clothes. Only, it didn't work too well."

"We both agreed it was an accident. It's not like we planned it. So to get back at Rod for messing with our family, we decided to frame him. After all, we'd seen him talking to her at the gas station moments before," Phil explained.

"You followed us?" I asked, remembering leaving my sister at the station so she could hang out there a little longer. I hadn't seen Rod there that day, but if she was in love with him, she would have tried to keep it from me.

"Sure did." Phillip laughed. "God, we used to love fucking with you."

I remembered how many times they had tried to run me off the road on my bike with grandfather's truck. If I told on them, they'd find me alone and sucker punch me in the gut. So, I stopped telling on them.

My cousins were so arrogant, they actually believed they had all the time in the world to confess to their crimes. And I did want them to confess to everything. I knew my phone was still in my pocket, most likely still on the call with the 911 operator. It was just a matter of time before help arrived. I only had to stall them from shooting us.

Whatever happened now, there was no way they'd get away with murder again.

"Imagine our surprise when Rod left the gas station that day and spent the next hour mowing a yard for the whole damn town to see. Then he headed out to dinner with his parents across the island. His alibi was rock solid. Yours, dear cousin, not so much." Derrick shrugged.

"It was fun watching you squirm though." Phil laughed. "God, our dads were so pissed. Everyone in the family was sure you'd done it. Even dear old grandpa thought you were guilty, at least for a while."

"What changed?" I asked.

"Dumb ass over here slipped up," Derrick growled out, motioning to Phil. "He mentioned something about losing his ring that last summer when Sherry died. Told his dad that he thought he'd lost it in the pond that summer. The fucking idiot."

"My dad broke down and told your dad, who in turned told dear old grandpa last year," Phil said.

"I think it's why he had a stroke. Too bad it didn't finish him off back then. Maybe then we would have gotten something in his will," Derrick said. "How was I to know he'd recover and put two and two together? He's old," Derrick shouted.

"After that, our dear old grandfather moved back here and started calling us and asking for more details of that last summer," Derrick said. "Asking me where I was, where Phillip was, when Sherry went missing."

"It wasn't until he hired you and we heard that he'd cut us out of his will that we understood he knew what we'd done," Phillip said.

"Then, one day, while snooping around upstairs, I over-heard the two of you talking about finding Sherry's diary," Derrick said. "I knew that bitch always wrote that shit down. Everything we'd done to her in the past. Whenever I used to visit your place in the city, I'd sneak upstairs into her room to jerk off in her underwear." He and Phil chuckled. "She liked it when we did that. We'd always read her diaries and tear out all the pages where she spilled about all the fun we had together, our little secrets."

"When we couldn't find her last diary, we asked around," Phil said, leaning on the counter.

I remembered Melissa mentioning someone asking her about it earlier that evening. She'd thought it was my uncles. It hadn't been. No doubt it had been one of my cousins.

"So you broke in and destroyed her room looking for it?" I asked.

"Sure. Still didn't find it though." Phil sighed.

"Is that why you killed our grandfather?" I asked, feeling my anger spike again.

"No," Derrick answered. "I killed him because I'd been following him for a while. He met with Rod on several occa-sions. Then one day, after he collapsed on the beach, I watched as he met Rod at the bank. I'd heard Rod bragging to you at the diner about how he'd found something of ours. I knew instantly what it was. So I followed the two of them when they went into the bank and when they came out, our dear old grandfather was crying. I knew he had the proof. I followed him home, and he confessed to me that he had proof and my ring. I knew he must have found Sherry's diary. He said the proof was all locked up in the safety deposit box. He swore that I would never get my hands on it and even tried to pull the whole "if anything happens to him or either of you two, that the police would get their hands on it" bullshit. But I'm too smart for those tricks. I hit him over the head with my gun. I thought about shooting him, but he was already dead. I guess I hit him too hard. Then I went over to Rod's place and shot him in the head as he worked on his truck. Dumped his body in the same damn pond we dumped Sherry in. Course, they haven't found him yet," he added with a chuckle. "When they do, they'll see the note we left in his pocket where he confessed to killing Sherry all those years ago. How he had faked his alibi and after all these years just couldn't take the guilt and had shot himself."

"Enough," Phillip barked, straightening up. "Like we said, we saw you two going into the bank earlier today. The old man gave everything in the safety box to your whore, so where is the ring and the diary?"

I growled at the name they called Chloe, but held still, since the gun was still trained on me. At this distance, I doubted even Phillip would miss.

On the beach it had been dark, but here, under the lights of the kitchen, I knew he wouldn't just graze me.

"Do you really think you can waltz in here, get the evidence, then what? Kill us?" I laughed, causing Phillip to point the gun at my head again.

"We did it before," Derrick pointed out.

"And I'm so surprised that you two idiots were able to bungle your way through it and not get caught. This time, though, there's so much evidence." I pointed to Derrick's bloody chin, Phil's fat lip and black eye. "There's no way you're going free this time."

"We will clean up after and explain it away. Everyone always knows we're always fighting each other." Phillip motioned between him and Derrick. "Where is the diary?"

In the next moment, I watched in horror as a tan-colored furry blob rushed through the back door and latch onto Phillips hand, the one holding the gun.

Byron's teeth sank deep into my cousin's arm, causing him to howl with pain as blood splattered everywhere.

A gunshot echoed in the kitchen, and the glass door shattered into pieces.

"Police!" several people shouted. "Drop the weapon and get down on the ground."

Seconds later, Derrick's body hit the ground. I watched for a moment as he writhed violently, his eyes rolling into his head. There were two taser prongs sticking out of his chest.

Phillip ignored the warnings and continued to try to fight Byron off. The dog was refusing to release Phillip's arm and was emitting a low growl. He sounded satisfied.

"Byron!" Chloe yelled as more officers stormed in the room from all directions.

The dog released my cousin's arm and rushed over to Chloe, who hugged him to her chest for a moment. Then they both crawled towards me.

"Lane?" she cried and held onto me. "They killed them."

I held her, feeling extremely light-headed. Now that

both of my cousins were lying face down on the dining room floor, being cuffed and read their rights, I finally felt all the aches.

When they rolled Derrick over, I noticed he'd soiled himself. For some reason, that made me smile, then laugh.

"Lane?" Chloe cried again as I started to tilt sideways and pass out.

For the third time that night, I woke up to a mixture of light and darkness above me. Then Chloe's face appeared as memories of what had just happened flooded in.

"Hey," I said softly.

"Hey." She smiled. "We're on our way to the hospital. They let me ride in the back with you."

"Cool." I nodded.

"It's the second time I've been in an ambulance," she pointed out with a grin.

"Cool," I said again, making her smile even more. "Byron?" I asked.

"He's getting checked out. Did you know that our neighbor is a veterinarian?"

"No, that's cool. Think you could lean down here and kiss me?"

Chloe looked up and then smiled when the EMT nodded. When she brushed her lips across mine, I knew everything would be okay.

"You're my everything," I said, closing my eyes. "When we get out of here, I want to take a trip south with you. You've mentioned a few times that you wanted to go to Napa." When she was quiet, I opened my eyes. "Will you go to Napa with me?"

She nodded and I saw a tear slide down her cheek.

"Hey." I reached up and wiped it away. "Don't worry, when I can, I'm planning on asking you to marry me."

She smiled. "I'm not worried. I'm happy."

"Tears are a funny way of showing that," I said with a smile.

"Hormones." She shrugged. "Remember, I'm pregnant."

"I remember," I said with a smile. "While we're at the hospital, maybe they can confirm that for us."

"That's a great idea."

She pulled back as a phone rang. "It's your parents." She held up my phone.

"Answer it if you want. I'm done dealing with my family for a while." I closed my eyes.

The following morning, I woke to a bright hospital room. The surgery to remove the bullet embedded in my side, just under my rib, had taken more than three hours. They'd stitched me up, inside and out, and now I was itching for answers.

I'd gotten a lot of them last night, but there were still a few left over that I wanted.

Chloe had spent the night lying next to me in the bed. Her pregnancy test had come back positive.

We were going to have a baby.

We were going to be a family.

She'd disappeared for a while that morning and had come back with breakfast for the both of us. Even though it was hospital food, I enjoyed eating it with her.

I'd gotten a text message from our neighbor, Jimmy Evans, who assured us that Byron was healthy and happily enjoying his mini vacation with his own two dogs. He told us we could pick him up when we returned home and not to worry about him.

Shortly after we finished breakfast, my parents strolled in, followed by Officer Whitlock, Alex, and Detective Langford.

"I thought it prudent that your family be here," the detective said, setting a file down on the hospital tray. Then he looked around the room. "You two had a productive time last night." He motioned to Chloe and me.

"Tell me their confessions were overheard on the 911 call," I said.

"They were. Heard and recorded." Detective Langford smiled. "I've listened to them about a dozen times." His smile slipped. "I thought you'd like to know, we pulled Rodney Clarkson's body from the pond about an hour ago. Just like your cousin confessed. It was damned close to where they pulled your car out too."

I swallowed. "That SOB was rough on me like my cousins, but he was trying to change. He hadn't killed anyone."

"We'll have to send flowers and our condolences to Lindsey," Chloe said, taking my hand in hers.

I nodded. "Go on," I told the detective.

"If we'd just had the ring, there wouldn't have been enough evidence to convict the two of them. However..." He held up Sherry's diary. "Thanks to you telling us where this was hidden, we have our first real evidence." He flipped the book open to the last page.

"I didn't want to skip to the end," Chloe said softly. "I was going to finish reading it tomorrow." She shook her head. "Today, I mean."

I squeezed her hand. "Go on," I told the detective again.

He shook his head. "What's in here will only cause more pain." He shut the book and looked to my parents. "This"—he tapped the book— "along with their confessions and the bullet we'll pull from Rodney and the one they pulled from Lane, will be enough to send them away for good." He closed the folder. "Oh, this is yours." He handed my grandfather's letter back to Chloe. "It's a copy, but I figured George would have wanted you to read it none the less."

"Thanks," Chloe said, holding onto it.

"So, that's it?" my mother asked. "They killed my baby and killed George and Rod to cover it up?" She held onto my father.

The detective nodded. "Not too bright, if you ask me. There could have been a dozen reasons why that ring ended up in the pond. There wasn't any DNA evidence on Sherry tying them to the crime. No witnesses. No solid evidence. If they had just stayed quiet, they would have gotten away."

"Those two were always idiots," my father growled out.

"Well, we'll leave you to your recovery," the detective said. He motioned to the two officers.

"We just stopped by to see how you're doing," Officer Whitlock said. He motioned to my parents. "If you need anything..." He shook my hand then my father's and left.

"When this is all over, we're going to have to hang out," Alex said, shaking my hand. "Now that you'll be living on the island full time." He winked at me. "Chloe." He nodded at her, then left.

"What does he mean now that you'll be living on the island full time?" my mother asked, tears streaming down her face.

I had no doubt my parents were happy that their daughter's killers were caught. Still, part of me hated them for believing all these years that I'd done it. How they had treated my cousins, the real killers, so much better than their own innocent son... I was done with them. At least for now.

I pulled Chloe down next to me and held onto her hand.

"I've put the townhouse and the house on Beaker Street up for sale. Robert and Reba will have to find someplace else to squat," I added with a smile. "Chloe and I are staying here. After a quick trip to Vegas to get married, followed by a longer trip to Napa for our honeymoon, we're heading back here to open a restaurant and raise our first kid, who will be arriving in about eight months. Maybe we'll add one or two more kids and dogs to the mix along the way. But one thing is for sure, we will live happily ever after."

The entire time I was talking, my parents stared at us with open mouths.

They both started complaining at the same time until their voices were so loud, I almost had to cover my ears.

Suddenly, there was a loud whistle, and everyone turned towards Chloe, who stood up and placed her hands on her hips.

"I think you're both mistaken. We're not asking your permission," Chloe said as she took my hand in hers. "We're telling you and if you don't like it, there's the door."

I smiled up at her, then pulled her down and kissed her. "You are my family," I said.

She smiled back. "And you are mine."

Chloe

I stood on the hill overlooking the green fields filled with long rows of grape vines with Bryon sitting at my feet, whining for attention. My mind was too occupied with the sheer beauty in front of me to break my gaze for the animal that I loved.

"Here," Lane laughed and bent down to pick up the dog's green ball and toss it a few feet away, sending Bryon scurrying off in play. Then Lane's arms wrapped around me and I sighed, leaning into his chest. "Well?" He asked. "What do you think, Mrs. Robinson?"

I turned into him and leaned up on my toes to kiss him.

It was a dream come true. I had enjoyed the sights and sounds of Los Vegas, for a while. We had been married the second night we were there, in a small chapel on the main strip. Then, Lane had shown me around the city. He'd taken me everywhere. Spoiled me. After a week, however, I was ready for the quiet.

As we drove through the dessert, heading towards the vineyards, something settled deep inside me. That longing

I'd always felt, the isolation, it was gone. Replaced with peace and so much love that when I thought about what I'd almost lost, it hurt.

"I think," I smiled. "I'm going to never want to leave." Lane chuckled. "Then you'll miss out on your big day. In less than a month, New Hope will open it's doors back on the island. Unless we go home, the doors will open without you."

I smiled and then laughed. "Okay, you talked me into it. I'll go home for that."

Taking my hand, we started walking down the hill towards the little cottage that would be ours for the week. Bryon happily ran circles around us.

"Can this really be happening?" I asked when we stopped at the edge of the vineyard.

Lane kissed me. "It is real, and thank god too. I believe that I'm the luckiest person alive."

"No," I shook my head quickly. "I am." I paused and laid a hand over my growing belly. "We are," I corrected with a smile.

The Pride Series

Finding Pride

Discovering Pride

Returning Pride

Lasting Pride

Serving Pride

Red Hot Christmas

My Sweet Valentine

Return To Me

Rescue Me

A Pride Christmas

The Secret Series

Secret Seduction

Secret Pleasure

Secret Guardian

Secret Passions

Secret Identity

Secret Sauce

Secret Obsession

Secret Desire

Secret Charm

Secret Santa

The West Series

Loving Lauren

Taming Alex

Holding Haley

Missy's Moment

Breaking Travis

Roping Ryan

Wild Bride

Corey's Catch

Tessa's Turn

Saving Trace

Christmas Holly

Maggie's Match

The Grayton Series

Last Resort

Someday Beach

Rip Current

In Too Deep

Swept Away

High Tide

Sunset Dreams

Lucky Series

Unlucky In Love

Sweet Resolve

Best of Luck

A Little Luck

Christmas Wish

Silver Cove Series

Silver Lining

French Kiss

Happy Accident

Hidden Charm

A Silver Cove Christmas

Sweet Surrender

Second Chances

Entangled Series – Paranormal Romance

The Awakening

The Beckoning

The Ascension

The Presence

The Calling

The Chosen

The Beyond

Haven, Montana Series

Closer to You

Never Let Go

Holding On

Coming Home

The Hard Way

Pride Oregon Series

A Dash of Love

My Kind of Love

Season of Love

Tis the Season

Dare to Love

Where I Belong

Because of Love

A Thing Called Love

First Comes Love

Someone to Love

Fools in Love

FindingLove

Wildflowers Series

Summer Nights

Summer Heat

Summer Secrets

Summer Fling

Summer's End

Summer Wish

Summer Breeze

Summer Ride

Distracted Series

Wake Me

Tame Me

Save Me

Dare Me

Stand Alone Books

Twisted Rock

Hope Harbor

Raven Falls

Angel Bluff

Day Break

For a complete list of books:

http://JillSanders.com

ABOUT THE AUTHOR

Jill Sanders is a New York Times, USA Today, and international bestselling author of Sweet Contemporary Romance, Romantic Suspense, Western Romance, and Paranormal Romance novels. With over 90 books in eleven series, translations into several different languages, and audiobooks there's plenty to choose from. Look for Jill's bestselling stories wherever romance books are sold or visit her at jillsanders.com

Jill comes from a large family with six siblings, including an identical twin. She was raised in the Pacific Northwest and later relocated to Colorado for college and a successful IT career before discovering her talent for writing sweet and sexy page-turners. After Colorado, she decided to move south, living in Texas and now making her home along the Emerald Coast of Florida. You will find that the settings of several of her series are inspired by her time spent living in these areas. She has two sons and off-set the testosterone in her house by adopting three furry little ladies that provide her company while she's locked in her writing cave. She enjoys heading to the beach, hiking, swimming, wine-tasting, and pickleball with her husband, and of course writing. If you have read any of her books, you may also notice that there is a love of food, especially sweets! She has been blamed for a few added pounds by her assistant, editor, and fans... donuts or pie anyone?

facebook.com/JillSandersBooks

twitter.com/JillMSanders

amazon.com/Jill-Sanders/e/B009M2NFD6?tag=jillm-com-20

bookbub.com/authors/jill-sanders

instagram.com/jillsandersauthor

tiktok.com/@jillsandersauthor

www.ingramcontent.com/pod-product-compliance
Lightning Source LLC
Chambersburg PA
CBHW031308210726
48287CB00005B/1461